BARON
of
RAKE STREET

#2 Sisterhood of Secrets

BY
JENNIFER MONROE

WOLF PUBLISHING

Baron of Rake Street by Jennifer Monroe

Published by WOLF Publishing UG

Copyright © 2022 Jennifer Monroe
Text by Jennifer Monroe
Edited by Chris Hall
Cover Art by Victoria Cooper
Paperback ISBN: 978-3-98536-039-0
Hard Cover ISBN: 978-3-98536-040-6
Ebook ISBN: 978-3-98536-038-3

WOLF Publishing - This is us:

Two sisters, two personalities.. But only one big love!

Diving into a world of dreams..
   ...Romance, heartfelt emotions, lovable and witty characters, some humor, and some mystery! Because we want it all! Historical Romance at its best!

Visit our website to learn all about us, our authors and books!

Sign up to our mailing list to receive first hand information on new releases, freebies and promotions as well as exclusive giveaways and sneak-peeks!

WWW.WOLF-PUBLISHING.COM

ALSO BY JENNIFER MONROE

The Sisterhood of Secrets

There is far more for the women at Miss Rutley's Finishing School than an education, for their secretive headmistress will assure her pupils find the happiness they each deserve.

#1 Duke of Madness

#2 Baron of Rake Street

#3 Marquess of Magic

BARON

of

RAKE STREET

PROLOGUE

Chatsworth England, 1825

The large oak tree that grew in the front garden of Mrs. Rutley's School for Young Women had great meaning to Emma, Lady St. John. It was where she and the other girls who attended the school had made an important pledge. Now as a wife, a mother, and a baroness, she had arrived this day to honor that promise.

The carriage had stopped moments ago, and the driver waited patiently at the open door as Emma composed herself. The letter had arrived several days earlier, requesting that she return to the school as soon as possible. Her emotions ran high, and she needed them under control if she was to face what was ahead of her.

For Emma, there had been no hesitation in leaving Redborrow Estate, even though she and her husband had plans to throw a party in just four days. Her children, now grown, were curious as to how a letter from the headmistress of a girls' school could possibly command a baroness to come running and ignore her responsibilities to her family.

Although Emma had made every attempt to be open with her children, there were some things she simply could not share with them. At least, not before she spoke to Mrs. Rutley.

Alighting from the carriage, her lady's maid, Beatrice, followed behind. Emma's eyes fell on an exquisite white carriage with gold trim. A smile came to her face, for the insignia on its door was that of the Colburn family, which said that her dearest childhood friend, Julia, Duchess of Elmhurst, had already arrived.

Sighing, Emma returned her gaze to the wondrous oak. Like everything in life, the tree, rumored to be nearly three hundred years old, had aged. Enormous limbs spread across a great expanse, and its thick trunk was dotted with dark knots. Memories flooded Emma's mind, and she was filled with fondness of remembering her life on these very grounds.

Twenty years. Had it truly been that long?

"My lady?" Beatrice whispered. "Is there anything I can do for you?"

Emma turned to the young lady's maid, who had been in her employ only three months, and smiled up at her. It was not that the maid was exceptionally tall, but Emma was far shorter than most women.

"I don't believe so," she replied. "I would like some time alone. You may walk around the grounds after you've unpacked if you'd like. The servants' entrance is around the back. I'm sure someone there will be able to direct you to where we'll be staying."

Beatrice nodded, bobbed a quick curtsy, and hurried away.

After giving very much the same instructions to the driver, Emma walked over to the tree. The shadow of the overhanging branches cooled the air as she walked around the broad trunk, a hand trailing across the bark. Deep ridges like small riverbanks felt rough beneath her fingers until she reached an exposed section.

The letters **EH**, which had once belonged to her, Emma Hunter, had been carved into the tree's flesh beside **JW**, those of Julia Wallace. Nine sets of initials had been carved there that day, a suggestion made by Ruth Lockhart, the most adventurous of all the girls. A makeshift contract promising if any one of them should call for help, all would come, no matter their circumstances.

Now, however, Emma could not help but wonder if all the girls—nay, women—would indeed come. She had kept in touch with some, but others had stopped replying to her correspondence years ago. Life had a strange way of shifting one's path, and all too often, promises could not be kept no matter how hard one tried.

Walking away from the tree, she turned to study Courtly Manor, which had been her home for four years during her youth. The white paint was a bit weathered, and the black trim could use a fresh coat, but otherwise, the house was exactly as she remembered it.

As she approached the portico, the door opened and a familiar face greeted her.

"Ah, Miss Emma, you haven't aged a day!" Age had not affected the portly cook, either, except for the mop of silver hair that had replaced her once coffee-colored tresses. The smile and rosy cheeks remained the same.

"It's so good to see you, Mrs. Shepherd," Emma squeaked. The cook's strong embrace was another thing that had not changed. "It's been far too long."

Mrs. Shepherd took a step back. "It certainly has. I was just..." Her eyes went wide, and she gasped. "I forget that you girls have proper titles now!" She grasped her skirts to drop to a curtsy, but Emma placed a hand on the cook's arm to stop her.

"You'll always be Mrs. Shepherd to me, and I'll always be Emma to you." Looking past the cook, Emma added, "And Mrs. Rutley? How is she?"

"Stubborn, crafty, seeing the positive in all this," Mrs. Shepherd said. "She hasn't changed one bit. Come in and go see her."

Emma followed the cook into the small foyer. It was as if she had stepped back in time, and her memories came to life. Dozens of girls moved about, hurrying to their respective lessons. Ruth, Diana, Jenny, every one of her friends was there...

"Are you all right?" Mrs. Shepherd asked, bringing Emma back to the present.

Shaking her head to clear it, Emma stared at the empty foyer. "Yes, I'm well. Is Mrs. Rutley in her bedchamber?"

Mrs. Shepherd nodded.

"Then I'll go to her now." Emma ascended the staircase, a pounding behind her ears that matched her heartbeat. Taking a right, she walked down the corridor until she reached Mrs. Rutley's room.

She closed her eyes and drew in a calming breath. Did she truly wish to see her once vivacious headmistress lying in her sickbed?

Is that not why you made this journey? she chastised herself. No matter what she found here, no matter how sick Mrs. Rutley was, she had a duty to the woman who had been such an important part of her life.

Squaring her shoulders, she gave the door a gentle knock. When it opened, her heart filled with joy upon seeing Julia for the first time in seven years.

"Emma!" Julia said, throwing her arms around Emma. Then she held Emma at arm's length and studied her. "Look how beautiful you still are!"

"As are you," Emma said. Then she lowered her voice and glanced toward the bed. "And Mrs. Rutley? How is she faring?"

Julia gave her a small smile as she took Emma's hand. "I believe she would like you to tell her a story. And if you don't mind, I would like to listen as well."

A story? What sort of story could she, Emma, possibly tell? Her life since marrying had been busy, certainly, but it was no different from every other woman with a family and home to maintain.

Mrs. Rutley's hair, once thick and dark, was now sparse and gray. Sinewy arms protruded from the sleeves of her nightgown. Emma's heart ached at seeing her headmistress in such a terrible state, and she wished she had a way to help her somehow.

"I don't need to see with my eyes to recognize a confident woman," Mrs. Rutley rasped as she opened her eyes. "Hello, my dear. I'm so happy you came."

"Oh, Mrs. Rutley!" Emma whispered as she lowered herself onto the edge of the bed. "I came as soon as I received your letter. I was determined to honor the vow we made."

The headmistress smiled. "I had no doubt that you would. And now that you're here, I must make a request."

Emma nodded. "Of course. I'll do whatever I can to fulfill any request you make."

"A great romance took place here," Mrs. Rutley replied. "A story about a young woman who fell in love with a baron. Yet he was not just any baron, was he?"

Emma could not help but give a small laugh. "No, he certainly was not. His reputation was nearly in ruins, as was his estate. But in the end, all was put to rights."

Mrs. Rutley laid a thin hand on Emma's arm. "Tell me your tale, for although I witnessed it firsthand, I would like to hear it from you."

Emma nodded, and the memories once again filled her thoughts. Where should she begin? The first time she saw Andrew, Lord St. John, and he had winked at her? Or perhaps when she and Julia had encountered him in the alleyway just outside the gaming hell off Rake Street, and he had demanded the price of a kiss for passage?

No, she knew the exact place to begin.

"It was the day after Julia left Chatsworth forever. Diana had moved into my room. It was a downpour, and I heard that the Baron of Rake Street was in your office."

CHAPTER 1

Chatsworth, England 1805

Miss Emma Hunter was alone. Well except for the rain, which had not stopped since the previous day. She found herself feeling even more miserable because her best friend, Julia, was gone. Not that she was unhappy for Julia, for that was untrue, but that did not mean Emma would not miss her. Julia had found love with a duke, and her reward was to return home to prepare for the wedding.

After completing her morning classes, Emma and the other students at Mrs. Rutley's School for Young Women were given an hour to do as they pleased. Emma chose to return to her room to wallow in her sorrows. This proved to be a foolish idea, for she could not stop herself from staring at the empty bed across from hers.

With Julia now gone, where did that leave Emma? She had become accustomed to having someone there, a friend to whom she could express her fears. Or share her dreams. Depending on the day, it could be either or both. Now it would be neither.

Her main concern at the moment was that her father had announced he was considering selling her hand to a man thrice her age.

If they did indeed come through on the agreement, Emma and the gentleman old enough to be her grandfather would begin courting come January, once the season began.

Archibald, Viscount Egerton, and her father, Sir Henry Hunter, made it clear that the courtship would be short-lived before the reading of the banns took place. With it now being the month of October, Emma had three months to put a stop to the plan her father had for her and set her own future.

Yet, how did a woman with no personal means achieve such a thing? She had been advised by Ruth Lockhart to run away. Though the idea was enticing, Emma knew that with no money, such an act was impossible. She knew how difficult it was to be poor, but destitute would likely be how her life would end.

There had to be a solution to her problem, and Emma prayed she would find it soon. If not, Lord Egerton would come to claim her hand and whisk her away to a life that could not be less than abominable.

Who she was destined to marry was not the only complication in her life, however. The second of her problems appeared when the door opened, and the cruelest girl Emma knew entered the room.

"I find it fascinating that Julia somehow tricked a duke into marrying her," Abigail Swanson said as she leaned against the frame of the door. Her bright red hair was piled atop her head, held up with more than a dozen red and blue paste jewel pins. "And yet, for all her talk of friendship, she has abandoned you here, so that an old man may claim you as his bride."

Blood pounded behind Emma's ears as Abigail leered down at her. Being of a short stature, Emma was often seen as an easy victim for some of the girls, especially Abigail. Yet Emma had never been comfortable confronting those who wronged her, so she oftentimes found her confidence matched her height. Who would be intimidated by someone who couldn't look her in the eye?

But oh, how Emma would have liked to give the girl a right smack!

"Julia did no such thing," Emma managed to say, although her heart beat in her chest so hard the entire school should have heard it. "She and the duke fell in love."

"I do wish you'd speak up," Abigail snapped. "It's why no decent man looks your way."

What little boldness Emma had been able to muster disappeared completely. Why did Abigail have to be so harsh? Emma had done nothing to provoke such treatment. Yet whenever they encountered one another, Emma felt no older than twelve, rather than her eighteen years. Why could she not have been born self-assured like Julia or brave like Ruth?

"Abigail Swanson," Diana Kendricks said as she entered the room, several dresses draped over an arm, "you have no room to talk. Your father must offer an above-average dowry for any man to even consider you." Abigail turned her glare on Diana, but the latter gave her no chance to respond before adding, "I believe your father offers far too much for your hand in marriage. A three-legged goat and half a bottle of the cheapest spirits would be plenty."

"The two of you are just jealous," Abigail retorted as her nose threatened to touch the ceiling. "Father has money to spare and, therefore, has no need to worry about how he spends it." She then returned her attention to Emma. "Your parents are poorer than those who sweep the floors of the shops in the village. At least a gentleman who marries me will have both a title and wealth, not the illiterate man you're destined to wed."

Had she forgotten that the man asking for Emma's hand was a viscount? Apparently so.

"None of us knows what the future holds," Diana said. "I'd be careful with your predictions, or you just may find yourself working as a scullery maid!"

Abigail snorted before storming out of the room.

Diana walked over to the bed that had belonged to Julia and laid the dresses across it. "You really should learn to stand up for yourself, Emma. Especially against such a beast as Abigail."

"I know I should," Emma said as she returned to her place on her bed. "It's just that I get so nervous. What she says is true. My father may be a baronet, but he cannot even afford to host a party. What gentleman of means would ever consider me as a viable prospect? Just the one who's older than the great oak tree!"

Indeed, her parents were poor. They had used all their savings to send Emma to the girls' school in the hope she might find someone who could help dig them out of poverty and, hopefully, climb the social ladder. Even if it meant only rising a couple of rungs above where they were now.

Diana sighed and shook her head, sending her blonde curls bobbing to and fro. "I came to ask if you would consider allowing me to take Julia's bed. But if you would rather have Abigail as your companion, I can leave." She rose and walked toward the door.

"No!" Emma said a bit too loudly. "I mean, stay, please."

Diana grinned, and the two embraced. Although Julia would always be Emma's best friend, Diana came close. Sharing a room with her would be wonderful.

"Why do you wish to leave your old room?" Emma asked.

"I love Ruth, I truly do, but she can be maddening sometimes. Her endless tales of romance, highwaymen, thievery are simply far too much for my ears. And to be honest, I knew you would be sad now that Julia's gone. I want to be here for you. We did make a promise, after all."

"Thank you," Emma said, her worries easing. "I'm glad to have you here." She glanced at the dresses Diana had brought with her. "Shall we get your other things?"

"Let's wait," Diana replied. "Ruth is speaking with Theodosia, and I don't want to interrupt them. Why do we not speak of Julia? I already miss her dearly, although she's been gone only a day."

"Do you think her wedding will be impressive?" Emma asked.

"She's marrying a duke, so I would say it will be," Diana said. "I imagine her dress will be quite extravagant, and the guests will likely be served a breakfast of the finest food and drink as a part of the celebration. What sort of wedding gift do you suppose His Grace will purchase for her? I know! What if he gifts her a grand estate of her very own?"

Emma nodded. Although she knew Julia cared nothing for material possessions, her new husband would likely shower her with all sorts of lavish gifts. Emma would not have minded if her husband were a cobbler, as long as he was not as ancient as Lord Egerton. Just thinking of the viscount made her stomach ache.

"And what about you?" Diana asked, giving Emma a sympathetic pat on the arm. "Have you formulated a plan of escape, so you will not be forced to marry the viscount?"

Were her thoughts so easy to read? The truth was, she had hoped that she would have the same fortune that befell Julia and find someone she could fall in love with. But her hopes as of late were falling by the day.

"No," Emma replied, sighing. "And I have only three months before time runs out. My family can offer nothing in the way of a decent dowry, nor are they in the peerage. Unless I meet someone who cares not for those things—someone other than Lord Egerton, that is—my fate is sealed."

"What about Lord St. John?" Diana asked with a mischievous grin. "Surely you've taken the first step in securing a courtship with him."

Emma's cheeks felt as if hot coals had been placed against them, and she fell back onto the bed. Last month, she and Julia had taken a shortcut through an alleyway that went past a gaming hell. There, the infamous Lord St. John had stumbled upon them. His reputation was that of a rogue and a notorious gambler. Therefore, he had earned the moniker *Baron of Rake Street*.

As strange as it might have seemed, Emma cared nothing for what others thought of him, for she knew no man who was as handsome as he. In fact, he was so dashing, he could make a woman's mind become the consistency of porridge by simply speaking to her. Yes, his clothing had been rumpled, and his breath smelled of spirits. His jaw may have had more than a day's worth of stubble, but still, her legs had gone weak.

What had caused Emma to toss aside all her training, and every ounce of her sensibility, had been the man's request for a toll to move past him—a kiss as payment. She should have given him the rough side of her tongue, but instead, she had closed her eyes and prepared to pay the toll he requested.

And pay she did.

Rather than being the gallant gentleman he should have been, he had leaned forward and pressed his lips to hers. Her heart soared as she relished that kiss; her entire body becoming so buoyant, she wondered if she would float away.

Julia had not been very pleased with Emma's behavior that day, of course, but Emma did not care. Lord St. John was so handsome, she would do the same again if the opportunity so presented itself.

Smiling at the memory, Emma said, "Though it was a wonderful kiss, one I would hope to have again, he will never court me. He's very handsome, and the women who seek his attention are too many to count. And they're beautiful and far taller than I."

"Your height has nothing to do with anything," Diana said, her hands on her hips and a frown on her face. "You really must stop putting yourself in such a terrible light. You have far more to offer than others taller than you."

"I suppose so," Emma said, though she did not truly agree. Was it not her short stature that drove women such as Abigail Swanson to be so unkind to her?

Diana smiled. "Perhaps we can search for him while we're in Chatsworth on Saturday. Many of the *ton* enjoy spending time in the village during the weekend."

"I would like that," Emma replied with a grin.

The door opened, and Jenny Clifton peeked into the room, her long chestnut braid falling over her shoulder. "You'll be late for our French lesson if you two don't come now."

Emma considered what Diana had suggested as she followed her out of the room. Perhaps she could indeed search out the baron. This time, however, she would not allow him to kiss her as easily as he had during their last encounter. She would forgo any unladylike actions, so she could ask him a single question. Would a baron as handsome and wealthy as Lord St. John consider marrying a woman as poor as she?

<hr />

Andrew, Baron St. John was bankrupt.

Only twenty years of age, he had taken the family fortune left in his control and lost it all in games of chance. What had begun as a weekend streak of luck had turned into many months of drunkenness and gaming until the early hours of the morning.

Very well, he was not yet completely destitute, but it would only be a matter of months before he was. It was not that long ago when one Mr. Johnathan Blackwell, solicitor, had met Andrew in private.

His words had been few but to the point. "I've been warning you for months. The profits on your holdings were dwindling even before your father's death. Unless you make some drastic changes, the estates will fall."

Andrew had felt the weight of the world on his shoulders and an immediate desperation take over him. Desperate times called for desperate measures. Which was why he found himself sitting outside Mrs. Rutley's School for Young Women at this late hour.

That and a request from his mother. Would her old friend, Agnes Rutley, be willing to attend a party hosted by Andrew and bring along two of her most promising students? Something about giving the girls an opportunity to gain experience in such social functions or some other form of ridiculousness.

Andrew had purposefully not sent the invitation, and he would have gotten away with his deception if his mother had not outright inquired into her friend's reply. This compelled him to lie and say that with all he had to do to prepare for the party, it had simply slipped his mind.

He'd been forced to send the invitation late. Doing so, however, had allowed him the opportunity to accomplish a task that was far more important. One that could help him get back on his feet. Or so he hoped. Andrew had added a note that he would like to stop by the school in person.

As he listened to the rain pound on the roof of the carriage, he reached into the pocket of his coat and produced a silver flask. "For courage," he mumbled as he took a rather large swallow, grimacing at the burning sensation that erupted as the rum flowed down his throat.

As his thoughts returned to the present, he added, "And the extra courage I'll need to see this through." He took another long pull and shook his head without thought that he likely resembled an English mastiff after a bath.

Due to his precarious financial situation, he had been preying upon women of means in an attempt to replenish his accounts. Some he had adulated, others—those he had been unable to charm or who were too old to romance—he convinced to invest in fictitious schemes.

One story was the raising of funds for the poor wretches of the rookeries to help orphaned children. What he was doing did not sit well with him. In fact, he had tried to do right. He had sold a small parcel of land and meant to use the funds toward putting his estate to rights. Yet the allure of doubling his money at the gaming tables had been too much to resist. With that money gone and his estate even worse off, Andrew was a man nearing his tether. He either lied to get what he needed or saw everything come crashing down around him.

"If I may, my lord," Hodge, his driver, said when the door to the carriage opened, "you asked me to remind you of my wages. Will they be paid this week?"

Hodge had always been a loyal servant. The shame of being unable to pay him bothered Andrew. Yet how could a baron tell anyone, let alone his driver, the truth?

Andrew smiled and clasped the man on the shoulder. "Not only will they be paid, but you'll see a bonus as well." He paused for dramatic effect. "You know, as soon as my investments clear, I believe it's time for you to receive an increase in pay. Do you not agree?"

Hodge beamed. "Thank you, my lord."

Andrew gave the man's shoulder a tap and smiled, almost believing his own words. "Now, let's see if this Mrs. Rutley has the money I lent her. I'll not be so charitable in the future to those who do not repay on time." The headmistress owed him nothing, but he had to lie and maintain appearances.

That thought nearly made him laugh. Appearance had been quite important to Andrew as of late. He had lied for its sake so much over the last months that he had lost count as to how many stories floated about him amongst the *ton*.

He shook his head. One day, those lies and rumors would return to haunt him.

But that day is not today, he assured himself.

Squaring his shoulders, he approached the portico, knocked on the door, and waited. He had met Mrs. Rutley several years earlier, although he had been drunk at the time. He attempted to conjure up an image of the headmistress, but he remembered very little about her appearance.

The door opened to a rotund woman wearing a warm smile flanked by round, rosy cheeks.

"Mrs. Rutley?" he asked, perplexed. He might not have remembered her appearance well, but she had certainly added on weight. Quite a lot, in fact.

The woman chuckled. "No, my lord. I'm Mrs. Shepherd, the cook."

"As I suspected," he said, donning the smile that rarely failed to earn any woman's trust. Following Mrs. Shepherd into the foyer, he glanced around, seeing no one. Were there not students in residence? "The house is very quiet. Are the girls already abed?"

"That they are, my lord," Mrs. Shepherd replied. Her eyes narrowed. "Locked away securely in their rooms where they are safe." Andrew was unsure how to take this response, but before he could inquire, the cook started down a nearby corridor and added, "Mrs. Rutley's in her office. I'll show you where it is."

He had to admit that he was disappointed with the fact that none of the young ladies were present. Many of the girls, he knew, came from families of lesser means, but rumor said that others were far better off than some of the lesser nobility. To him, the value of a potential bride's dowry was more important than her station.

He had learned from a friend during a game of hazard that the wealthy ones were often sent away for the simple fact their parents wished to rid their home of their children. If this was true, those daughters would likely have a healthy allowance. And many young women in similar situations looked upon the world with sadness, giving him an excuse to comfort them. From there, their purse strings would be within easy reach.

The door to what Andrew assumed was the office was open, and after indicating he was to enter, Mrs. Shepherd walked away. But not before giving him a stern glare. He could almost hear her thoughts. *Baron or not, you'd better be on your best behavior!*

Mrs. Rutley—yes, he remembered her now—stood at a window,

and when she turned, Andrew could not keep from grinning. Although the headmistress was nearing the age of fifty, she was strikingly handsome. With her advanced age, her mind would be slow, making her an easy mark.

"My lord," Mrs. Rutley said, offering him a small curtsy before walking around her desk. "It was an honor to receive the invitation to your party with your letter requesting to speak with me. I've been eagerly awaiting your arrival to learn what you have to say."

Andrew closed the door and turned to focus on the woman before him. He had included in the invitation his interest in speaking to her about a matter that could only be discussed in person. And judging by her smile, like other women, she would not be able to resist his charms.

"The honor is all mine, Mrs. Rutley," he said, taking a step toward her. "Though, I do wonder if a woman with your obvious youthfulness is not actually a student pretending to be the headmistress. Surely, you cannot be Mrs. Rutley." He took her hand in his and kissed her above the knuckles.

"You are too kind," she said. "But I'm afraid I'm much too old to believe you could possibly confuse me with one of my students."

The twinkle in her eye made Andrew stifle a groan. He had misjudged her. She would be far more difficult to seduce than he had first believed. Well, he was not one to surrender easily. He would simply have to resort to his original plan.

"Please, have a seat," Mrs. Rutley said.

Andrew sat in one of the high-back chairs facing the desk. "Mother came to me less than a week ago with such worry, I thought we'd lost another relative." He sighed. "What I learned was she had meant to invite you to our party and had forgotten, as she often does. Though this is quite short notice, I do hope you'll attend."

Mrs. Rutley chuckled. "Helen has always been a bit forgetful," she said as she sat in the chair behind the desk. "But surely you have not agreed to invite the likes of me and my students to one of your parties? I assume the guest list includes members of the aristocracy. I'm just a simple headmistress of a girls' school and, therefore, have a much lower standing."

If Andrew gave his mother the credit, he would likely lose what little footing he had. Therefore, he had to convince this woman that the idea was his. "The truth is, the training you offer the young women who attend your school is renowned, and I would be honored to have you and your students at my home." He leaned forward. "You could extend this invitation to those who are in the greatest need of this kind of experience, perhaps those preparing for the next Season."

He said this with a wink, hoping to draw a smile. Yet none came. Was she made of stone? Though Andrew was not vain, he knew few men could compete with his looks. Perhaps she was far slower of mind than he had come to believe.

"I appreciate your suggestion, my lord, and already have two students in mind." She shifted in her seat, relaxing back in the chair and placing her hands in her lap. "Your letter also spoke of an opportunity you believe might interest me. A business proposition, I assume. If so, I'm curious as to what that may be."

Andrew smiled. The seed he had planted in that correspondence had sprouted into curiosity. Good. Now he would carefully water it. And if all went well, he would see it grow into a healthy crop and then reap a wonderful harvest.

"Indeed, this proposal will be quite beneficial to all who choose to participate," he replied. "You are among the first to whom I am making this offer."

"I'm honored to receive such a distinction, but why me? Although you and I are acquainted through your mother, we certainly cannot be considered friends."

Never had he misjudged a woman so completely. She was confident, straightforward, and sharp of mind—all qualities with which Andrew did not have time to contend.

He had met such women before, and in truth, they frightened him. One young lady in particular came to mind, the daughter of an earl who had the audacity to speak as if her intelligence was greater than his. Her quick wit and sharp tongue had made him concerned for the future of men like himself.

"Mother speaks very highly of you, Mrs. Rutley. I simply wanted a way to repay you for showing her kindness."

A small smile played at the corner of Mrs. Rutley's lips. "An invitation to a party and now a business opportunity? All because I have treated your mother with the kindness friends should show one another? I'm at a loss for words."

Andrew reconsidered. All was not lost. "Excellent," he replied. "This is an opportunity, certainly, though not exactly business."

"Very well, my lord. I'm listening."

"London is growing every day," he continued, maintaining the air of conspiracy. "The population is increasing exponentially, and the streets have become clogged with vendors and traffic. Carriages block the thoroughfares, and angry mobs march through the city, many asking, what about the poor?"

Mrs. Rutley went to speak, but Andrew lifted a hand to forestall her. "The poor are overlooked, Mrs. Rutley. There is no other way to say it. It's up to those of us with means to answer their cries for help. Therefore, we—I, along with those who agree to contribute—are looking to purchase six buildings across London to meet at least one of the needs of the poor."

"But I thought you wished to discuss a business investment," Mrs. Rutley said, frowning. "That is what your letter said."

Andrew gave her his best smile, the one he used to close every agreement he had been able to make thus far. "It is a moral investment, Mrs. Rutley. For every pound you are able to give, a thousand smiles are returned."

This was the point in the negotiations where Andrew would answer numerous questions and await the flood of gratitude for offering such a wonderful opportunity. It was also the moment he had to rein in his conscience. For every lie he told, another brick of his deceit was laid. If he wasn't careful, he would be unable to break himself from the prison he was constructing around himself.

Mrs. Rutley, her posture rigid, offered him a small smile and replied, "It truly is a lovely offer, but sadly, one I'll be unable to afford at this time. The school already donates to several different charities, either in the form of funds or items that can be used by those in need."

"We are speaking of a pittance, a few hundred pounds," he said.

Perhaps pittance was a poor term to use in this case. It was a vast sum, especially to a headmistress, but Andrew had overheard his mother speaking of the wealth this woman possessed. The money was said to have come from successful ventures of the estate and not from the school itself. But either way, from what he understood, she could afford what he was asking and much more.

"A pittance, my lord?" she asked with a raise of an eyebrow.

"Perhaps I am exaggerating just a bit," he conceded, still smiling, although he had to force it to remain. "I admit that it is quite a sum. Yet, isn't the peace of knowing children will not starve, or entire families will have a safe place to live, well worth the sacrifice? Of course, I can accept a small deposit, say twenty pounds? I can then wait to receive the rest if you need time to gather the funds. What matters is that enough money is collected to make the necessary purchases and get started on the project. The sooner that happens, the sooner people will have proper accommodations."

Quiet filled the room as Mrs. Rutley steepled her fingers and brought them to her lips. Andrew held his breath. Surely, she would not decline! He had learned enough about her to know that she had a kind heart, which made for easy prey.

Finally, she pulled out a desk drawer and removed a small box. "As luck would have it, I do happen to have twenty pounds on hand, and this is a very worthy cause. Are you certain you don't mind waiting another day or two for the rest?"

Andrew's eyes widened at the notes she held out to him. "Not at all," he replied as he rose. At one point, he had possessed tens of thousands of pounds and several estates. Now, the sight of a mere twenty made his heart thump with excitement. "We can discuss matters further at the party." He paused. "But please, don't tell Mother. I wish to surprise her once the first building is completed. I'm having it named after her. And if you happen to think of anyone else who would like to invest in such a worthy scheme, please send them in my direction. We cannot have too many benefactors, not when it comes to those in need."

He straightened, doing his best not to snatch the notes from her hand and quickly hiding them away in his pocket.

"I'll be sure not to ruin your surprise," Mrs. Rutley said as she walked around the desk and placed a hand on his arm. "It's a welcoming sight to see lightness appear in such dark times because of men like you."

Bile rose in Andrew's throat. Oh, how he hated when they said such things, for it reminded him of the desperation he was facing, the lies he freely told. The money he was willing to swindle from those who trusted him. But he was desperate, and he had no other means to right his wrongs.

All his schemes included some charitable aspect, so getting caught was less likely. It would be easy enough to claim the plans had fallen apart for one reason or another. That did not mean he had no plan to pay back every benefactor, for he did. In time. This was not how he wished to treat those who trusted him. For now, however, this was his life, and he had to accept it.

He didn't have to like it.

"Very good," he managed to say, unable to look her in the eyes. "I really must be going. And please, don't forget to bring the rest of the money on Saturday if you can."

"You've no need to worry, my lord," she said as she walked him to the door. "I'll not forget."

The foyer was no longer empty. Two young women, likely students if he were to hazard a guess, stood with their heads together. One had tight blonde curls and a pleasant shape many men would have given a second look.

The other was dark-haired, and despite her short stature, she was beautiful. No, that was not the correct term. Exquisite. She had a small, upturned nose, a heart-shaped face, and a hint of red in her cheeks that made his heart skip a beat.

He winked at her, just as he always did when he saw a lovely woman and, without another word, headed out the door. There was no time to concern himself with beautiful blue eyes.

Once outside, he sighed. This was not the life a baron should lead, offering false stories in an attempt to save his own estate.

Reaching into his pocket, he removed a small notebook and a stick of graphite. Entering the name of the headmistress and the sum she had given him, Andrew scanned the rest of the list. Since starting on this path, he had vowed to pay back every person from whom he had taken money. Every penny was accounted for, and once his estate was in order, this way of life would end.

But for now, he had no choice but to continue on as he had. Twenty pounds now and more to come on Saturday. And with the number of guests attending the party—and plenty of wine—his fortune would soon be returned to him.

One bold tale at a time.

CHAPTER 2

After dinner, Emma helped Diana collect the rest of her things from her old room and brought them back to the new. From brush handles decorated with pearls to fine jewelry and dresses made by renowned shops in London, Diana wanted for nothing.

"I believe we'll be the best roommates ever," Diana said. "And although we're already sisters because of the vow we made, I can see us growing even closer." Emma nodded, and Diana smiled. "You've not let go of that hairbrush since you took hold of it. Would you like to keep it?"

Emma looked down in horror at the brush that was clutched in her hand. "Oh no, I don't want it. I was merely admiring the handle. It's very beautiful."

Diana took the brush and snorted. "Father bought this for me, just as he has purchased every other fine gift." She turned the item in her hand and gave a sad shake of her head. "My family appears so perfect, does it not? We have as much money as any noble family, and gifts are delivered every other week. You would think I want for nothing, is that not so?"

A sense of sadness filled Emma. "Until you shared your secret under the tree, I had believed your family the happiest I've ever seen. Still, you have so many wonderful things, why would you not be happy?"

When the young women of the Sisterhood had sworn their oath, each had revealed a secret. Diana's had been that her father was an unscrupulous man, one who hurt her mother by having numerous affairs. Diana had expressed how his behavior tore at her heart. And rightfully so.

"I understand why you would think so," Diana said. "It's what everyone believes. They see me wearing my new dresses and spending exorbitant amounts of money. So, they say to themselves, 'I wish I could be like her, to live her life. Look how content she is. Surely, she suffers from not a single worry in her life.'" She heaved a heavy sigh. "During my time here at the school, I've learned one thing. Rich or poor makes little difference. Sorrow strikes us all and can be found everywhere. Well, except here with you, my friend." She placed the hairbrush in Emma's hand. "I want you to have this."

"Oh, no!" Emma said. "I cannot! It's far too valuable. Plus, will your father not be angry you've given away something he has gifted you?"

Diana laughed. "Father is always angry. I'm sure Mother selected it for me, anyway. And I have several just as ornate as that one. Please, take it or you'll make me sad." She jutted out her lower lip to emphasize her point.

Emma threw her arms around Diana with a laugh. "Very well, I'll keep it," she said as she walked over and placed it on the small vanity table that held what little she owned. "But know that I don't count you as a friend just because you're willing to give me things."

"I'm well aware of why we're friends, Miss Hunter," Diana said with exaggerated haughtiness. "I need someone like you to protect me from the likes of Abigail Swanson!" This had them both laughing until tears leaked from their eyes.

The door opened, and Emma glanced up to see Unity Ancell and Theodosia Renwick enter. The two were inseparable and acted like twins, despite the fact they were unrelated. Both had brown curly hair, high cheekbones, and large brown eyes, but Theodosia was the taller of the two.

"I've the most horrible news, Emma!" Unity said.

Emma's heart began to race. Had her parents brought Lord Egerton here? No, it was far too early for such a call.

"The rumor concerning Mrs. Rutley is true!"

"Which rumor?" Diana asked. "There are so many."

What Diana said was true. Despite how wonderful the headmistress was, certain girls at the school chose to tell tales about her. One said that Mrs. Rutley sold girls into marriage and collected a percentage of the profits from the dowry the suitor received. Another said she left the school at midnight to meet various lovers. Emma, however, believed the stories had been created as an excuse for the others to gossip and therefore paid them little heed.

"You've heard of the Baron of Rake Street, have you not?" Theodosia whispered. "Well, he's currently ensconced in the office with Mrs. Rutley, and at this late hour, they certainly cannot be discussing the weather!"

The memory of the day she had allowed Lord St. John to kiss her bounded into Emma's mind, bringing with it the same warm feelings that intimacy had kindled.

"I'm sure he has a perfectly good explanation as to why he's calling," Emma said. "Ladies, do you not remember what Julia said? We can no longer speculate on idle gossip, especially when it concerns our friends."

Unity sighed. "Yes, you're right. It doesn't matter what they are doing."

"Exactly," Emma said.

"If she's having a romantic tryst with the baron," Theodosia added, "it's none of our concern. And I'm sure it will not include a kiss, either."

Emma worried her bottom lip. Indeed, it was no concern of hers. He had kissed her, yes, but that did not mean they were courting or that he had any designs on her. She might find the baron quite handsome with his chiseled jaw and mysterious dark eyes, but he was a bachelor—and a member of the aristocracy—and therefore free to do as he pleased.

Yet, what harm would it do to see what he and Mrs. Rutley were doing? Just to put the rumors to rest, of course.

"Diana, will you come with me, please?" Emma asked, adding as much disinterest into the request as she could. Which meant little.

The mop of blonde curls bounced when Diana gave a vigorous nod. "You two remain here," she said to Theodosia and Unity. "We'll return with a full report."

At the top of the stairs, Emma pulled Diana by the arm. "We're not going to outright spy, are we? That's much too unladylike. What if we simply pass by her office? If we happen to overhear any conversation, so be it."

"Indeed," Diana said thoughtfully. "And if I got a sudden pain in my foot and needed to rest? That would be a very appropriate excuse to stop wherever that happens."

Smiling, they bounded down the stairs. In the foyer, Emma froze.

Like a hero from a romance novel, Lord St. John came walking toward her. He had several days of stubble growing on his jaw, and his dark wavy hair was as unruly as the rumors said he was. He was tall and handsome, and when his gaze fell on Emma, her legs turned to jelly.

Would he remember her name? When he had spoken it the last time they met, it had sent pleasant shivers down her spine.

What would Mrs. Rutley think if he gathered her in his arms and demanded another kiss? What if he professed his undying love for her?

Sadly, he did neither. She was rewarded, however, with a small smile and a wink that made her head spin.

In a daze, it was not until she heard the echo of the door closing that she returned to reality.

"What are you two doing here?" Mrs. Rutley asked with a raised eyebrow. "I hope you're conducting yourselves with dignity."

"Oh yes, we are," Diana replied. "You see, my foot was hurting. We had no plans to listen in on your conversation with the baron!"

Emma groaned. Now they were in for trouble.

Mrs. Rutley shook her head. "I've been meaning to speak to you about something important, anyway. Lord St. John has invited me to a party on Saturday."

It was as if Emma had been stabbed in the heart. So, the rumors were true! Although she did not know the baron personally—well, except for the impromptu kiss they had shared—a sense of melancholy washed over her. And anger at her headmistress. Did Mrs. Rutley not see that she, Emma, admired Lord St. John?

Oh, how could her headmistress do something so dastardly? Plus, she was twice his age! What was she doing chasing men so young?

"Emma?" Mrs. Rutley said, concern filling her tone. "What's wrong?"

"Nothing. I'm well." The words were forced, but she could do little about that.

Mrs. Rutley's lips thinned. "It does no one any good to lie, not to your friends but more importantly, not to your headmistress. Now, what problem has you so upset?"

With a heavy heart, Emma sighed. "He may not be a man with a wonderful reputation, but I've become... enamored with Lord St. John. But now, it seems you've caught his eye. Ruth was right. He sent a carriage for you last month, did he not? I did not want to believe it at first, but now I can see that she spoke the truth."

Now, Mrs. Rutley's lips nearly disappeared. "First of all, the carriage did indeed belong to the estate of Lord St. John. And yes, it did come for me."

The knife in Emma's heart drove in deeper. Why did fate deign to have her meet a gentleman who stole her heart only to lose him to someone else? It just was not fair!

"Come with me to my office, and I'll explain. Not that I should have to, mind you, but I'll do so, nonetheless."

With heavy steps, Emma followed Mrs. Rutley to the office. There, she and Diana took a seat in the chairs in front of the desk.

"Helen, Lady St. John, is the baron's mother and has been a very good friend of mine for many years. She wrote to me last month, asking me to call to her house and was kind enough to send a carriage to collect me."

Emma sat up, hope filling her. "Then you have no romantic interest in him? In the baron, that is?"

Mrs. Rutley laughed. "I've warned you about rumors, Emma. Do you truly believe everything you are told? Surely you have learned that most of what you hear about others is false."

Emma shook her head. How silly of her to believe such terrible gossip! Julia would have given her a terrible tongue lashing if she had been there!

"Good," Mrs. Rutley said. "Now that we have cleared that up, we can move on to other, more important topics. This party to which I've been invited, I'm to bring two guests. Lady St. John thought it would be the perfect opportunity for two students of my choosing to practice what they've learned here. Therefore, I've chosen the two of you to join me."

What had first appeared to be a disappointing evening had become one of the best! Emma's mind raced as she considered what she would wear and how she would style her hair. Then there was the matter of Lord St. John. Would they be given the opportunity to speak? Would he remember her?

Would he kiss her again?

"I chose the two of you because of how dedicated you are to your studies," Mrs. Rutley said. "I pray you'll not disappoint me." Why had she looked at Emma when she said this?

Emma felt a blush creep into her cheeks. "No, Mrs. Rutley. I promise to be on my best behavior."

Diana echoed her.

When they returned to their room, Unity and Theodosia had been joined by Jenny.

"Did you see him?" Unity asked. "What did he say?"

"Is it true about Mrs. Rutley?" Jenny asked as she pulled at her braid, a strange habit she had whenever she was upset or nervous. Or excited.

Emma sighed. "The baron's hosting a party, and Diana and I will be attending."

This was followed by a squeal and a barrage of questions. Emma and Diana took turns answering.

"But isn't the baron a known rake?" Jenny asked, frowning and giving her braid another firm yank. "Are you not worried?"

Emma could not help but grin. "Oh, he's quite mischievous, I'll admit. That's why he winked at me when he was leaving. But it's nothing more than a bit of banter. And as to worrying? You seem to have forgotten that Mrs. Rutley is a very wise woman. Why would she allow me to attend the party of a man who was a true scoundrel?"

Andrew wondered if the cool days of autumn would never come as he strolled through the gardens of Apple Green Estate. The air was unusually warm in the bright sunshine on this Friday afternoon.

Or perhaps it was his nerves wreaking havoc as he forced himself to listen to Miss Hestia Morton and her simpering voice that made the hairs on the nape of his neck stand on end. She was not much to look at, either, with her overly sharp nose and eyes that were too close together. Even her hair was unsightly, for it reminded him of the color of dirty straw. The word lovely could never be used to describe Miss Morton, not in his opinion. Perhaps some man out there would see her as such, but he most certainly did not.

Her father had insisted on arranging this encounter, the second in as many weeks. The only reason Andrew had agreed was because of the wealth the man possessed. Perhaps it was unfair of him to use her in such a dastardly fashion, but he had little choice.

Again with the desperation, he chastised himself. Well, he was who he was.

"When Papa said he had given you permission to call on me again," Miss Morton was saying, "I admit that I was quite pleased." They came to a stop beneath the shade of a tree. "I knew then that you found me suitable."

Andrew smiled as her chaperone appeared in the corner of his eye. She had discreetly turned away, allowing them a bit of privacy. "Miss Morton... Miss Hestia, if I may?"

Miss Morton's cheeks went red as she nodded. "I would be honored to have you address me by my Christian name."

"The honor's all mine, I assure you," he continued. "And I would not say that you are suitable. No, I believe the correct term I would use is 'perfect'." Her blush deepened, and he leaned in to whisper,

"Would it be too bold if I were to utilize the word 'beautiful' as a way to describe you?"

Lying had become second nature to him by this point in his life. Not a skill he was proud of. He had not enjoyed his penmanship lessons as a child but did them out of necessity, nonetheless. That was all this was to him—a necessity.

To him, beauty came in the form of the dark-haired young woman he had encountered at the school. Now, there was a lovely woman, one with whom Andrew would not think twice about having a conversation. Or a kiss.

Miss Morton let out a sigh, breaking him from his thoughts. Her eyes held that dreaminess he had hoped to accomplish today. Now, he would see if his time with her had not been in vain.

Taking a step back, he said, "Two nights ago, Lady Florence nearly begged me to call on her."

"I'm not acquainted with her," Miss Morton said with a frown. "How did you respond to her request?"

Andrew paused to allow worry to settle over her. Soon, she was smoothing the skirts of her yellow dress and adjusting her gloves. When he had seen her suffer enough, he said, "That although I'm not yet courting anyone, there is one I am quite interested in pursuing. Once I have completed my negotiations with several investors in London, of course." He took a step closer. "Just think what the two of us can do if we were to do business—*or whatever*—together."

Miss Morton clasped her hands in front of her. "I'll certainly consider what you asked me concerning the investment, my lord." A frown crossed her lips. "I must admit, I'm a bit worried. When I mentioned to Papa about the new housing for war orphans in London —just in passing, of course—he said he hadn't heard anything about it."

That had been the particular tale he had told Miss Morton. A network of new buildings was being constructed for children who had been orphaned by the ongoing war with France. He had hoped to convince her that she could do her part by investing in an organization with many prominent members of society.

Andrew nodded sadly. "Yes, many men who are not involved in

charity work say such things." He made a point of glancing behind her. "And that small bag your chaperone holds. Does it contain the funds I requested?" His heart was pounding. The money he so desperately needed was within his grasp. He could make no mistakes now. "The transaction is nearly complete and yet you hesitate? Do you not trust me?"

"It's not that..."

Andrew took her by the elbow and led her behind a nearby hedge.

"My lord? What are you—"

Before she could finish, Andrew pulled her in his arms and pressed his lips to hers. She gave little resistance and was soon returning the kiss with as much eagerness as he gave. When he pulled away, she let out a small sigh.

Upon hearing footsteps, he took a step back just as the chaperone came around the corner, her dark eyes that matched her hair taking in both of them.

"Well, thank you for the lovely stroll," Andrew said as if the kiss had not taken place. "Unfortunately, I must go. I promised Lady Florence I would call if prior arrangements failed. After all, I must put others before myself."

He began to walk away, and as sure as the sun rose every morning, Miss Morton reached out and grasped him by the arm.

"The housing for them, my lord?" she asked. "That will be the return for my investment?"

"No," Andrew replied, "it will be far more. It's the peace you'll have knowing that small children will have food and a warm bed. Charity is not for everyone, my dear Miss Morton. But if you do not trust me, then you keep your money. No, I insist. I'll find someone else who cares for others before herself. Good day to you."

"No, wait! Miss Trudeau, bring me my bag," Miss Morton said before signaling to her chaperone. A moment later, she placed the small silk sack in his hands. Its weight said it held more than just money. "It contains every farthing I have as well as several pieces of jewelry you can sell. And when you speak to the others, tell them that Miss Hestia Morton pledges all she has."

With a sigh, Andrew pressed the bag against his chest where his heart was located. "I'll tell them that you are a lady of charity and dignity, Miss Morton. Sleep well knowing that so many children will be safe because of your generosity."

The chaperone rolled her eyes, but Andrew pretended not to notice. What that woman thought of him made no difference whatsoever. Only Miss Morton's opinion mattered. At least for the time being.

"I'll send word soon enough," he continued. "Don't despair if it takes me several months to contact you again. I must travel to foreign lands and assist my fellow countrymen. Just know that in the face of danger, with my life at stake, I'll think of you when I need hope."

"Oh, my lord," Miss Morton breathed, placing a hand on his arm. She stood on the tips of her toes and kissed his cheek. "Let that be a reminder of me when trouble arises."

Andrew nodded and, with a quick smile, hurried away. Excitement coursed through his veins as he entered the house and made his way toward the front door. How much money had the daughter of a well-to-do wool merchant given him?

Once outside, he poured the contents of the bag into his hand. A quick count said there was nearly two hundred pounds, several gold rings with fine emeralds, and a ruby necklace. Pulling out his note-book, he made a quick note of what he had received. As the guilt gnawed at him, Andrew made an extra notation below her name. "Reimburse quickly." Removing a single note, he put the rest in the pocket of his coat and made his way to the carriage where Hodge waited.

"I forgot to give this to you earlier." Andrew handed the driver the note. "Your wages plus a small bonus."

Hodge's eyes went wide. "You're too kind, my lord," he said. "Thank you for your generosity. Do you wish to return home now?"

"You know," Andrew said as he placed a foot on the step of the carriage door, "I'm feeling rather lucky today. Take me to Rake Street. I would like to get in a few rounds of hazard before the party tomorrow."

He stepped into the carriage, and when the door closed, he let out a sigh. Although he was happy to have secured the money, a small twinge of guilt still pulled at him. He hated that he was forced to lie, and tricking others was not who he truly was. Yet somehow, he had to right the many wrongs he had done before anyone—especially his mother—learned the truth.

There were those in London who would not hesitate to give him a proper walloping. Not over a charitable story he had told, for Londoners would have caught him out as a scoundrel the moment he opened his mouth. No, while there, he had borrowed money from men far more unscrupulous than he. And promptly lost it at the gaming tables.

But London was faraway. His concern now was focused on the local women such as Miss Morton and others as trusting as she. Of course, if they learned he had hoodwinked them, they would likely want to get in a good hit as well.

Yes, he had chosen to use Miss Morton, and that did play into his guilt. But it was the hope he had given her that they could possibly share in something more than money that made it far worse. His intention was not to hurt her, but he had to do whatever he could to save his estate. Once he did that, he would put a stop to this outlandish behavior.

All he needed was one good night of dicing to double the amount he had. Then he could pay the staff and avoid the worry in his mother's eyes. Andrew longed for the day he could stop with the games of chance and the lies and honor the promise to himself that all would be repaid.

As the carriage moved, he leaned back against the bench, his mind on the party tomorrow. There would be plenty of women in attendance to entice with his clever quips and get more money.

He found his thoughts returning to his visit to the school and the dark-haired girl who had caught his eye. She was shorter than most, but her beauty made up for that. He had a nagging feeling he had seen her somewhere before, perhaps even spoken to her, but he could not remember where.

Then an idea came to him. What if she came from a wealthy family? Would she be one of the two Mrs. Rutley invited to attend the party with her? If so, he would find out what he could about her. To have both beauty and wealth would be fine qualities, indeed.

When he had winked, her lovely blush had not escaped his notice. Neither did her plump lips that begged to be kissed. Andrew had no doubt that he could easily kiss her a thousand times and enjoy every moment of it.

He grinned as he thought of the many young women at the school. Perhaps his mother had been wise in asking that Mrs. Rutley bring some of the students. In fact, Andrew could throw more parties, asking the headmistress to invite different girls each time. The possibilities of the small fortunes he would acquire were endless!

Reaching for his flask, he took a heavy drink. The future was bright with promise, and soon, his estate would be returned to its former glory.

And if the dark-haired girl was part of that plan... With a sigh, he leaned back and allowed her image to fill his mind.

CHAPTER 3

Laughter, cries of victory, and curses of defeat filled the air in the gaming hell. The Rake Street Gaming Hall was located in an alleyway off the main street of the village with a spattering of rundown taverns around it. Although the true name of the street was Drake Street, it had earned the name Rake Street long before Andrew was born, due to the type of establishments the area offered.

When the same moniker was ascribed to Andrew, he found himself reconsidering his actions more than once. Who wanted to be known as a chronic gambler who lost more often than he won?

On Rake Street, if a man had the funds, he was not turned away. With little in the way of entertainment so far from London, the nobility took sport where they could find it. Which made the establishment one of the few places where those with titles met without concern that the man they might be betting against was a cobbler. Although, the latter rarely remained at the hell for long. Once a man's funds ran out, he was encouraged to leave. At times, forcefully.

Although men were the majority at Rake Street, a woman from time to time also could be found there. Most were prostitutes plying their trade, but there were a few who had a knack for one game or another.

The problem was few men, especially gentlemen, wished to take money from such opponents. Those of the feminine gender who won received far less attention than those who lost, for few men were willing to admit they had lost to a woman.

Andrew had come this evening with the sole purpose of having a few drinks and going home. "No gaming tonight," he had promised himself. He was strong enough to resist; he was certain.

Yet with each cheer, each bout of laughter, and so many men bragging about their wondrous luck, his resistance to the games began to wane. It was not long before his drunken mind rationalized that tonight would be the night he would emerge the winner. Then, he would see that every person he had wronged was compensated.

It was the familiar exhilaration, the expectation of success, the certainty of winning, that had made him stumble his way to the tables more than an hour ago. And like so many times before, his plans had gone awry.

With his head aching, heart racing, and worry knotting his stomach, Andrew watched as another baron, Lord Thrup, sent his dice tumbling across the table. Upon seeing the dice stop to reveal a total of nine, Andrew let out a choked groan.

"It appears you lose again, St. John," Lord Thrup said as he took the last of Andrew's money. "Two hundred pounds and some wonderful jewelry for my wife. I do thank you." He was far too smug in Andrew's opinion.

His plans had been to pay the servants' wages with the small fortune he had received from the simpering Miss Morton. Then, he'd double, or even treble, the money he received from the head mistress. Over the past nine hours, however, he had watched it all slowly slip away. How did one go from possessing enough to pay a month's worth of expenses to being broke just before sunrise the next day?

Anger raged inside him as Lord Thrup counted the notes, a smirk on his lips. With a nod, he turned and walked away to join a small group of friends, leaving Andrew to agonize alone.

Two older gentlemen sat at a nearby table laughing, playing a card game Andrew did not recognize. Well, he was in no mood to learn a new game.

Rising from his chair, Andrew shrugged on his coat. In the past, the proprietor had been willing to extend him credit when his funds ran out, but after too many late repayments and Andrew's propensity to argue, that privilege had been denied.

"St. John," a familiar voice called out.

Andrew turned as Henry, the Earl of Walcott, joined him. A silver-haired man of sixty, Lord Walcott, like Andrew, took great joy in spending time at the gaming tables. Andrew had been acquainted with him for many years. It had been only in the last few months that he had been playing at the gaming hell. Unlike Andrew, however, the earl often won.

"Leaving so soon?" Lord Walcott asked. "Did the dice not fall in your favor?"

Andrew pulled his flask from his pocket and undid the cap. "I'm afraid not," he replied, forcing a grin. "But after ten straight days of winning, I suspected that my luck would eventually dry up." He threw his head back and took a long drink from the flask. When he returned his gaze to Lord Walcott, he was surprised to find a look of pity on the man's face.

"Maybe it's time you began a new hobby," the earl suggested. "Besides, the Season is almost upon us. Is it not time for you to begin the arduous process of searching for a bride?" He lowered his voice and elbowed Andrew. "That should occupy your time quite well. Though, you don't have to wait that long if you choose someone sooner." He barked a laugh.

Between the rumors of his love of gaming and his rakish ways—oh, very well. Perhaps they were not all rumors! Regardless, Andrew had hoped, like his peers, he could postpone the inevitable. He would have been quite content to wait at least another five years before marrying. A man needed time to enjoy himself and not be burdened with a wife. But now, more than ever, he needed a bride who came with a sizable dowry. And soon.

"You're a very wise man, Walcott," Andrew said with a wry chuckle before taking another sip from his flask. "The issue is that the available young women in this area come from families with little means. But alas, unless I marry the daughter of a servant or one of those who attend the girls' school, I have no choice but to wait until the Season begins."

Hearing himself speak the words aloud caused his worry to increase tenfold. Waiting to find the right bride was not what concerned him, however. Rather, it was a question of whether his estate would survive until then. Who would be willing to give his daughter's hand in marriage when he, Andrew, had nothing on which to support her? His title could only get him so far.

"Some of those young women who attend the school come from minor nobility, you know," Lord Walcott said.

"So I've heard," Andrew replied. "I admit I was surprised when I learned that a handful of the girls come from wealthy merchant families. The problem I see is that they send their daughters away in hopes of landing a titled husband."

Lord Walcott laughed. "I would say that is likely true. But can you blame them? Have you considered that by marrying one of those young women, you may just have an answer to your money troubles?"

"I'll have you know that my finances are just fine," Andrew snapped. How dare this man make statements about the state of Andrew's financial situation! What business was it of his? What's more, how did he know? "My investments grow stronger every month, and my coffers are full to overflowing. As a matter of fact, I have several ventures awaiting my approval that will only further increase my wealth."

"Of course, your estate is strong," Lord Walcott replied, although his tone said he did not believe a word Andrew had said.

And why should he? Andrew had blathered like a whining child!

"Well, I have matters to which I must attend. See you tonight?"

Andrew could only nod. His mother had invited the earl to the party since he was an old family friend. Andrew hoped he would remain quiet about Andrew's finances. This begged him to question how many other guests were speculating about his current fiscal standing. What if others were discussing the various stories he had been telling as well? Were there angry husbands now searching for him, realizing their wives had been swindled?

Andrew's confidence faltered as he considered that perhaps his plans had not been as brilliant as he had first thought.

Sighing, he turned his gaze on a woman in a green dress with a neckline that exposed too much bosom. He was well aware of how she made her money. She was speaking to a man Andrew recognized as a footman from a marquess' estate. If memory served him correctly, the footman was married.

For all his rakish ways, Andrew held on to at least some sense of dignity. If a woman was spoken for, he kept away. There were some societal rules, no matter how desperate he was, that he did not violate.

Frustrated that his crumbling estate was a topic of conversation amongst his peers, Andrew exited the hell, his pockets empty. With dejected steps, he walked to where Hodge waited by the carriage.

"Coin, milord?" a voice asked from the shadows, causing Andrew to jump.

A man sat against the wall in clothing so tattered that Andrew wondered how it held together. With a dirty face covered in stubble and many missing teeth, the man reached an old, gnarled hand to Andrew. "Mercy?"

What sort of troubles could this beggar have possibly endured to end up begging for coin in an alley? Did he, too, once have an estate in trouble? Had he chosen to engage in similar activities as Andrew, gambling away all he owned for the hope of landing a great deal of wealth? Or had he taken a more honorable stance, chosen not to swindle others, and *that* had led him to where he was today?

Reaching into his pocket, Andrew produced a few coins. It was not much, but perhaps the man would put it to a better use than Andrew had planned.

"Thank ye, milord," the old man whispered as he received the coins.

Hurrying to the carriage, and without a word to the driver, Andrew pulled himself into the vehicle and dropped onto the bench. Propping his head against the wall, he forced himself to think of the days and weeks ahead.

The start of the Season was too far away to wait to find a bride, which meant he would now be forced to look for one locally. The problem was that with the various rumors circulating about him and the dozen or so women he had wooed as of late, the pickings would be sparse.

There was Mrs. Rutley and her school. Perhaps that old fool Walcott was right. Was there a student at the school whose family was aching to tie themselves to a titled family? If so, maybe he could fulfill his needs while at the same time fulfilling theirs.

Yes, that would make it a perfect match.

Light was breaking over the horizon when the carriage pulled up in front of Redborrow Estate. Andrew stifled a yawn as he entered the foyer, looking forward to dropping into bed. Then he paused at the sight of his mother waiting at the bottom of the stairs, her usually carefully coiffed graying chestnut hair hanging down to her waist in long waves. Her arms were crossed over her dressing gown, and her face said she had been waiting for him for many hours.

He had always adored his mother and would have words with anyone who spoke against her. And he had. One night at the gaming hell, a man had suggested that Andrew should wager his mother. Andrew had become so enraged that he had not realized his fist had connected with the man's nose until he heard the man's agonizing wail and saw the flowing blood. He likely had broken it. But Andrew did not care. The man had it coming to him with such talk!

Andrew and his mother had always had a close relationship, but that had changed as of late. There was no doubt who was at fault—he was. If only she knew that he was doing all he could to right the wrongs, in the only way he knew how.

"Andrew," she said through a clenched jaw, "why must you spend your nights at such an establishment?"

So, she knew where he had gone. He should not have been surprised. "Mother?" he asked, offering her his best smile and most innocent look as she walked toward him. "I have no idea what you mean. I've been with Lord—"

His mother grimaced and pulled away. "Your breath reeks of alcohol. And don't think I have not heard the wagging tongues of the *ton* and how much time you spend playing games of chance. Do not lie to me, for I know exactly how you have been spending your time."

"The *ton* spreads rumors simply to keep their lips moving," Andrew said with a forced laugh. "Surely you don't believe them."

"I know very well the condition of this estate, Andrew," his mother snapped. "We're in near ruin."

Andrew's heart froze. How could she have known? The accountant would not have spoken to her, not after Andrew had threatened to move his accounts elsewhere if the man breathed a word to anyone—especially his mother.

"Running from your problems will do nothing to solve them, my son."

"Again, more rumors spread by those who are jealous," he replied with a wave of his hand. "I really must get to bed. I'm exhausted." He went to move past, but her voice stopped him.

"The gardeners came to me this afternoon. They say they have not yet been paid."

"Such impatient men," Andrew said, a foot on the bottom step and his back to her. "They know very well that Monday is when the staff receives their wages."

"According to them, they have not been paid in three weeks. I've also heard the servants whispering very much the same. Don't lie to me, Andrew. Have you lost *all* the money?"

Turning, Andrew looked at his mother. If he told her the truth, that he had indeed lost everything, it would crush her. Therefore, he decided to do what he did best. He lied.

"They're right, Mother. I've not paid them, but not for the reasons you believe. There was a mistake in the packets, a mistake I made. I informed the gardeners of this and even offered them a bonus for their patience."

When his mother looked away, guilt tore through Andrew. Oh, how he hated lying to her! But if he wished to protect her, he had no choice.

"Then I'll inform the others that all will be worked out by Monday," she said in a voice he had to strain to hear.

"You see, all is well and will remain so," Andrew said, stifling another yawn before giving her a quick kiss on the cheek. "Now, I must get some sleep if I'm to be refreshed for the party this evening. And please, don't worry so much. It will only make you ill, and I would hate for that to happen." At least he had told her one truth.

Once in his room, he closed the door and heaved a heavy sigh. There was no doubt he would need a bride. And soon. Hopefully, tonight he would find someone suitable, one with a sizable dowry. Perhaps he could get an advance before Monday, so the servants would not create an uprising and walk away from their positions. If that were to happen, everyone would know the rumors were true and that his estate was indeed in ruins. *That* he could not allow. For his mother's sake as much as his.

The carriage trundled down the road toward Redborrow Estate, Emma sitting beside Diana and Mrs. Rutley on the bench opposite. Emma wrung her white-gloved hands in her lap. The week had been fraught with worry, excitement, and every other emotion possible. This was the first party she would attend as a woman, for as Julia had often reminded her, she was no longer a girl. That knowledge did little to ease her shattered nerves, however.

Diana had allowed her to choose one of her dresses, as Emma had nothing worthy of a party given by a baron. After spending a day modifying the bottom hem, she now wore the lovely cerulean blue gown made of the finest muslin with far too many buttons down the back. Intricate white lace hung to a point at the middle of her back and lined the hem of the puffed sleeves. Never had she worn anything so marvelous in her life!

"I saw you received a letter from your parents yesterday," Mrs. Rutley said, breaking Emma from her thoughts. "I presume all is well?"

Emma nodded. "Mother says they are very much looking forward to January when they will collect me, so we may travel to London."

The truth was, Emma was frightened out of her slippers, for the letter was a reminder of her future with the man to whom she was betrothed. She had never considered she would have the opportunity to go to London, but because of Lord Egerton's position, he had insisted.

"Lord Egerton," Mrs. Rutley said as if she had read Emma's thoughts. "I'm sure he is looking forward to you completing your schooling, so he can marry you. Have your thoughts on the matter changed?"

Emma jutted out her chin. "No, they have not," she said. "I have no desire to marry such an old man. Oh, why can I not find a man willing to court me and ask for my hand before they arrive? It happened with Julia. She was meant to marry Lord Howe, but in the end, she fell in love and married a duke. Can the same not happen to me?"

Mrs. Rutley sighed. "Julia's situation was far different from any I have witnessed before. I must admit, I doubt we'll see a repeat anytime soon. It's that rare."

Emma's heart dropped. Mrs. Rutley was the wisest woman she knew. If she believed Emma's chances were nil, it was the truth.

"Besides," the headmistress added, "even if a man came forward hoping to court you, do you believe I could allow you to do so given the fact that you're already spoken for?"

"I don't mean any disrespect," Diana chimed in, "but you allowed the duke to call on Julia, even though her parents had already chosen a husband for her. Surely you can extend the same privilege to Emma?"

Bless Diana for always speaking her mind.

The carriage slowed and came to a stop. "Again, those were different circumstances," Mrs. Rutley said. "Julia did not reveal that they were courting until well after the fact. If I had known beforehand, I would have put an immediate stop to it. But what can I do when an arrangement is made without my knowledge?" Her eyes had a strange twinkle as she said the last. "Now, remember that your behavior tonight must be impeccable. You not only represent yourselves, but you also represent the school and your parents."

"Yes, Mrs. Rutley," Emma and Diana said in unison as the door opened, and a footman waited to offer them a hand to step from the carriage.

Redborrow Estate was a grand house with gray brick and white-trimmed windows. It had a high-pitched, sloped roof, a generous portico, and a manicured front garden. At least a half dozen carriages lined the drive, and as soon as theirs pulled away, another took its place.

Emma followed Mrs. Rutley to the portico, through the front door, and into a foyer filled with hushed whispers. She could not help but smile. Never had she seen such a wonderful array of gowns of golds, blues, reds, and greens. The handful of women there displayed lovely hairstyles held with delicate pins or extravagant combs. Emeralds, rubies, and diamonds set in lavish jewelry sparkled in the light from the hundreds of candles in the extravagant crystal chandelier above them.

An equal number of men stood near them, all adorned in fine suits that had been carefully brushed and shoes polished to a sheen.

Emma searched for the baron but could not see him, much to her dismay.

"Ladies," Mrs. Rutley said, "allow me to introduce you to the baroness, Lady St. John. This is Miss Emma Hunter and Miss Diana Kendricks, and they are so very pleased to have been invited."

Emma's heart skipped a beat. This was the baron's mother. It would do Emma well if she impressed her.

Lady St. John was of the same age as Mrs. Rutley with silver mixed with her dark hair. She had likely turned many heads in her youth with her slender nose and high cheekbones. Emma had no doubt that even in her advanced years, she still drew more than one man's gaze.

"I'm so pleased you came," Lady St. John said. "Agnes has told me much about you both."

"Thank you for extending an invitation," Emma said. "You have a lovely home, and I—"

Her words were cut off by a deep voice. "My friends, I apologize for the delay."

Emma turned with the rest of the guests toward the staircase and nearly fell against Diana. Lord St. John was descending the stairs, wearing an impeccable dark-blue coat and tight-fitting breeches. His face no longer was stubbled, and his hair was now carefully brushed. Never had he looked more handsome. When he stopped midway and brushed back the lone dark curl from his brow, Emma thought she would faint.

"I received a letter an hour ago from Lord Montague, who, as many of you know, has been residing in Africa."

Many in the crowd nodded and murmured agreement. But why had Lady St. John pinched the bridge of her nose?

"Although he wished to be here with us this evening, he extends his regrets that he'll be unable to attend. I realize many of you were looking forward to hearing the many anecdotes he was to share, but, alas, the negotiations with the rulers in the Cape Colony have not gone well. The French grow in power as Britain wavers on the brink of defeat. In fact, it's why he has requested my aid in this matter. You, my friends, shall be the first to know that, come January, I'll set sail for that country to give what aid I can."

As those around them spoke words of encouragement and praise, Emma leaned closer to Diana and whispered, "You see? He's not a rake but rather a man of adventure. And to think he'll go all the way to Africa to help in special negotiations!"

Emma had always wished to travel, to see foreign lands, and experience new customs. And if given the opportunity to go anywhere meant she would not have to marry Lord Egerton, that would only sweeten the situation. For a moment, thoughts of marriage to Lord St. John crept into her mind.

Together they would set sail to the continent, visiting the lavish houses of the nobility of Europe. After that, they would go to the Orient and meet one of their great emperors. Perhaps they would even travel all the way to the Americas!

She was so caught up in her thoughts that she started when Diana whispered, "Emma, it's our turn!"

With wide eyes, Emma realized that everyone was filing down a long corridor just past the staircase. How long had she been standing there lost in her own imagination? Quite a long while since they would be among the last, given their lack of title.

When it was their turn to enter the ballroom, Emma could not help but gape at the luxurious surroundings. Stark-white walls with gilt trim surrounded tall, thin mirrors reflecting the light of a dozen large chandeliers. Eight recessed archways, also mirrored, lined the walls, each topped with gilt-framed paintings of colorful flower arrangements in bronze and silver vases. Gilded patterns even lined the otherwise white domed ceiling.

Music rose from a far corner where a small orchestra played a pleasant tune. The guests made their way to various tables set up with a variety of refreshments. It was not long before the hushed tones rose to normal levels and then to peals of laughter.

"I suggest we enjoy a sip of wine," Mrs. Rutley said. "And I do mean a sip. It does no young lady any good to become intoxicated at any time, but especially not at a party."

Emma and Diana nodded as they took a glass from a passing liveried footman. Despite her short stature, not a single person gave Emma a second glance, much to her pleasure. Perhaps it was only she who was obsessed with this deficiency.

They followed Mrs. Rutley to a place on the far wall to observe those in the middle of the room.

Emma could not help but search out Lord St. John again. She soon found him talking to a young lady and an older woman Emma suspected was the girl's mother, for she appeared an older version of her daughter. Both had the same shade of golden-blonde hair, although the mother had streaks of gray in hers. They also had similar heart-shaped faces and pouty lips that any man would find attractive.

The younger woman laughed at something the baron had said, and Emma felt her jaw tighten. She could recognize an insipid laugh! She straightened her back in hopes that he would notice her.

"Your back will crack if you stretch much more," Diana teased. "Are you looking for someone in particular? Perhaps a certain baron?"

"I see him, but he does not see me," Emma replied. "It's times like these that I truly wish I were taller."

"Nonsense! Your height makes little difference to anyone. It's your beauty that will catch his attention. None of these other women can compare to you."

Emma's cheeks heated. "Thank you," she said, a surge of confidence rushing through her. Their conversation turned to the various fashions of the other guests.

"Can you imagine wearing so many ruffles?" Diana whispered as one older woman walked past them, the ruffles on her gown making her seem twice as wide as she was tall.

Emma laughed. "No, but I do love the blue color of the fabric."

Lady St. John returned to speak with Mrs. Rutley once more, and the headmistress turned and said, "I would like you to remain here. I must go for a short time. If you do need to go anywhere, you are not to do so alone. Is that clear?"

Emma and Diana voiced their agreement, and Mrs. Rutley walked away, Lady St. John at her side.

"Remaining here is far too boring," Diana said. "Let's walk over to the refreshment table. Perhaps we can overhear something of interest on our way."

Indeed, as they circled the crowd, Emma overheard a gentleman speaking to another about his wife and her "tendency to complain the night away." Another man was boasting about a tryst he had with a woman with such detail that a flush of embarrassment washed over Emma.

Yet it was the young woman and her mother Emma had seen speaking with the baron earlier that caused her to stop.

"I don't care what you want," the older woman was saying. "The baron will look at no woman without a sizable dowry."

"But Mother," the younger replied with a soft whimper, "what if he's different? Mary said there is a new generation of men who wish to marry for love and care little for wealth."

"I'm sorry, Constance, but a man such as Lord St. John will only marry a young lady equal to his station. As much as it would please both of us, that woman is not you. I'm sorry."

Well, that sealed her fate. What Constance's mother said was true, and it spoke volumes to Emma's situation. She was doomed to marry Lord Egerton, who was far too old to be interested in a dowry. She should have been pleased to become a viscountess, but even that could not ease her dismay.

Why would Lord St. John even look her way when her parents could offer him nothing? He was like every other man—interested only in what he could gain through a marriage of convenience. Oh, how cruel fate was!

Diana signaled to Emma to join her along the wall. As Emma lowered herself onto one of the chairs, the sense of dejection increased. All she wanted to do was leave!

"What's wrong?" Diana asked. "What has made you so sad? Is it because the baron has yet to speak with you? Don't worry. I'm sure he'll come by soon enough. He is the host, after all."

"No, he's likely never to notice me," Emma replied. "I overheard a woman speaking to her daughter, and what she said confirmed my worst fears. I'm far too poor for Lord St. John to even consider me as one he would call upon, let alone marry. All I can do now is resign myself to the fact that I'll never marry for love." She sighed. "At least I will no longer be poor."

Diana grasped Emma's hand. "You don't know for certain that Lord St. John has no interest in you or that he only wishes to marry a wealthy woman. Perhaps he is more interested in finding a lovely wife."

Emma snorted in a most unladylike fashion. "That's not the way of things. Nothing will ever change for someone like me." Her gaze fell on Lord St. John, who was speaking to a simpering blonde woman. "Look at the lady with whom he speaks now. She wears the latest fashion, and the ring on her finger is likely worth more than my father receives in a year. I cannot compete with someone like her."

"Having money changes nothing," Diana said. "Look at me. Next year, I'll be returning home to begin the arduous process of entertaining possible suitors, but I don't wish to do that. I want to find a gentleman in my own way and experience this love I've heard and read so much about."

The baron walked away from the blonde woman, and Emma let out a sigh. "I don't care what you say. If my father were rich, or if he made good investments, life would be so different. My story would not be filled with sorrow but happiness, instead."

"Oh?" Diana asked with raised brows. "And how different do you truly believe your life would be? Tell me as if it were that way now." She said the last with a mischievous smile.

"That's silly," Emma said.

"It is not," Diana replied firmly. "Is that not how many dreams become reality? By speaking of them as if they were true? Go on, tell me about this wonderful life you lead."

Emma turned to face her friend. "My house is the largest within twenty miles and the envy of all the *ton*," she said, picturing the wonderful manor house she would own. "My father makes his fortune in mining, and three years ago, he purchased a fleet of ships that he docks in Dover, so he could begin a hearty shipping trade. He owns farms, hotels, inns. There's nothing in which he does not have some sort of investment. Come this Season, I'll be adorned in the finest jewels, and every eligible bachelor will attempt to woo me because I'll have the largest dowry in all of England!"

"How wonderful!" Diana said. "Now, Miss Hunter, you must have a dozen suitors vying for your attention given these facts."

"A dozen?" Emma scoffed. "Why, I had a dozen just last week!"

In her excitement, her voice had risen to the point that several people nearby glanced in their direction. Then her heart leapt into her throat when a figure loomed over her.

"Miss Hunter," Lord St. John said. Oh, but he had the most handsome smile! "Where have you been hiding? I've been searching all evening for you."

CHAPTER 4

A Lord Montague had indeed traveled to a foreign continent, that much was true. Andrew, however, had never met nor corresponded with the man. The tale of the voyage to Africa had not sparked enough interest with his guests, much to his disappointment. Three of the ladies who had been willing to even broach the subject only wished him luck, then turned a deaf ear when he attempted to mention the possibility of investments there.

He downed another glass of wine before motioning to a passing footman to exchange his empty glass for another. Scanning the crowd, he searched for anyone willing to speak to him, someone who would listen and sympathize with his situation. Or at least the situation he wished to present to them.

His mother had been speaking with Lord Walcott earlier, but now he could find neither of them. Not that either would be of any help, but he hoped to steer clear of both of them for the time being. The last thing he needed was for his mother to overhear him cajoling someone into a business agreement he had no intention of fulfilling. And the earl would only lecture him as he had at the gaming hell. Neither appealed to Andrew in the least.

Mrs. Reynolds and her daughter, Constance, had their heads

together, tittering like a couple of wrens. He had invited them at the last moment to learn the truth about their financial situation. Rumors stated that Mr. Reynolds was either nearly broke or vastly rich, depending on who was telling the tale.

Andrew downed his wine, though his head was aching from over-consumption already. But he needed it to beat down the guilt that tried to creep into his mind while he placed the empty glass on a nearby table. As he approached the two women, he caught sight of his mother on the other side of the room. He hoped she would keep her distance until he learned what he could.

"Good evening, ladies," he said, taking first the hand of Mrs. Reynolds followed by that of her daughter and kissing their knuckles. Miss Constance looked very much like her mother, only twenty years younger. They shared the exact shade of golden blonde hair and brown eyes and had facial features that could have been near-mirror images. Any man would have been as pleased to have the older woman vying for his attention as much as the younger.

Except Andrew. He found what constituted beauty these days boring. What he wanted was something different. Such as a pair of deep blue eyes, dark hair, and a button nose...

He shook his head. There was no time for fancies. Much more urgent matters had to be dealt with first.

"Are you enjoying yourselves?" he asked.

"Indeed, we are, my lord," Mrs. Reynolds replied. "Constance and I were just saying that the wine is exquisite. I don't believe I've ever had better."

"I'm pleased to hear it," Andrew replied. "I had it shipped from my personal vineyard in France." He leaned forward and lowered his voice. "I usually reserve this blend for more important occasions—such as weddings." He winked at Miss Constance. "But I thought my guests deserve the best."

The truth was that he had won three dozen of the bottles off an old man in a game of cards two weeks earlier, one of the few times he had won in some time.

"And you, Miss Constance?" he asked, giving the daughter his best grin. "Are you enjoying yourself this evening?"

"Oh, yes. Very much so, my lord," Miss Constance cooed. "The wine is perfect, the music lovely. I've never attended such a grand party."

This was the perfect time to steer the conversation toward the information Andrew was seeking. "And Mr. Reynolds?" he asked. "I hear he's involved in important negotiations, something about stakes in a farm near Yorkshire? Is that where he is tonight?"

"Oh no, my lord," Mrs. Reynolds replied. "I'm afraid there were complications with the... contracts? What I understand is limited." She flicked out a fan and began flapping it in short, quick movements at her breast. Her giggle made her sound as if she were the daughter rather than the mother. "What do women know of business?"

Although Andrew nodded, inside he grimaced. Complications in business typically meant that one lacked the funds to complete the transaction, which said that Mr. Reynolds was as broke as he.

"I see a dear friend I have not seen in a very long time calling me over," he said, giving the two women a smile. "Have a very pleasant evening."

With a quick bow, he hurried away, scanning the room for someone —anyone—to whom he had yet to speak. Then his gaze fell on two women sitting beside the far wall, one quite familiar.

Were they not the young ladies Mrs. Rutley had brought with her from the school? Although the young woman with the blonde curls was quite pretty, the dark-haired woman caused his heart to thud in his chest, just as it had the last time he had seen her.

"Let's see if Walcott was correct," Andrew whispered. "Are there women from that school who come from money?"

As he made his way toward them, he was but two arms' length away when the dark-haired woman spoke in a carrying voice, and what she said made him grin. Ships? Hotels? Her father was wealthy! Quite wealthy, apparently. Wealth and beauty? He would feather his nest with this one!

Approaching the two young women, he searched his mind for the name of the dark-haired girl. Surely, he would have learned it at one point. One of her enchanting beauty would not have passed by without him asking. Luck was on his side when her companion gave it to him. What a pity he had nothing on which to make a wager.

"Miss Hunter if I recall?" he said. Oh yes, she was beautiful with her rosy cheeks and flawless skin. And she seemed taken with him, given the way she gaped up at him. "Where have you been hiding? I've been searching all evening for you." He took her gloved hand in his and kissed above the knuckles before taking half a step back.

"M-my lord," she whispered. "I'm Miss Emma Hunter, and I've been here, waiting for you." Her eyes widened. "That is... I've been here waiting to speak with you." She did have a lovely smile.

"I've been hoping to speak with you, as well, Miss Hunter," Andrew said. "When I left the school on Monday, I happened to gaze upon your beauty. Although it was our first encounter, I must admit the moment has remained with me. In truth, I was pleased to learn you would be attending this evening." He lowered his head and gave her a bashful smile, a trick that had worked dozens of times in the past.

"But that was not the first time we've met, my lord," she said.

Andrew grimaced. Where had they encountered one another before? He would have remembered such a lovely young woman!

"The alleyway?" she asked. "Do you not recall?"

His mind raced as he searched for any such memory. Then shock overcame him. A month ago, perhaps even two, he had indeed encountered Miss Hunter in the alleyway off Rake Street. He had been quite inebriated and demanded a kiss as a form of a toll.

"I-I do remember," he replied, cursing himself inwardly. Of all the foolish things he had done in his life, that had to be the worst! He had ruined his chances with this woman before he had even begun!

"Forgive my boldness," she said, her cheeks turning a delectable pink, "but I've thought about that moment every day since. When I was invited to your party, I could not have been happier."

"You're not angry?" he blurted and then coughed. "That is... I've thought of you, as well, Miss Hunter."

She dropped her gaze. "Do you recall what you said to me that day?"

Curse the gods and the luck they brought! He used far too many colloquies with far too many women to recall a single incident!

"I do," he replied, forcing a smile. "And although we broke societal rules by speaking of a kiss we shared, I'd enjoy hearing the words from your lips." At least he was a quick thinker!

"You told me I was beautiful, and I should be pleased to be kissed by a baron."

Andrew did not recall saying such a thing to Miss Hunter—or any other woman, for that matter. How many times would he allow his tongue to speak without thought? It was the liquor, of course. Such forwardness would get him in trouble one of these days if he were not careful! At least out in public as he apparently had that day.

"Therefore," Miss Hunter continued, "I must ask if those words were true, or did you say them simply to steal a kiss from me?" The blush now covered her entire face, and her breath came in short gasps. Yet she wore a playful smile that made him grin.

"I'll admit, only to you, that the kiss was my feeble attempt to gain your favor, and for that, I apologize." He then leaned in closer and lowered his voice. "Though, I would never recant my opinion about your beauty, even if I were to face the gallows, for it was merely truth."

Andrew considered his next move. Outright asking about her father's various business affairs would be far too obvious. No, he needed a better way to garner that information.

"Miss Hunter, would you allow me the honor of calling on you?"

"I'd love nothing more," she replied. Then her smile dropped. "Oh no, Mrs. Rutley would never allow such a thing. You see, I'm—"

"Too shy to ask our headmistress," her companion said, leaping from her seat. "Forgive me, my lord, for interrupting. I'm Miss Diana Kendricks, and Miss Hunter does not like to be a burden on others. That's why she's afraid to ask our headmistress."

"I see," he said, although he found her reasoning odd. "Well yes, I understand. What if I were to speak to Mrs. Rutley this evening? Would you agree then?"

"No!" Miss Hunter shouted. Then she cleared her throat. "I'm afraid you cannot. As a part of our training, she will only accept cards on our behalf. If you don't mind sending one, that is."

"Of course," Andrew replied. He glanced across the room. His mother and Mrs. Rutley were together. That would not do. He needed to speak to the headmistress alone, to discuss their investment. "I'll send a card first thing tomorrow. Now if you'll excuse me, I must go and speak to a man about a matter of business."

He gave the two young women a bow and hurried over to his mother. "Excuse me, Mother, but the students who arrived with Mrs. Rutley wish to speak to you about your décor."

"Oh? Well, is that not wonderful? Which items of décor exactly?"

"I'm not sure," he replied with a quick wave of his hand. "You know that sort of thing always confuses me. Please, go speak to them. I would hate for them to leave feeling as if they were ignored." He gave her his best smile. "Don't worry. I'll keep Mrs. Rutley company until you return."

When his mother was gone, he directed his attention to the head-mistress. The schemes he had developed for the charity houses in London would haunt him forever if he did not end it now. But this woman had control over the life of Miss Hunter—at least for the time being—and he needed to keep in her good graces.

"Mrs. Rutley, I had hoped to speak to you concerning the invest-ment we discussed earlier this week."

"Of course. Did you wish for me to bring the money to you, or would you prefer to collect it from the school? I cannot seem to recall."

Andrew tightened his grip on the stem of his wineglass. A few hundred pounds would do wonders for his debts in the short-term, but the Hunter fortune would save it in the long.

"Sadly, my other investors have had a change of heart as to where they wished to build," he replied, "and we could not reach an agree-ment. Therefore, I pulled out of the negotiations. I'll return what you gave me next week."

"Yes, of course," Mrs. Rutley replied. "What a pity. It seemed not only a lovely investment, but a wonderful way to help those in need."

Andrew's gaze fell on Miss Hunter. "Indeed, it was, but I will not mourn the lost opportunity. I've found something far better and shall refocus my attention on that instead."

Mrs. Rutley smiled. "You know, rather than returning the money, why not keep it and give it to a charity of your choosing? That way I can feel as if I've done my part for those in need, and you will not have to fuss over finding the right time to call."

Unable to keep from beaming, Andrew replied, "I think that a marvelous idea, Mrs. Rutley. And you can trust that it will indeed be given to a very worthy cause."

Worthy cause, indeed. His.

Emma found herself unable to concentrate on her lessons as she sat listening to Mrs. Barbara Gouldsmith. Even two days after speaking with the baron, she found her mind on him and him alone. She was still mystified that one moment, she thought he would never look her way and in the next, he was all but begging to call on her.

The lie concerning Mrs. Rutley's preference that cards be sent did not sit well with Emma. Her intention had not been to deceive, but after Diana had lied for her, she decided that one more small fib could not hurt. The risk was well worth the reward.

Now all she had to do was convince Mrs. Rutley that having him call was in Emma's best interest.

"Miss Hunter," Mrs. Gouldsmith snapped, "may I ask why you're not tasting your soup?"

Emma's eyes widened when she realized that eight pairs of eyes were focused on her. "I'm sorry, Mrs. Gouldsmith." She picked up the spoon, dipped it in the empty bowl in front of her—remembering to push it away, not bring it toward her—and brought it to her lips, all in one fluid motion.

As the students continued their mock practice, Mrs. Gouldsmith resumed her lecture on how to comport oneself at the dining table. "You'll soon learn that, as you make your debuts in society, many engagements are gained or lost at the dining table. What man wishes to marry a woman with bad table manners? Only a barbarian or high-wayman would accept such atrocities."

Emma kept a steady pattern, and her gaze fell on Diana, who sat across from her. She, too, appeared as bored as Emma felt. Just because many of the students came from families of lesser standing did not mean they were not taught dining etiquette. Believing all lower-class families ate like animals was as boorish as the tutor claimed their eating might be.

"Very good, ladies. Now, place your spoons thus on your bowl to demonstrate that you have finished."

Each girl followed the tutor's directions. But when Jenny's spoon made a resounding *clang* on the bowl rather than the light *clink* expected, Mrs. Gouldsmith gasped and snapped, "No, no, no!"

One would have believed Jenny's *clang* had murdered someone!

"Now you've drawn the attention of every other guest at the table, and the gentleman whose interest you worked so hard to draw is likely embarrassed. He will now wish to cast you aside and turn his attention to the more cultured young lady on his opposite side."

Emma shook her head in disbelief. Mrs. Gouldsmith had always been one for grand tales about young ladies who had made the slightest of mistakes and society had somehow shunned them for it. Thankfully, for many of the students, this was their final lesson, an exam of sorts that was to last the entire week.

Jenny gave the tutor a sweet smile. "My apologies, Mrs. Gould-smith, for the imperfection with my spoon." She then turned to Diana beside her and batted her eyelashes. "And to you, my darling Stephen, for driving you into the arms of another woman. I pray she does not sneeze and ruin your wedding ceremony!"

The girls burst out laughing, but Mrs. Gouldsmith was not as amused. "That is quite enough rebellion for one day. Miss Clifton, I would like you to come with me, please. I believe a talk with Mrs. Rutley is in order. The rest of you are dismissed."

"Poor Jenny," Diana said as the pair left the room. Emma was surprised the tutor had not led the poor girl by the ear. "Although, I suspect Mrs. Rutley will likely laugh as heartily as the rest of us did."

Emma nodded. "If not more. But not until after Mrs. Gouldsmith has had her rant and left the room." Mrs. Rutley was far too kind to punish someone over a clink of a spoon. It was that kindness that Emma hoped would have Mrs. Rutley agree to allowing Lord St. John to call.

"Would you like to take our food outside?" Emma asked as they headed toward the sideboard that held a variety of cold meats and cheeses. "It is far too lovely to remain indoors."

Diana gave her a sniff. "Perhaps you're waiting to see if a letter arrives from the baron," she said. Then she winked. "I don't blame you, for if it were me, I'd likely be blue with anticipation."

Collecting their food, they carried it out to the shady area beneath the great oak. Several of the other students sat scattered about the grounds, all seeming to have the same idea.

"At last night's party," Emma said, "when I told Lord St. John that Mrs. Rutley only accepts cards, I felt guilty for lying. Do you suppose that in matters of romance it's all right to speak falsehoods? As long as they are small, of course."

Diana pursed her lips as she broke off a small morsel of bread. "You were not the only woman to lie, you know. I, too, stretched the truth a bit. So yes, in matters of romance, I see no problem with it."

Emma sighed. "Even if he does send a card, Mrs. Rutley will refuse him. She knows my father has already made an agreement with Lord Egerton." She shivered. "What do you think?"

Before Diana could respond, a shadow fell over them. Emma looked up and was relieved to find not Mrs. Rutley but rather Ruth Lockhart standing over them. With bright red hair and a mischievous smile, Ruth was always a wonderful source of entertainment. And trouble.

"What you must do is conceive a story so grand that Mrs. Rutley will have no choice but to allow him to call. Lord St. John is a known rake, and you're spoken for. It doubles the reason for Mrs. Rutley to deny his request."

Emma sighed. Ruth could cause a great deal of trouble, but she was a good friend and—more importantly—she was right. Ruth took a seat beside Diana, and the trio ate in silence. After several minutes, Emma was no closer to a solution. Nor did she have an inkling of one.

"Perhaps you can forge a letter from the man to whom you're betrothed," Ruth said. "In it, you can say that he's found another woman and no longer wishes to marry you."

Diana shook her head. "And if her parents visit, Mrs. Rutley is bound to mention it, which will get Emma into a great deal of trouble."

Emma tore off a bite of bread and popped it in her mouth. "There has to be a way," she said. "I just haven't thought of it."

"I've got it!" Ruth said with such emphasis that Emma's heart began to race. "He can call on Diana rather than you!"

Emma frowned. "This is no time for teasing, Ruth. I'm being serious."

"As am I. Diana has had no suitors, nor is she courting. Therefore, she can have a gentleman caller. You, Emma, can act as her chaperone, but the truth is that you'll be the one speaking to the baron. That way, Mrs. Rutley will never know."

For a moment, Emma considered this plan. And the more she thought on it, the more she liked it. It truly was a wondrous scheme. And the only one that was logical. They certainly would tell a few small lies in the beginning, but this was romance and therefore justified.

Then she realized that the decision could not be hers. "Diana? Would you be willing to do this for me?"

"I'd love nothing more!" Diana exclaimed. "Whatever we can do to save you from marrying Lord Egerton, I'm happy to do my part."

Emma threw her arms around her friend. "Oh, thank you!" she said, then she turned to Ruth. "And thank you. Sometimes your ideas can be frightening, but they are always wise in their way."

Ruth rose and brushed off her skirts. "Just be careful," she said. "Lord St. John is not known for his respect for women."

Emma considered the warning. There was no denying that rumors about the baron and his exploits, more so toward women, were questionable, to say the least. Yet Emma saw a different man, one who was cultured, kind, and unselfish. Even if there were a hint of truth to said rumors, she needed a way to escape the life she was being forced into with Lord Egerton. If it meant the man who rescued her had a few blemishes, then so be it.

Looking up at Ruth, she replied, "I will, I promise."

As Ruth walked away, Emma shook her head. "They are rumors and nothing more. Even so, I'm sure any antics have been exaggerated."

Was she attempting to convince Diana or herself?

"You know how these things are," Diana said. "Mrs. Rutley has said it all too often. What starts out as a small grain of truth grows taller with each passing tale. Regardless, it is evident the man is smitten with you and no other."

Emma heaved a happy sigh. "Did you see his enthusiasm when he spoke to me last evening?"

"How could I miss it?" Diana asked with a laugh. "The two of you were smiling as if you'd won some sort of prize, and I'm still unsure who the true winner was."

Emma laughed as she and Diana returned to the school. There was indeed a contest, one that had many women vying for the attention of the baron. And thus far, it appeared that Emma was in the lead.

CHAPTER 5

I n the days that followed, a number of things fell into place, much
to Emma's delight. The card the baron had sent, requesting to
call on Friday, was intercepted. Diana received permission to
allow him to call. And Emma wrote the letter to accept his request. Of
course, he was under the impression that he would be calling on Emma
rather than Diana, but that made little difference since both would be
present. It was the perfect scheme!

Now, it was Friday afternoon. Lessons were finished for the day, and
several of the girls who lived close by had returned home for the weekend. Those who stayed behind were either in their rooms or out for a
stroll before they had to dress for dinner.

As luck would have it, Mrs. Rutley had gone out earlier that
morning and was not expected to return until the evening. This would
allow Emma plenty of time to explain to the baron as to why she had
instructed him to ask for Diana.

As they sat in the drawing room, Emma wrung her gloved hands.
Lord St. John was to arrive at any moment, and she prayed that Mrs.
Shepherd would not run him off the property.

"Don't be so nervous," Diana said. "You'll have a lovely stroll
around the gardens, but what's important is that you enjoy yourself."

Emma sighed. "You're right, but what if he realizes that I'm far shorter than he recalled? After all, I remained seated when he spoke to me at the party. Or what if in this trickery, he realizes that you're far more beautiful than I?"

Diana gasped. "Don't say such a thing! You're very beautiful and have drawn the attention of far more men than me. I cannot compete with the likes of you, nor would I want to."

"I'm sorry," Emma said, releasing a heavy breath. "I'm afraid my confidence, although improving, still wanes at times."

Diana patted Emma's hand just as a knock sounded on the front door. Muffled voices made Emma glance at the drawing-room door, and when it opened, Mrs. Shepherd entered, Lord St. John behind her. It was as if all the air had been removed from the room, and all Emma needed to survive was his handsomeness. Although his coat and breeches were well-pressed, the shirt he wore beneath appeared rumpled.

"Lord St. John," Mrs. Shepherd announced with a frown. She placed her hands on her hips. "If you want to take a walk through the gardens, that's fine. But nowhere else." Then she gave a belated, "My lord."

Diana and Emma stood and dropped into a curtsy. "Yes, Mrs. Shepherd," they replied in unison.

The cook narrowed her eyes, and for a moment, Emma worried she would decide to join them. That was the last thing she needed. Mrs. Shepherd following them around the gardens with her frying pan hidden behind her back. There was no doubt the cook would use it if the need arose.

Mrs. Shepherd appeared ready to say something but then snorted and withdrew from the room, much to Emma's relief.

"It's so wonderful to see you again, Miss Hunter," Lord St. John said. "Though, I must admit I'm a bit confused as to why you asked me to call on your friend rather than you."

"Please sit," Emma replied, giving him her best smile. "You see, Diana, that is Miss Kendricks, comes from a very strict family that wishes for monthly reports on what gentlemen call on her. Although she's become acquainted with one in particular, he's currently away on business and not due to return for several months. I believed that Mrs. Rutley had already made her report, saying that she has indeed met their wishes, but I learned that she had not. Therefore, we used our meeting as a means to keep Diana from disappointing her parents. Really, it makes little difference to us, except that Diana is the chaperone rather than I. I hope you don't mind."

Emma held her breath. Would he be repulsed by her lie? Would her dishonesty send him running away, never to call on her again?

"There's no need to concern yourself, Miss Hunter," he said, smiling. "Though I strive not to lie, circumstances arise from time to time when I must. As to your dilemma, Miss Kendricks, I understand all too well the pressure one's parents can put on their children. My mother does very much the same. And now I've been forced to feign interest in women simply to appease her." He turned to look at Emma and smiled. "But my days of pretending are now over."

Emma swallowed hard, and her heart pounded in her breast. If the baron requested to carry her away at this moment, she'd agree.

"Now," Lord St. John said, "shall we speak here, or would you rather take a stroll through the gardens together?"

Emma wanted nothing more than to walk beside the baron rather than sit across from him. To place her hand on his arm. To feel the heat of his body next to hers. To enjoy another wondrous kiss...

Such thoughts were unladylike, but oh, how she enjoyed them!

"A walk would be lovely," Emma replied. "But you should take Miss Kendricks's arm if we are to continue with this ruse." How she despised having to say that!

They exited the room and walked down the corridor that led to the back veranda. There, Mrs. Shepherd was waiting, staring at them like a hawk ready to swoop down and collect its prey.

Once outside, Emma glanced over her shoulder. "I would like to apologize again for the confusion we may have caused you. It was not my intention to lie, but—"

"Think nothing of it," the baron interrupted. "As I said, I understand far better than you realize the reason you were driven to conjure a story. It was a sacrifice for a friend. I'll admit that I've done it several times myself. And always for a good reason." He looked away. "Forgive me. Let's speak of pleasant things. There's no need to discuss the woman who betrayed me."

Emma's heart went out to him. Who was he thinking about to have such a look of pain cross his eyes? Well, it made little difference, for she, Emma, would never do anything to cause him so much distress! If that woman who hurt him to such a terrible degree were to appear at this moment, Emma would give her a few choice words!

When Lord St. John gave a heavy sigh, Emma wanted nothing more than to console him.

He glanced over his shoulder and then offered her his arm. "Please, Miss Hunter, walk with me. I'm sure we'll be safe now that we are out of sight of the house. While suffering terrible memories, a man needs a strong woman at his side. No offense to you, Miss Kendricks."

Diana smiled. "Oh, none taken, I assure you, my lord."

Her hand trembling, Emma placed it on his arm, pleased when Diana dropped back behind them. What a wonderful friend she was! All her life, Emma had wanted to walk beside a gentleman, and here she was, doing just that. What wonderful sensations such an encounter brought forth, as if she had discovered a treasure chest hidden deep beneath the soil.

A shiver ran down her spine as she took in his masculine scent, a light woodsy smell mixed with oranges—and an undertone of liquor she chose to ignore.

"Did you enjoy yourself at the party, Miss Hunter?"

"Oh yes, my lord," Emma replied. "The food, drink, everything was wonderful. And your mother is a true lady. I admire her greatly. And then there was you, of course. You made the evening all the better by simply allowing me to speak to you."

What had come over her? Perhaps it was she who had been drinking, for she felt as giddy as Ruth acted after consuming too many glasses of rum.

As they passed a bed of lovely yellow Lemon Queens, Emma's attention fell on the firmness of his arm muscles beneath the sleeve of his coat. What did they look like when they were not covered in cloth?

"Three times," the baron said, coming to a sudden stop. "Three times I attempted to summon the courage to speak to you, and I could not. Then I overheard you speaking about your father and the admiration you have for him for his business affairs and great wealth. It was then that I thought, 'if she admires her father for those traits, surely she would admire me for the same.'"

Emma's heart froze. Her father's wealth? What made him believe her father was...

She nearly groaned aloud. He had overheard her telling a story, one told to Diana in jest! And he believed it was true. Oh, what would she do now? Not only would he leave her standing in the middle of the garden, but he would likely never call on her again!

"My lord," she said, looking up at the man she had admired from afar for some time, "I know nothing about the wealth you possess, nor would I admire you for it." Realizing what she had said, she quickly added, "That is... I do admire you for your ability to conduct business, but that would not be the most important thing I admire. You seem a man of adventure, and the fact you are journeying to Africa... Well, I admit that I would enjoy participating in such an adventure."

The baron smiled down at her. "I may have to delay the journey," he said. "Something else has caught my interest that is far more valuable than trade."

Emma could only pray that it would rain and cool off the heat that rose inside her. Perhaps she should have brought an umbrella, but a bonnet should have sufficed!

"Speaking of business," Lord St. John said. "It appears your father has seen a great deal of success. Has it always been thus?"

Stifling a frown, Emma could not help but wonder why he wanted to know more about her father. Granted, he had overheard her speaking so foolishly with Diana, but he was likely far wealthier than she pretended to be. Yet if she told him the truth, that she was poor, he would likely leave and never return. And that thought frightened her far more than the lies she'd told.

"My father was once poor," she replied. "But through several sound investments and other means, he's become quite wealthy. So much so that he has to be reminded of how many estates he owns." She groaned inwardly. Well, if she was going to tell lies, she might as well make them grand!

To her pleasure, his smile widened. "His story sounds very much like mine." They came to a stop once more, this time near a small outbuilding in which the gardeners stored various tools of their trade. "I must admit I'm quite shy and don't enjoy speaking about myself."

Emma could not help but laugh, and he tilted his head.

"What do you find so humorous?"

No one else was nearby, so Emma replied, "You certainly were not shy when you requested that kiss."

Lord St. John laughed. "That was the courage of the drink, Miss Hunter, I assure you. How else could a man approach a woman of your obvious beauty, otherwise? Surely, you have a vast number of suitors, do you not?"

"I'm afraid not," Emma replied, dropping her gaze. "You see, I'm poor..." She gasped, realizing what she had just said and quickly added, "In height, that is."

The baron frowned. "Poor in height? You mean men pass you over because you do not stand as tall as other women?"

Emma nodded, pleased that this would surprise him.

"Well, then those men are fools, Miss Hunter. For your height is like everything else about you."

"And what is that, my lord?"

"Perfect."

Never had Emma's heart soared so high as it did at that moment. Her head spun as they continued their stroll, and her feet somehow entangled with her skirts. With a cry, she lurched forward. If he had not grasped her arm so tightly, she would have fallen flat on her face.

"You should watch your step," he said, sending her heart melting. "The path is uneven here. Here, allow me to put an arm around you to keep you steady, at least until the way is once again safe."

Emma could only nod, for words refused to leave her throat. When he placed a hand in the small of her back, her heart thudded in her chest. The man was bold! And oh, how she loved it! As long as Mrs. Shepherd did not make a sudden appearance, she would allow herself to enjoy his closeness.

"Tonight, I must meet with some investors, but I would like to call on you again if I may."

"I would like that," Emma replied. She found keeping her mind on the conversation difficult, for her thoughts kept going to where his hand touched her. What would it be like to have no fabric between his hand and her back?

Now, *that* thought should have set her hair on fire!

"When would be best for you?" she managed to ask, surprised that the question had not come out as a squeak.

"On Sunday, after I've returned from the orphanage, let's go on a carriage ride." Then he grinned as his arm left her back, causing her to miss it immediately. "Or rather, I'll call on Miss Kendricks and hope you'll be her chaperone. I would like to show you the estates I own in this area. Perhaps you can tell your father about them."

What an odd comment, she thought. Then she considered how all men were the same with their boring talks of hunting, business, and other matters. Regardless, she found herself replying, "I'll be sure he learns of them, my lord. And I'd be very pleased to see your estates." He could show her the rocks on his property for all she cared. Any reason to be close to him was just fine with her.

"I still have a few minutes before I must leave," Lord St. John said. "I'd like to hear more about you. Tell me about your life before you came to Mrs. Rutley's school. I imagine it was very fascinating."

Emma beamed. No man had ever shown an interest in her life before! And although she had sworn never to lie again, she did just that, weaving a tale so grand that she hoped she could remember its details if she were asked to tell it again.

Andrew had never heard such a story in all his life. Yet, with each word that passed her pouty lips, he never doubted that she spoke the truth. He was well aware that Miss Hunter was not attempting to entice him with her beauty—at least not on purpose—but he could not help but take in her feminine form.

What would it be like to hold her in his arms? To feel her head against his chest? To feel the smoothness of her skin against his. To inhale the natural fragrance of her hair. Of her body.

"It was then," Miss Hunter said, breaking him from his thoughts, "that I understood one thing. Although Father promised me passage to America, and that Diana could come with me as my companion for a year, I found I preferred to remain here and benefit from a young lady's education. I can always take a ship at another time. Whenever I like, in all honesty, for he has told me as much." She smiled at Miss Kendricks. "But I would miss so many of my friends. Plus, how could I choose only one to take with me? I would hate to disappoint the others."

Andrew had once heard of a man whose uncle—unbeknownst to anyone in his family—had invested his entire savings in a mine. When that uncle died, he left his nephew an unexpected great fortune. That was what stood before Andrew now, a chance at a very great fortune, indeed!

"The way you think of your friends is inspirational," he said. "I, too, am often ridiculed by my peers for the amount of time and energy I put in to helping others. Today, I've learned that the woman before me does the same."

Miss Hunter sighed, and again, Andrew's heart skipped a beat. What was wrong with him? He had to focus on the task at hand, not her feminine allure!

"Do you suppose your father will approve of me?" he asked as he offered her his arm.

She smiled. "Oh, he most certainly will. But let's speak of him later. For now, I wish to know more about you."

A sliver of fear stabbed Andrew. What could he tell her? That he was broke and thus his only reason for requesting her company? That he was attracted to her father's money as much as he was to her?

He paused. Did he wish to continue lying to this woman? For some reason he could not explain, he did not.

You fool! he chastised himself. *Do you truly wish her to know how your failures in life increase with each passing day? That your mother looks at you with shame in her eyes?*

No, he had to keep up the ruse or lose her completely.

As they strolled down the cobbled path, Miss Kendricks following behind them, Andrew racked his brain for another tale he could fabricate. The problem was that he could not recall which he had already told her. What if he repeated himself, and she caught on to his true self? That would not do at all.

Then his eyes caught movement of a rather large form hurrying down the steps of the veranda. "It's the cook!" he said in a hushed whisper. "Miss Kendricks, quickly!"

Miss Hunter and her chaperone exchanged places just as Mrs. Shepherd rounded the corner of a hedgerow.

Andrew placed a smile on his lips and turned to Miss Kendricks as if they had been in deep conversation. "Hearing you speak of your education is a delight... Oh, Mrs. Shepherd! What a pleasant surprise." What on earth did she plan to do with that frying pan?

As if hearing his thoughts, the cook replied, "Clearing the garden of pests. You see, if I can bop 'em before they try anything, they usually won't come back."

He had an odd feeling that she was speaking of him, but that, of course, was silly. Any sane woman would never strike a baron, especially a cook. Surely Mrs. Shepherd knew her place better than that.

Still, the way she eyed him made his stomach feel as if it were filled with stones.

"Forgive me for interrupting, my lord. I'll just be off to take care of business." The cook offered him a perfunctory curtsy and hurried away.

"Mrs. Shepherd does spend a great deal of time patrolling the grounds," Miss Hunter said, remaining behind him and Miss Kendricks. "I would not worry too much about her or her words, but we must remain vigilant, nonetheless."

Before Andrew could respond, he heard the voice of Mrs. Shepherd shout, "There you are! You think your act of chivalry can fool me, do you?"

Andrew swallowed hard. Perhaps it was time he was gone. "I appreciate the time we've spent together, but as I said earlier, I do have matters of business to which I must attend." When he caught sight of Mrs. Shepherd peeking around a nearby bush, he took Miss Kendricks's hand and brought it to his lips. Although he looked at Emma as he added, "Until next time." Then he bowed to Emma, wishing he could kiss her hand—or preferably her lips—but did not dare. "Miss Hunter." He then waved at the cook. "Thank you, Mrs. Shepherd."

With a huff, the cook stormed past them. Had she truly believed he could not see her? It was a relief when she entered the house, allowing him one last word with Miss Hunter.

"And I do hope I can see you again."

Miss Hunter smiled. "Although this has been a most unusual day, with the particular request we made of you, I do hope you will call on me again."

Andrew pulled at his cravat. Oh, but he could have watched her bat her eyelashes and push out that bottom lip into that lovely pout all day!

No! He had no time for fantasies of love and romance. He had an estate he had brought to ruin and needed to save.

"I can assure you, Miss Hunter," he said with an alluring grin, "I'll call so often that you'll grow weary of my company."

"How could I ever want you to stop calling?" she asked with wide eyes. "I enjoy your company far too much for that."

Oh, yes, he had no doubt that his future was secure. Nothing could stop him from getting what he needed to get his life going in the correct direction once again.

And having it happen because of a woman who took his breath away only made the game all the more enticing.

CHAPTER 6

Andrew strode light-footed down the alleyway on Rake Street, wearing a smile as wide as the sky. Not only was Miss Emma Hunter a great beauty—by far the loveliest creature he had ever seen—but she was also wealthy.

Well, her father, Sir Henry Hunter, was a wealthy baronet, but that wasn't all Andrew cared about.

The added bonus was that many men preferred taller women. Andrew, however, cared nothing for the woman's height or her shyness, evident by her downward glances earlier that day. No, all that interested him was getting on with his wooing of the young woman, which was proving far easier than he would have ever imagined.

While she discussed her life, tendrils of selfish hope tickled the recesses of his mind, distracting him. Andrew pushed it away, thus allowing him to listen. Women enjoyed speaking of themselves, but they preferred when a gentleman listened, and so that was what he did.

Miss Hunter had lived a life of luxury. Dozens of horses of her own spread out over six estates. So many dresses and gowns that she had an entire bedchamber dedicated to wardrobes to hold them. A boat at every major port in the country.

Yes, Sir Henry was a very wealthy man, indeed! A kind, charitable man who was known to reward even his servants with small token gifts. If he held a servant in such high esteem, how much more would he hold the man who married his daughter?

"Baron or not," barked Jenkins, the man who guarded the door to the gaming hell, breaking Andrew from his thoughts, "no more credit for ye." With bulging arm muscles and a crooked nose that said it had been broken more than once, he was not one to be trifled with.

Smirking, Andrew withdrew a bundle of notes from the inside pocket of his coat. Several days earlier, he had arranged the selling of a painting he had purchased for himself before his father's passing. Not enough to take care of past-due wages, the temptation to double or even treble its worth was too much to overcome. Plus, selling it would have no effect on the coffers of the estate. Nor his mother.

Andrew returned the notes to his pocket. "I've asked for credit only once, and I'm treated as if I have the plague." He took out a coin. "For you, my friend." Reaching out, he meant to place it in the man's rather large hand, but the scowl Jenkins wore made him pull it back.

"In with ye or leave," Jenkins growled as he stepped aside.

Andrew snorted as he entered the parlor of the gaming hell. A tall, burly barkeep glared from behind a long bar that ran along the back wall. A dozen tables sat haphazardly around the room, the light from the wall sconces gleaming off their sticky tops.

Caroline—Andrew had no idea her surname, nor did he care— sauntered over to him, her hips moving provocatively beneath a purple gown cut so low it threatened to expose certain parts of her body that should remain covered.

Andrew wanted to run.

"Well, if it isn't the Baron of Rake Street," she purred as she ran a finger across his chest. Brushing a blonde curl from her shoulder, she looked him over as if she were choosing a particular cut of beef. "My lord, I often wonder why you give me such a look of disgust."

"You are imagining things," he said. "It was the porridge I ate this morning that has my stomach upset, is all."

Her laugh had a lightness to it as she placed a hand on his arm. "My lord... rumors abound that you've had dozens of women, yet you shun me?" She gave him a sultry pout. "What am I to think except that I repulse you?"

Where those rumors originated, Andrew did not know. Yet like his financial woes, words had been spoken. Although he was far from a saint, Andrew had no interest in a woman who shared her bed with any man willing to pay.

"Caroline, I'll let you in on a little secret." He lowered his voice. "I've met a woman, one of such beauty that she makes a man consider his life and what it means to him."

For a moment, an odd sensation trickled through him; one he had never felt before. A sort of twinge in his stomach that sent heat through his limbs. Perhaps the porridge had been bad after all.

"My heart is with her," he continued. "And that is why I must refuse any offers from any other women."

A sudden image of Emma appeared in his thoughts, and he shook his head to fling it away. He had to be losing his mind. She was merely a means to save his estate, not some sort of love interest!

"I've never heard anything so beautiful," Caroline said breathily.

He had to fight the urge to take a step back. Could one become drunk off the breath of others?

"But if you change your mind," she continued, "always know that I'm here." She kissed his cheek and walked away.

Andrew sighed with relief. He was here to make money, not to pay to bed a harlot!

Although he was glad to rid himself of Caroline, he could not help but wonder at the odd feelings that had come over him while thinking of Miss Hunter. Perhaps it was the anticipation of the wealth she would bring with her.

Could it have been her beauty that had made his thoughts tumble over one another?

No, that was ludicrous. He was not so simple-minded.

"St. John!" Andrew turned toward the familiar voice and found Lord Walcott sitting alone near an empty fireplace. "Come have a drink with me."

Andrew glanced toward the door that led to the main gaming room. "I'm here to play hazard, not to engage in conversation," he said with a surliness he could not explain. Why did this man irritate him so? "Perhaps later, after I've won."

"You don't want to go in there," Lord Walcott said. "Come here and have a drink with me, instead."

Andrew sighed. It would do no good to argue with the earl. Sitting in the dark-blue high-back chair facing Lord Walcott, he tried not to sulk. On the small table between them sat two glasses and a decanter of brandy. Had Lord Walcott been expecting him?

"Thank you for the kind invitation," Andrew said. As Lord Walcott poured him a drink, Andrew eyed him. "Why did you suggest I not join in the game?"

The earl replaced the stopper and pushed the glass toward Andrew. "There's a man in there whose luck is even greater than mine. And with your current propensity for losing, I thought it would not bode well for you to lose more."

"I'm quite good when it comes to games of chance, thank you very much," Andrew snapped, snatching the drink from the table and downing it in one gulp. "I appreciate the advice, but it's not needed. And I'll have you know, I rarely lose."

Lord Walcott smirked. "I've been thinking of you as of late, young St. John. You are aware that I was friends with your father, are you not?"

"I am. But Father's gone now, and I find speaking of him imprudent."

The fact was that Andrew was ashamed of where his life had gone after the estate fell to him, but he would not reveal that to anyone, not even a man who had been a good friend to his father.

"St. John." Lord Walcott paused. "May I call you St. John?"

Andrew snorted. "Only if I may call you Walcott."

"Of course," the earl said with a light chuckle. "You may as well. After all, we would be better as roommates as often as we see one another here. I was about your age when I lost my father, and he left me an estate in near ruin. I found the responsibility of running the estate and finding a bride quite arduous. I often thought of simply running away from it all."

Andrew nodded. How often had he considered fleeing to a place no one would know him? Somewhere he could start anew. Too many to count.

"I sought pleasure in places such as this. Or with any woman who would have me—or who would take my money. But I came to realize an important lesson in the end. True pleasure does not come from money dishonestly earned, nor from meaningless encounters. I found that the work I completed, honest work, gave me far more pleasure.

"As I put more energy in the smaller transactions, the holdings I'd been able to retain began to grow. Soon, everything returned to its proper order. I began avoiding places such as this and instead focused my time elsewhere." He laughed. "It was well I did, for Mary never liked the time I spent gambling."

Andrew felt a tightening in his stomach at the grief that crossed the earl's face. His wife had died four years earlier, and it was clear the man still missed her terribly.

"I tell you this," Lord Walcott continued, "for there was a particular friend who also gave me advice back then, one who understood that I needed guidance. And I was glad I accepted, for it made all the difference in the world. Therefore, I'd like to offer you what was offered to me."

"I appreciate the gesture, but I need no guidance—"

"Yesterday," the earl interrupted, "I hired two new gardeners. Need I say more?"

Andrew hung his head in shame. At least the men had found new employment. "I paid them, but they demanded more."

"I said nothing about wages," Lord Walcott said. "Although, your admittance tells me much. I'd say your estate is likely nearing bankruptcy. If it has not reached that point as yet. Am I correct in saying so?"

Andrew clenched his fist. "If your purpose was to humiliate me, then you've succeeded." He glanced around to make certain no one was close enough to overhear. "Yes, it's nearly in ruins."

The earl set down his drink and leaned forward. "I'm here to help you. I'm currently in negotiations for a proposal from which I believe you can benefit as much as I. The investment will be high, but I believe it will right your estate and perhaps even give it the breath of fresh air it needs."

Andrew poured himself another drink. "What are these investments?"

"Inns, farms, and other interests I have. I believe you'll find them quite interesting."

"I'll think on it," he murmured, although the offer sounded appealing. Far too appealing. It somehow had the feel of the type of schemes he had put forth as of late.

"Good," Lord Walcott said with a firm nod. "We'll discuss it another night. Now, come. Let's watch this man and his dice that I told you about. You'll be glad I convinced you to stay away from him."

Following the earl from the parlor, Andrew entered the main gaming room. Various tables offered a variety of games of chance. Some men played cards while others used dice, including a man who sat in the middle of the room at the long hazard table. At least of an age with Lord Walcott, if not older, the man had silver hair and deep wrinkles around his eyes. A younger woman, no older than twenty, stood beside him, her gaze cast down.

"He brings his daughter?" Andrew asked in a whisper, although she likely could have been his granddaughter. "Why would anyone do such a thing?"

"That is not his daughter," the earl said. "That is his mistress. One of many, I suspect."

After several throws, Andrew shook his head. "You're right. He doesn't seem to lose often. How is that possible?"

"Some call it luck," Lord Walcott replied. "Others will swear that men such as he made a pact with Lucifer. I wanted to show you that men like him must be avoided. If not, one may find himself joining him in that pact with the devil."

The old man's opponent, the local blacksmith, dropped his forehead on the table and groaned. "My wife's going to kill me!"

A bout of laughter rose from the onlookers, and the man lumbered away, his shoulders drooping and his head downcast.

"Do you see how dangerous it is to play these games?" the earl asked. "Men have lost everything—estates, clothing, even wives. Don't think your title will save you from such terrible defeat."

Andrew sighed. What Lord Walcott said was true. He had lost plenty in this gaming hell. It was time he stopped.

"You're right," he said, clapping his friend on the back. "Come. Let's have another drink and let the money remain in our pockets."

Although Andrew had returned with Lord Walcott to the parlor, they spoke no more about business. Instead, they discussed a variety of topics, spending several hours together and enjoying one another's company.

When the earl announced it was time for him to go, he stood and offered Andrew a smile. "It's a rare occasion that a man leaves with the money he arrived with in an establishment such as this," he said. "I find it rather exhilarating."

Andrew glanced toward the loud cheers that erupted from the gaming room. The temptation to play hazard for even a few minutes was great. Then a thought came to him. Perhaps the earl was testing him. If Andrew could not restrain himself from wasting what little money he had, what kind of business partner would he be?

"I was thinking the same," Andrew replied. "Come. I'll walk with you to your carriage."

He walked past Jenkins, who said nothing, not even a fond farewell.

"Tell me," Lord Walcott said, "have you considered searching for a bride here in Chatsworth? Or will you wait for the Season to begin?"

"I admit that I have found a woman, although I'll not say who just yet. I will say that she is beautiful, pure of heart, and her father is rather wealthy."

"Ah," the earl said, grinning. "So, she has a rather large dowry?"

Andrew nodded. "She does."

"That is important to many men. I'd say I know few who haven't a care about what they'll receive from their betrothed's family."

"It's the way of things," Andrew said with a chuckle. He reached for his flask. "A woman is equal in worth to the size of her dowry. You know this."

Lord Walcott's smile had a strange sad tinge to it. "Many years ago, I understood it to be so. Then I met Mary. Her father was poor, at least compared to his peers. But I found that the pride I had in providing for her was far more rewarding than any dowry that came with her."

Andrew considered the man's words. Lord Walcott sounded like a young man Andrew had met in a tavern the previous year, a university student who spoke of love and honor. His speech had brought on a chorus of laughter from the other men who had been listening.

"If you don't mind me asking, did your wife come with a dowry when you married?"

The earl laughed. "Three horses. That was all. But I didn't care. She was the best gift I ever received."

Andrew frowned. "You are most certainly the strangest of men. Commoners certainly have no care for dowries and the like, but I cannot recall ever hearing a peer marrying for three horses."

"Why do you think so many suffer through unhappy marriages?" Lord Walcott asked, clasping Andrew on the shoulder. "Well, we'll talk soon about this matter I mentioned earlier. For now, I need to sleep."

As the earl walked to his carriage, Andrew took another drink from his flask. Although his friend had not said it outright, he spoke as if he married for love. A noble sentiment, surely, but Andrew knew that love could not save a failing estate. Only money could.

Shaking his head, Andrew headed to his carriage where Hodge greeted him. "Well, my lord. Your spirits seem rather high. I take it you won?"

"As always," Andrew replied. "My luck is so great that I've decided to leave while I was far ahead."

"That's wonderful to hear, my lord," the driver said as he held the door for Andrew.

Leaning back against the bench, Andrew considered the advice Lord Walcott had given him. Although Miss Hunter came from a wealthy family, would he marry her if she were poor? No. He had an estate to save. Only a woman of means could help him do that. Such a pity.

Once he was home, he entered the foyer to find his mother descending the staircase, a candle glowing in the holder in her hand.

"What are you doing up so late, Mother?" he asked.

"Interesting," his mother replied. "I was just wondering who would arrive at such an hour. For I know my son never returns before the sun rises."

Her tone left his mouth dry, and guilt tore through his heart as she came to stand before him. What could he possibly say to appease her? After all, what she said was true. He was likely her biggest disappointment.

Her lips thinned. "I've been meaning to speak to you about the party," she said. "Why did you announce that Lord Montague requested your aid?"

Andrew forced surprise onto his features. "For the very reason I said. I know it's unlike me to brag, but I felt it was important enough to do so."

She clearly did not believe him. "But you've received no correspondence. How else would he have contacted you?" She shook her head. "Why must you always create elaborate lies rather than be truthful?"

He wished to tell her that he was terrified of their estate collapsing. That his father had been a good man but left an estate already in financial trouble. That his mother would likely have to live with her sister, where they would drink tea and discuss Andrew's failures.

"I don't lie—"

"Lord Montague died two months ago," his mother snapped. "The family returned yesterday and have announced plans to hold a memorial in his honor. You spend your days spreading tales and your nights on Rake Street. Do you think this is prudent behavior for a baron?"

"I was discussing the possibility of an investment," he said. When his mother looked away, anger filled him. "You don't believe me?" His ire grew when she did not respond. "Lord Walcott and I will be coming to an agreement in the near future, a business agreement."

A smile crossed her lips. "Are you really?" she asked. Andrew nodded, and her smile widened. "How wonderful. I pray that whatever success you need comes, for we are now without a butler."

It was as if she had struck him in the stomach. "Morris left?"

His mother nodded. "He did."

Andrew pulled the wad of notes from his pocket and thrust several toward her. "Here. Take this and make the appropriate payments." When she had taken the money from him, he hurried past her to hide his shame.

"Andrew," she called after him, "The estate is in trouble. There are those who can help us."

He stopped halfway up the staircase. "The estate is fine," he said without turning to look at her. "You worry too much."

Ignoring her further attempts to engage in conversation with him, he hurried to his room and closed the door. His mother was right to be concerned, for everything was crumbling around him.

Yet there was hope. Whatever business arrangement Lord Walcott offered had to be enough to save the estate. And if that fell through, it did not matter. For he already had a plan in place that he would pursue regardless of the outcome of Lord Walcott's proposition. Miss Emma Hunter.

Although there were gentlemen who had ignored the lovely young woman, Andrew would not. He would win her over and have her tell her father that Andrew was the one for her. But how would he ensure his victory? To keep calling on her would take far too long. What he needed was a location away from the school and the meddlesome cook, who would surely interrupt them just as she had before.

Then he recalled a place that he had enjoyed in his youth; one he was certain Miss Hunter would come to love. One that would make her his.

CHAPTER 7

Sleep evaded Emma as her mind churned with thoughts of her outing with Lord St. John. When Sunday finally arrived, she and Diana had spent two hours dressing and doing each other's hair in preparation. Emma felt as if she were preparing to meet the King.

"You should wear this to impress him," Diana said.

Emma's eyes widened as her friend offered her a gold ring with a large sapphire. "I can't wear this!" she gasped. "I'll be nothing but an impostor owning something so valuable. What if I lose it?"

Diana sniffed. "You're not an impostor," she said, pushing it over Emma's gloved finger. "And you mustn't hide it. You want him to notice it. Plus, if the baron is to believe that your family is one of the wealthiest in the country, you must look the part."

Emma nodded, although guilt tore through her. What had begun as a fantasy had turned into a mountain of lies. What would Lord St. John say when he learned the truth? What would he *do*?

"I don't like to lie," she said as she turned the ring on her finger. "I'm considering telling him the truth today."

"That's a terrible idea," Diana said, clasping a gold chain around Emma's neck. "If he were to learn the truth now, you may frighten him away. And you don't want that, do you?"

Emma heaved a heavy sigh. No, she certainly did not want that! "But I cannot continue to deceive him. One day, he'll learn the truth, and he'll never speak to me again."

Diana took Emma's hand in hers. "From all you've told me, the moment you first saw him, you've felt something for him. Is that not true?"

"Well, yes. It began the day Julia and I encountered him in the alleyway off Rake Street. Then when he winked at me..." She sighed again. This time it had a dreamy note to it. "I cannot stop thinking of him and how he makes me feel inside. I've never felt my heart soar so high or my body become so alight with heat." She whispered the last, her cheeks burning for admitting aloud such a thing. "Should I tell him how I feel?"

"The purpose of these outings is to see where those feelings lead," Diana said. "Once you've determined whether they are real, you may tell him. By that time, I'm sure he'll share your admiration, and the tale you told will no longer matter. After all, how can people in love be angry over a tiny lie?"

Emma worried her bottom lip. What choice did she have? Perhaps what Diana said was true. Once Emma was better acquainted with the baron, once she had a better understanding of his feelings for her, perhaps then she could reveal the truth. Love could heal any wound she may have caused. At least, that was what all the romantic novels said.

"Very well, I'll not tell him the truth for now. This is for romance, after all."

"You could not be more right," Diana said with a wide smile. "In romance, the woman is always allowed a bit of leeway with the facts."

Feeling a bit better, Emma nodded. "But I shan't wait too long to reveal the truth, for it would be wrong to deceive him for longer than necessary. No marriage can be built on fabrications." She laughed. "Listen to me discussing marriage when we scarcely know one another!"

"And why not?" Diana asked as she turned Emma toward the mirror. "After all, you are quite the prize. I mean... look at you!"

Her white day dress embroidered with azure flowers and green vines, as well as the lovely jewelry Diana had insisted she borrow, made Emma feel beautiful and regal. "I've no doubt that the baron will approve," she replied honestly. "Perhaps if I'm lucky, he'll ask to court me today."

For a moment, Emma imagined the baron doing just that. Of course, the request would take a bit of time, but she had no doubt it would come at some point. And not only would she accept, but he would also write to her father to ask for her hand in marriage. How could her father refuse? Not only would she get what she wanted, but her father would as well—his daughter married to a member of the *ton*.

Then after the New Year, they would marry, and all her problems would disappear.

"Why would the baron ask to court the chaperone?"

Emma's heart nearly burst from her chest as she turned to find Mrs. Rutley standing in the doorway. Had she been so entranced in her fancies that she had not noticed the headmistress's arrival? Apparently so.

Mrs. Rutley entered and closed the door behind her. "It appears the two of you have created a charade to dupe me," she said in a clipped tone.

Words stuck in Emma's throat. If she admitted they had, she would lose any chance at earning Lord St. John's admiration, and she did not want that to happen. But what other excuse for her behavior could she give? If it had not been for Ruth, she would not have had the current complicity she and Diana shared.

"The fault was mine," Diana said. "I take full responsibility. Emma was against it, but it was only because of my persistence that she agreed to take part. The guilt lies with me."

Emma stared at Diana. She could not allow her friend to take responsibility for her misbehavior. "That's not true. It was I who asked Diana to lie on my behalf."

The headmistress's lips thinned. "It appears that both of you chose to participate in this betrayal," she said in a quiet voice. "But what concerns me most is why you felt the need to do so. Many of the students have gone on outings in the past, and as long as they have a chaperone, I have no issue with it. You should know this."

Emma dropped her gaze again. "Yes, but they are students who are not spoken for. Since my father has made an arrangement with Lord Egerton, I knew you would refuse any request I might make."

If the disappointment on the headmistress's face were not enough to make Emma's heart clench, the words that followed most certainly would be.

"Lying comes easy to some young ladies at this school," Mrs. Rutley said. "But I would never have guessed that I would be forced to add either of you to that list."

Guilt washed over Emma for lying to the woman who had always given her such wonderful support. "I'm sorry, Mrs. Rutley. I truly am. I meant no harm."

"Nor did I," Diana added, her eyes downcast.

"Well, what's done is done," the headmistress said. "But now I'm in quite an odd predicament. I spoke to your parents—and Lord Egerton —the last time they visited. It was my understanding that although he had indeed shown interest in marrying you, he stated quite clearly that he wished to wait for you to complete your schooling before making a final decision. Therefore, if one were to argue your situation, you are spoken for but not fully."

Mrs. Rutley knitted her brows in thought. "Yet, I also know that allowing the baron to call on you without your parents' permission would be an insult to them in light of the situation with Lord Egerton. I must say, you have certainly tied my hands."

The room fell quiet for the second time in as many weeks, and dread filled Emma. She did not want to marry Lord Egerton! But no matter what she did, either lying or being truthful, her fate was sealed.

"Mrs. Rutley," Diana said, breaking the silence of the room, "is it not true that you've sought permission from several of the other parents in various ways? I understand that some agreed to allow their daughters to have gentlemen callers when the student first arrived. That way, if they do happen upon an acceptable suitor, they can learn more about one another while under your careful eye. Yet, there have been times when you've written to gain permission, in those instances when a previous agreement was not made. Am I correct in saying so?"

"I suppose so," Mrs. Rutley replied with a frown. "What are you saying?"

"Would it not be possible to do the same with Emma's parents? I mean, writing to get their permission? Surely that would clear up any confusion about the situation. Until then, you may use what you already know—that the viscount has yet to propose—and allow the baron to call on her. I'll be happy to act as chaperone. You know I can be trusted to see they behave themselves."

A surge of hope coursed through Emma as Mrs. Rutley pursed her lips in thought. Would she agree? Or was Emma destined to remain home today?

"Very well, I'll write the letter today and see it sent right away. When your father replies, whatever he says will be honored. Until then, I see no problem with Lord St. John calling on you, Emma."

"Thank you, Mrs. Rutley," Emma said. "And I'm sorry for lying."

"It's not the lies we tell others that are often the most harmful," the headmistress said. "But rather those we tell ourselves. I'll consider a punishment for both of you later, but for now, you may go to the drawing room. Lord St. John is waiting for you."

Emma and Diana went downstairs, and indeed, the baron was pacing the drawing room.

"My lord," Emma said, dropping into a curtsy. Diana followed suit.

"Ladies," Lord St. John replied with a small bow. His eyes locked on to Emma's, and her heart pounded. Then his gaze dropped. "The jewel on your hand pales in comparison to you."

Emma swallowed in an attempt to add moisture to her dry throat. He certainly had a wonderful way with words!

"Now," he said, smiling as he offered one arm to Emma and the other to Diana, "let's be on our way. I have much I wish to show you."

⁓

For the first hour, Emma feigned interest in the various fields, farms, estates, and other properties Lord St. John showed them. Most he had inherited, but some he had purchased since his father's death. Although the baron possessed a vast wealth just in his properties alone,

Emma found she was not all that impressed. What she hoped was to learn more about the man, not what he owned.

Her mind went to her talk with Mrs. Rutley earlier. Would the letter truly be sent today? If so, how would her father respond? Just the thought of him not allowing another man to call made her stomach clench. For if that was his response, it meant that Lord Egerton had made his decision. A decision she could not face.

How she wished to tell the baron the truth about this mess they had created! But she feared that doing so would ruin what little they shared. She wished to enjoy her time with him for as long as she could. Who knew what would happen tomorrow?

"When I go to London for the Season," he was saying as the carriage slowed, "I have plans to purchase another house there. After all, it can be rented to families spending the Season in London when it's not in use."

Emma frowned. "But you spoke of leaving for Africa soon. How will you attend the Season if you're not here?"

"I'm surprised you have yet to hear the terrible news," Lord St. John said. "Sadly, Lord Montague died several months ago. His family sent a letter, but alas, it was delayed, so I only learned about it this morning. And to think all this time he lay dead without me knowing."

"My condolences at the loss of your friend," Emma said. She went to say more, but her stomach nearly rose to her throat as the carriage tipped precariously backwards. "What's happening?" She grasped the edge of the window to keep from tumbling onto his lap. Not that she would have minded...

He chuckled as he grasped for the arm-strap above him. "This is the surprise I mentioned earlier."

"What? Toppling over in a carriage?"

This made him laugh outright. "No. Just wait and see. It's well worth the discomfort, I assure you."

When the road—if they indeed were on a road—evened out, Emma sighed with relief. Wherever he was taking them was located atop a very steep hill, but he had instructed her not to draw the curtains. Without the ability to see where they were going, she had not the slightest idea what the surprise could be.

Soon, they came to a stop, and the baron said, "Here we are. I believe you'll find it well worth the journey. We've traveled nearly five miles from the school."

A sense of panic seized Emma. After the encounter with Mrs. Rutley, she had hoped they would remain closer to home. But when Diana gave her a wink and whispered that all would be well, Emma slackened the grip she had on her skirts. Yes, she had nothing about which to worry.

The carriage door opened, and Lord St. John exited. He offered his hand, first to Diana and then to Emma.

When Emma alighted, she gave a gasp. "It's lovely!" she whispered as she soaked in her sunlit surroundings. Below them lay a patchwork of green fields as far as the eye could see, dotted with copses of trees and a long stream snaking through the land.

"I've never seen such a lovely view," she said breathily.

"Come with me," urged Lord St. John. "I wish to show you something."

Emma's brows rose. "There's more?"

He laughed. "Indeed, there is. Come."

"I believe I'll wait here," Diana said, a mischievous smile playing at her lips. "I'm quite afraid of high places."

"Are you sure?" Emma asked.

"Oh, yes, quite sure."

"If you wish," Lord St. John said. He seemed pleased they would be alone. Emma certainly hoped so.

He led her on a path that zigzagged up a short hill.

"I've not been here but a few times over the past two years," Lord St. John said wistfully. "It's one of the last pieces of property I own."

Emma frowned again. "But I thought you owned many properties. Are they not what we spent most of the day seeing?"

"Oh, I meant the last of the properties my father purchased before his death. I come here perhaps twice a year when I can."

"For what purpose?" she asked.

A rock loosened beneath her foot, and she grasped hold of his arm to keep from tumbling down the hill. Her head became light at the firmness of the muscle beneath the sleeve of his coat.

"Be careful, Miss Hunter. The way can be treacherous if you don't watch your footing."

"So I noticed," Emma replied, giving him a grateful smile.

When they reached the top, they turned left toward a ridge that overlooked the valley below. The stream collected at the edge of the land, creating a pool far too large to jump over. In the middle lay a square stone, allowing for one to step across with ease.

"Now, do mind your step, Miss Hunter," the baron said. "The stone will not move, but it can be slippery."

"Thank you," she murmured.

Then she summoned all her courage and did something she would never be caught doing. She slid her arm from his and took hold of his hand. He came to a sudden stop and looked down, seemingly unsure as to what to do. Perhaps the move had been far too bold.

Embarrassed, she considered pulling her hand away, but then he closed his around it. This made her happier than she could have ever imagined!

As they approached the precipice, he asked, "So, have I impressed you, Miss Hunter?"

Emma peered over the edge. A wondrous waterfall flowed down the cliff wall. The water splashed into a pool at the bottom, leaving the surfaces of the rocks that surrounded it glistening in the bright sun. Small purple and yellow flowers blanketed the grass that surrounded it, giving the area just the right amount of color.

"Indeed you have, my lord. I must make a confession. This is my first outing with a gentleman, and I can say with all honesty that I could not have wished for a better place to visit." She glanced at their intertwined hands. "Nor have I felt safer."

Her heart was pounding in her chest. She did feel safe with her hand in his, and she relished the idea of never letting go. His grip was firm and strong, yet it was the heat of his touch that sent a shot of electricity up her arm, despite the gloves she wore.

She took a moment to glance at him and was pleased to see him smiling.

"I knew that if I wished to impress you, I would have to avoid taking you to the usual tiresome places. It appears I made the right decision."

Emma laughed. "With respect, my lord, you already impressed me. That may sound strange since I have yet to know you well."

"Then it's about time you did," he replied. "Ask me anything you would like, and I'll do my best to answer honestly."

Emma's thoughts were filled with so many questions, she could have chosen any and learned much. But she knew which she wished to ask first. "I must admit that I find it... strange that you invited me today. After all, you're very well known. Surely you have dozens of women at your disposal."

"I suppose I do, but they are not you. Every one of them pales in comparison when measured against your beauty."

Clearly, she had asked the question incorrectly. How did a lady go about inquiring of the rumors she had overheard without offending a baron?

"Such words," she said, choosing her own carefully, "are oftentimes used by rakes in order to woo women. I don't believe this is true of you, of course, but..." She allowed her words to trail off.

Lord St. John barked a laugh. "Is this your way of asking about the rumors that are circulating about me, and my propensity to use my charm on various ladies?"

Feigning shock, Emma shook her head. "No, of course not!"

"I'm sure you've heard the name that has been bestowed upon me, the Baron of Rake Street? I have no idea who dubbed that title on me, but as I've frequented that area often, I assure you that my time there is spent gaming on occasion and nothing more."

"I believe you," she said. The baron would not lie to anyone, especially not her. "That is what impresses me about you. You speak with authority and honesty. Both are admirable traits. I certainly wish I could demonstrate as much self-assurance as you do."

Lord St. John looked away. "You're very kind, Miss Hunter, but you are quite confident."

It was Emma's turn to laugh. "Then the rumors you've heard about me are false. I am incapable of speaking with authority, not because I'm a woman but rather because I fear scorn for doing so. Believe me when I say I lack the confidence to make even the simplest of decisions."

The baron laughed again, and Emma's cheeks burned from embarrassment. Was he mocking her? Her heart sank at the thought.

"Was it not you who reminded me of our kiss?" he asked. "Wasn't it also you who lied so I could call on you? It appears to me, Miss Hunter, that you are quite self-assured when you wish to be. The problem is, in my humble opinion, that you do not see yourself in the same way that I see you."

His words made her feel as tall as him, and she found herself wishing he would wrap his arms around her and pull her into his embrace.

"Thank you," she whispered. They returned their attention to the lovely waterfall, and her original question came to mind. "You mentioned that you come here often. May I ask why?"

"I'm a fool for forgetting!" he said, releasing her hand and reaching in his pocket. He produced several coins, choosing a copper and placing it in her hand. "You may believe it childish, but I often make a wish and drop the coin in the pool below. It's said that all who do so are granted their request, but only if the wish comes from their hearts. The waterfall knows when someone's request is reckless or selfish, so be very certain what you wish for is truly what you want for your life."

Emma glanced at the coin and then the baron. "I don't find it childish in the least. Even adults often make wishes, although we call them dreams instead." She turned to the waterfall. "I have so much I would like to wish for, but I'm not sure which one I should choose."

"There's no hurry," the baron replied. "Consider which would be the most important, make your wish, and then toss the coin. Perhaps it will come true."

Closing her eyes, Emma considered all she wanted. Material possessions were all well and fine, but she would not waste a wish on such things. She could wish to be taller. Or more confident. To have the arrangement with Lord Egerton ended. But no. Instead, she chose what was forefront in her mind. Above all, she wished that what she felt for Lord St. John would grow, and that he would return her admiration.

At this thought, pain tore through her heart for the lies she had told him. Admitting the truth, that her family was poor, would hurt him and drive him away. But there was one lie she had told him that she could admit to today.

"Before I make my wish, I must be honest with you about something." She could not look at him.

"Of course," he said.

Emma took a moment to gather her thoughts. What was leading her to open her heart to him? It was not the scenery, although the relaxing setting did not hinder her. Part of it was the guilt she felt, but perhaps it was the handsomeness of the man beside her that had muddled her mind.

When she looked at the baron, however, Emma knew what had caused it. He had. For a sense of trust came over Emma, a trust that she could tell him her worries, and he would somehow take them away. Never had she felt such a bond, especially with someone she hardly knew. Yet there was a familiarity about Lord St. John, as if they had been friends for many years.

"When I said there are no other men interested in me, I lied." A breeze blew a strand of hair across her cheek, and she pushed it back, her gaze remaining on the water below. "He's an old man, and I find the way he looks at me disconcerting, for his eyes are filled with lust." She took a deep, calming breath. "In January once my schooling is complete, if I meet the viscount's approval, my father will give him my hand in marriage."

A tear ran down her cheek, and she wiped it away before he could see it. "I'm sorry for not telling you sooner, but I hope you don't think less of me because I kept it from you." She then turned, whispered a wish to herself, and tossed the copper coin over the edge.

Emma faced Lord St. John. Searching his eyes, she wondered if she had upset him with her confession. With each passing second, her hope began to wane.

When the breeze once again sent the strand of hair across her face, it was the baron's turn to move it behind her ear.

"I, too, have lied," he said. "And I would like to confess it to you now."

CHAPTER 8

As Andrew listened to Miss Hunter's confession, one word spoke in his mind—motive. Her motive for telling him the truth, according to her, was that she did not want him thinking less of her. A perfectly good, sensible reason.

Yet, what were his motives with her? In truth, his purpose for pursuing her, for bringing her to this place, for lavishing her with compliments, was to earn her trust, so he could eventually ask for her hand in marriage. From there, he could somehow get a portion of her father's wealth. The compliments came easy, not because of his ability to lie without thought but rather because he did not have to lie. She was lovely, and that was the truth.

He had met plenty of beautiful women in his life. Most possessed the conventional beauty of the age. Blonde tresses, vivid blue eyes, a doll-like face, it had all become so... boring. Miss Hunter had a beauty that was all her own.

Despite his impression of her, however, Andrew was troubled. Miss Hunter had expressed little enjoyment of her surroundings. Oh, she had exclaimed at the extraordinary view and the wonderfulness of the waterfall, but he had expected that. None who saw it were left unimpressed.

What had surprised him most was that she seemed indifferent to the multitude of lands he had shown her, those he claimed to own but, in truth, did not. Instead, what seemed to attract her most was him. How was he supposed to feel about that?

Every woman he had encountered, every lady who had shown him even the slightest interest, had proven to be suspect in her motives. To the others, he would have been nothing if he were not a baron with holdings. They had no interest in the man but rather the title and the wealth they assumed went with it. To have a woman find *him* interesting, to find *him* the object of their admiration, was a pleasant change.

For the first time in his life, he felt a sense of true pride. Not for what he owned—or in his case, did not own—but rather for who he was.

Or for the man he could be. A man who did not desperately drink his worries away. One who kept his money in his wallet rather than donating it to the gaming hells. There were so many possibilities, so much he could accomplish. Above all, he wanted to have a woman like Emma beside him. And what a strange sensation that gave him!

A strong urge to protect this lovely young lady washed over him. He wanted to turn the world upside down for her, build bridges and erect buildings for her. He would forgo gaming and find a way to save his estate through rightful means, which would cause her admiration for him to grow.

He paused. Was he worthy of her admiration? Was he worthy of anyone's admiration—or dare he say love—especially from a woman who looked past the façade he had erected in front of him?

And what of this other man who was also pursuing her? That knowledge changed much. How could he admit his true motive when it would cause her to leap to the water below in an attempt to escape his company?

Well, perhaps that was far more drastic than how she would truly react, to be sure, but he was certain she would at least refuse to speak to him again. There had to be something to which he could admit without jeopardizing his standing with her.

The breeze blew a thick strand of her dark hair across her face, and he reached out to tuck it behind her ear. Just as when she had taken his hand, he found great joy in such a simple act.

Then an idea occurred to him. He could make a confession without admitting to all his shortcomings and therefore still be able to win her affections.

"I, too, have lied," he said. "It concerns Lord Montague and the journey to Africa. There was no letter from him. In fact, I have never met the man." He held his breath as he waited for her to return to the carriage at a run.

"Why did you tell such a tale?" she asked. Her voice held no anger, no placement of fault, only simple curiosity.

"I wanted to impress my peers." He heaved a deep sigh. "There, I've confessed a lie."

Miss Hunter smiled. "May I ask why you feel the need to impress others in such a way? Is it expected of a baron to travel great distances in order to increase his holdings?"

"It's that and much more," he replied. "Since my father died, I was thrust into a title I was not ready to accept. Please understand, I was ready in the sense of receiving proper training. But there were issues with the estate." He closed his mouth, having almost conveyed those issues. "It does not matter anymore. Rather, it is that I know those of the *ton* look at me in judgment, and I use such stories as a way to impress them."

Although Andrew had taken several sips of brandy from the flask before arriving at the school, he felt as if he had consumed an entire bottle. What else would explain the way this admission of guilt flowed so easily from his tongue? And how freeing it was to do so!

"So often," he continued, staring out over the great expanse of land before them, "all I wish to do is to run away and leave all my problems behind, in hopes they will simply disappear."

The only sounds were the trickling of the stream and the song of a nearby bird. Had he revealed too much? Even Lord Walcott, who spoke of marrying for love, would say he, Andrew, was a fool.

"The day I learned about this man who wishes to marry me," Miss Hunter said in a voice just above a whisper, "was the worst I've ever endured. You're not alone in wanting to escape your fate. At least you have never made the attempt."

Andrew turned to stare at her in shock. "You attempted to run away? Truly?"

She nodded. "I did."

"How far did you get before you returned? Or were you found and returned against your will?"

"I was no more than a hundred paces away from the school," she replied with a small laugh. "But my friends and the headmistress convinced me to stay and face whatever future awaits me." She turned and smiled up at him, and what a lovely smile it was, too. "Now I'm glad I did, for I would not have met you."

He drew in a deep breath. Oh, how her words made him feel like a worthy man! "You're very wise and brave, Miss Hunter. Perhaps one day I'll be able to face the future as you have."

"May I share another story with you?" she asked.

"Please," he replied, smiling. "I would like that."

"I heard of a baron who suffered greatly. There were many unsavory rumors about him, and the *ton* spoke his name with bitterness. But he was a wise man, one who gave me advice that I would like to share with you."

"Please, do," Andrew said. "For I cannot deny that I undoubtedly need it."

"The problem is," Miss Hunter said with a playful smile, "you don't see yourself in the same way I do. I see a strong, determined man, one who takes his position seriously."

Confidence flowed through Andrew at her words. How long had it been since anyone had seen him in such a favorable light? Since *he* had seen himself thus? Far too long. Yet in all of that, he cherished how she had used his own words concerning her and applied them to him.

He came to the sudden realization that a woman equal in wit was not a burden, but rather someone a man should seek as a companion. Truly this woman before him was special.

"It appears, Miss Hunter, that we are more alike than I would have suspected."

Her smile warmed his heart. "I agree, my lord. It appears we both have doubted ourselves, but I believe that—or rather I hope—as you continue to call on me, we learn how to stop such terrible thoughts."

Andrew could not help but grin like a young boy. She wished to spend more time with him, despite the fact he had confessed to lying?

He paused. How strange that he looked forward to calling on her again. And not to get to her father's money. He enjoyed her company as much, if not more, than she seemed to enjoy his! What a strange— yet wonderful—turn of events!

"I would very much like the same," he said. "In fact, it would be an honor if I were able to call on you often."

"That would be something I would greatly look forward to, my lord."

"And if we are to see more of each other, perhaps it was time that I address you as Emma when we are alone. May I?"

The pinkness in her cheeks only enhanced her beauty. "I would like that. And may I call you Andrew?"

He laughed. "Yes, of course. Now, Emma." Her blush heightened. "On Saturday, I've been invited to a party by Lord Cooper. I hadn't wanted to attend, but perhaps I will if you're willing to join me."

"Another party?" she asked, her eyes wide. "I would very much enjoy accompanying you. But I must first ask permission of Mrs. Rutley. Once I have garnered it, I'll send you a message."

He offered her his arm. "I do hope she agrees," he said, leading her back across the stream and toward the path that would return them to where the carriage was parked.

Life was certainly peculiar! He had brought Emma here to charm her, to gain her approval, so he could reap the benefits of her dowry. Now however, he had a foreign sensation of protecting her from both the slippery surface of a wet stone or a steep trail, as well as from a man he had never met who wished to marry her. Perhaps Walcott could help him save his estate and thus let his intentions with Emma remain as pure as she.

Five days had passed since Andrew had seen Emma, and he found it difficult waiting for Sunday to arrive. What had begun as a means to see his estate put to rights had turned into something that he was unable to explain. With every waking moment, she consumed his thoughts, and his desire to see her again left him feeling restless.

Although he had refrained from entering the gaming hell since their visit to the waterfall, he wished to speak to Walcott. And he knew where to find him. Loud cheers greeted him as he entered the gaming room in the late evening. Few were in attendance, no more than half a dozen, but the man about whom Lord Walcott had warned him sat at the hazard table as if he had not left since Andrew was there before.

By the wide grin the older man wore, he was doing very well. His female companion was not with him this time. Perhaps she had seen sense and ran away.

To his disappointment, he did not see Walcott. Preparing to leave lest the temptation to play became too strong, a chorus of laughs made him stop and smile. Just a few minutes more would do no harm. He had resisted thus far. He had already overcome that particular urge, had he not?

Well, there was only one way to test his resolve.

Andrew walked up to the table as another man lowered his head and hurried away like a dog with his tail between his legs. The least he could have done was show the tiniest morsel of honor and walk out with his head held high.

That thought nearly made Andrew laugh. How many times had he left in very much the same sense of defeat? Too many, he was sure, but because he was inebriated on most of those occasions, the number was likely ten times as high.

"A pity he lost," the silver-haired man said. "I actually liked him." He looked up at Andrew. "Are you familiar with this game?"

"Yes, of course," Andrew replied, puffing out his chest. "I play here quite often, although I've seen you here only once before."

"That's because I don't live here," the old man replied with a sneer. He reached a gnarled hand to grab the dice. "Care to wager in a game?"

Andrew licked his lips, and his hand went instinctively to his coat pocket. Lord Walcott had warned him that this man's luck was impenetrable, but perhaps Andrew would be the one to break through it.

But had he not put his ways of gaming behind him?

An image of Emma came to mind. She thought him better than he was, and now he could prove her right.

"I think I'll pass. But I do thank you for the offer."

The older man chuckled. "Many boys are cautious." He held up a note to inspect it and winked at Andrew. "But men take risks. It's quite clear in which category you fall."

Andrew clenched a fist. He was no boy! Perhaps he would be the one to break the old man's lucky streak. "Very well," Andrew replied. "I'll play."

"We'll roll for starters," the old man said, handing Andrew a die. Then he tossed the one he had kept for himself onto the table. "Three. Now, you roll."

Andrew smiled. Three would be easy to beat. He shook the die in his fist and tossed it. When it stopped, two pips were showing. Perhaps that would be his only show of bad luck.

"Looks like I get to start," the man said with a grin.

Andrew gave a grunt of agreement.

The old man stood and shook the dice in his fist. "Seven," he called.

Holding his breath, Andrew watched as the dice tumbled, hit the protecting wall on the side of the table, and landed to show a total of seven pips.

The man scooped the dice again and called out, "Eight!" The dice landed on a total of five, and the man grinned. "I do hope you don't roll a five."

Andrew put his fist to his lips and blew on the dice for luck. All he had to do was not roll a five, and he would be safe. The roll landed on six, and he sighed with relief.

Back and forth they rolled, each missing the five, until two minutes later, two pips landed beside three.

"Ah, too bad," the old man said with feigned sorrow. "You lose."

Cursing under his breath, Andrew pulled out more notes with trembling hands. His heart pounded, and a bead of sweat trickled down the back his neck. What made gambling so alluring? It had nearly cost him his estate and every farthing he could scrounge, and yet he desired to play more. Each time he entered the hall, with each bet he threw on a table, he was certain his luck would change.

Yet rarely did he walk away with any of the money with which he had arrived. Through it all, however, through all the loss, through all the devastation, there was a certain thrill knowing that, at any moment, he could emerge the winner. That he would win back all he had lost.

"Again. My luck will change."

"Of course it will," the older man said, although his smile said he did not believe the words.

With each toss of the dice, Andrew found his resolve weakening. His shoulders drooped, his chest tightened, his stomach ached, and his spirit was all but crushed. Lord Walcott had been correct. The old man had made a pact with the devil, for he won every toss except three.

Numerous brandies and eighty pounds later, Andrew hung his head in shame and turned to walk away. The old man laughed behind him, but Andrew had not the desire nor the will to even glance over his shoulder.

Outside, he cursed.

"Another day of losing?" Jenkins asked with a chuckle from his place by the door.

Andrew glared and removed the flask from his pocket. "That old man in there, if I didn't watch the attendant handle the dice, I would have sworn he was cheating somehow. How does one have such luck?"

Jenkins shrugged but offered no explanation.

Sighing, Andrew walked down the steps and into the alleyway. His stomach ached as if he had been punched, and he came close to vomiting. The thrill of tossing the dice had long since dissipated, and a familiar emptiness took its place. He had tried to walk away but, again, he had failed. Was this what his life had become? One failure after another?

The sunlight that washed over him as he exited the alleyway made him squint. The realization he had spent the better part of half a day gaming did nothing to improve his feelings of self-worth.

"Lord St. John!" a woman's voice called.

Andrew came to a stop and was surprised to see Miss Hestia Morton approach. His mind raced as he thought about the call he'd made to Apple Green Estate and the money and jewelry she had given him.

"I understood that you planned to be away for a while," she said. "What are you doing here?"

"Good afternoon, Miss Morton," Andrew said, giving her a smile she did not return. "I'm afraid that matters have changed concerning the issues with the Cape Colony. I'm no longer needed in Africa for negotiations, and thus I'm here, rather than there."

Was that the story he had told her?

Miss Morton frowned. "You told me nothing of Africa. Why would you be needed in matters of negotiation?"

Andrew glanced at the woman's chaperone, who eyed him with equal suspicion but made no comment. Had he been caught in his lie? Apparently so. What he needed was a way out.

"Are there truly war orphans?" Miss Morton demanded. "Or was that just a way to convince me to give you money?"

"There are many, I assure you," he replied.

Miss Morton pursed her lips. "Mother has been asking after you. She wants to know why you've not called. I told her that it was because you were away. Then I heard you hosted a party recently. You would have thought that with our recent attachment I would have received an invitation." Her voice was mixed with anger and sadness. "I do hope I will see you at Lord Cooper's party this weekend. I'm sure you've been invited."

Andrew went to nod but then stopped. He had promised Emma they would attend that party together. "I must ask that you forgive me, but I've a prior engagement. If it were for anyone but the orphans, I would consider attending. No, that is not true. If I were completely honest, the parties Lord Cooper throws can be quite tedious. I recommend you find a better use of your time and either remain home or go elsewhere."

"I understand," Miss Morton replied.

Andrew let out a relieved sigh. If this woman did not go to the party, he could spend his time there doting on Emma.

"When Mother asks again where my missing jewelry has gone, I'll simply have to be truthful with her. I see that my money is what is important to you and not me."

"Miss Morton," Andrew said, ignoring her companion's nod of agreement. "Hestia, please. There's no need for such bold statements. What time do you plan to arrive at the party?"

"The moment it begins," she said, and she raised a single eyebrow. "And I expect to see you there."

Before he could respond, she and her companion turned and walked away, her companion giving him a light smirk to show what she thought of him and his lies.

Of all the bad luck one could have! Now he would have to find a way to cancel with Emma, for he could not have her accompany him. She would expect him to keep her company, and rightfully so, but with Miss Morton vying for his attention, he would be unable to do so. Plus, he certainly could not have those two women coming together to discuss him. Oh, what a mess this was becoming!

As he continued his walk, he neared the butcher's shop.

"My lord," Mr. Finch said as he exited the shop, his meaty arms crossed over his chest, "I've been meanin' to speak to you."

"Finch, my old friend," Andrew said, giving the man his best smile. "How are you?"

The man's balding head reflected much more of the sun than the last time Andrew had seen him, and his brown eyes appeared darker than Andrew remembered. Otherwise, he had not changed much.

"I'm fine enough, my lord," the butcher replied. "But I've been wonderin' if you could help me with a problem I'm having with my Margaret."

Andrew swallowed hard as the image of the young woman with reddish-brown hair and a nose far too wide for her face came to mind. "I'm not sure what you think I can do about your daughter," he replied.

"Well, I think you can, my lord. You see, Margaret's been saving money for some time now. When I made mention of it, she said that she'd loaned it to a man—a gentleman, it seems—who said he was buyin' a gift for the King. According to her, those who contributed would be invited to a party of sorts to present it to him. Of course, that's only nonsense, since what nobleman would need money from the likes of a butcher's daughter to buy His Majesty a gift? Or to even invite her to attend the presentation of such a gift? Those sorts of stories may fool a naïve girl, but not me. Then I got to wonderin' what other things this gentleman's done to her. What do you suppose I should do with him once he's caught?"

Andrew nearly groaned in frustration. As he had done so many times before, he must have concocted the tale about buying the King an extravagant gift as a way to get money. Which drunken morning had that been? He remembered Margaret had been all too happy to pass over her meager savings. Andrew had awarded the young woman with a kiss that had left her sighing as he hurried away.

Yet there was a far bigger issue at hand. Quite literally. An angry father now wanted to avenge the daughter he believed had been wronged. The butcher would not dare strike Andrew in public, he was sure of it. But if he were to catch Andrew in a dark alley... well, that would be another thing altogether.

"It's an outrage, I agree," Andrew said, praying he was correct in thinking that Margaret had not given his name as the one who had taken her money. "Once this culprit's been ousted, we'll make him pay for his crime."

Mr. Finch flexed his arms. "When I'm certain of who he is, I'll teach him a lesson he'll never forget." He added a belated "my lord" which only raised Andrew's concern he indeed knew who had taken his daughter's money.

With a quick nod and a racing heart, Andrew hurried away in hopes he could reach his carriage before he was accosted by anyone else. As luck would have it, not ten paces from his vehicle, he caught sight of a lady across the street with whom he had shared a dinner. It was only after two glasses of wine and a few kisses that she had confessed that her husband had not left her as she had made it seem. Instead, she revealed that he had gone out of town for business and would be returning in less than a week. Andrew had no desire to interfere in a marriage and thus had fled immediately.

"Lord St. John," Lady Flemming called to him in a cheerful tone.

Andrew dropped his gaze and hurried to the carriage, calling up to the driver before the man could even step down from his seat. "Hodge, don't delay. Even if this woman requests that you stop, go!"

"Yes, my lord," the driver said.

Andrew leapt into the carriage, slamming shut the door, and the vehicle pulled away. Leaning back against the bench, Andrew rubbed the bridge of his nose. He would have to write to Emma and cancel taking her to the party. Then he would have to find a way to ease Miss Morton's anger. All while avoiding the ire of the entire village. Or so it seemed.

A short distance away, the carriage slowed and came to a stop, and Andrew leaned out the window. A line of carriages filled the street. Whatever was causing the problem was too far ahead to see.

"Wonderful," he growled. "Just wonderful!"

"My lord!"

Andrew could not stop his eyes from widening at the sight of Lady Flemming banging on his door. Surely, she had not chased after his carriage!

"We must speak, my lord," she said, gasping. She had indeed chased after him! Never had he seen such madness! "My husband is away for a fortnight, and I would like you to come to dinner tomorrow night. Oh, and I've some gifts for you." She handed two small boxes through the window.

He murmured his thanks just as the carriage lurched forward. Staring down at the boxes with their carefully tied ribbons, he grimaced. Although he had pledged to save his estate through honest means and not trickery, he wondered if it was too late. The number of people he had duped over the past months were many. In fact, there were three in London who, if they ever caught him, would be more trouble than he could ever handle. Although he had told Emma he had no intention on running away, he might just find himself having to do just that. Before they all came for his head.

CHAPTER 9

Mrs. Agnes Rutley sifted through the small stack of letters from parents who wished to have their daughters attend her school. Every year, she endeavored to maintain the attendance of those who were from wealthy families equal to those who were not. Achieving a perfect balance was never easy. But when given the chance to spend time together, those of differing classes found they had much more in common than they once believed. That in itself was an important lesson too few in the world had the opportunity to learn.

It would not be long before many students left for Christmas break. With the New Year came another group of new students to replace those who had completed their studies.

Every year was the same. Some of the girls were meek and quiet upon their arrival. Others were far too self-assured for their own good. Either way, they all received equal instruction. That was her job. Her duty was to love and protect them. Every one of them. And she could not imagine a different life.

She stifled a yawn. It was just past four in the afternoon. The students had completed their lessons for the day and were now changing for dinner. Perhaps it was time for her to dress, as well.

A knock on the door made Agnes look up before it opened, and Mrs. Shepherd came hurrying in.

"He's here, Mrs. Rutley!" the cook said in a harsh whisper.

"Who's here?" Agnes asked as she rose from her chair. Based on the woman's expression, it was either an angry parent or the King himself.

"That man! The one who's after Miss Hunter."

Agnes frowned. "Do you mean Lord St. John?"

"No! The other man." Mrs. Shepherd glanced over her shoulder at the door, a hand on her stomach. "He's in the foyer and has asked to speak to you."

"Then send him in," Agnes replied with a sigh. "And keep the girls from listening at the door. I don't want them snooping."

Mrs. Shepherd gave a nod and hurried away.

Agnes let out a sigh. She had met Lord Egerton only once and could not blame Emma for not wanting to marry him. Emma's reasons differed from hers in that Agnes found the man offensive. What gentleman eyed a girl young enough to be his granddaughter? Yet, it was more than repulsion that she felt for the viscount. He carried an evil aura about him.

"Mrs. Rutley," the old viscount said as he entered the room. A wisp of silver hair fell over his brow as cold, dark eyes moved about the room. He had an overbearing countenance that said he was accustomed to getting what he wanted. When he wanted.

"What a pleasure it is to see you again." He did not smile as he said this.

"Good afternoon, my lord," she said, dropping into a small curtsy. "Welcome back to the school. Would you like a cup of tea? I can have a tray brought up."

She reached for the bell cord but paused when the viscount replied, "No, thank you. I don't plan to stay long."

"Very well. What can I do for you? I admit that your arrival is somewhat of a surprise. Did I miss a letter announcing this call?"

Lord Egerton smirked. "May I?" he asked, pointing to one of the high-back chairs in front of her desk.

"Of course," she replied, walking around her desk to return to her chair.

The viscount glanced around as he unbuttoned his coat and sat. "I find it fascinating that there is a school especially for women. Tell me, who is its owner?"

Agnes smiled. "That would be me, my lord. A gift of sorts from my late husband. Of course, no woman truly owns anything outright, but it is I who am in control. I assume you're not here to discuss my life and property, so perhaps we should get to the point of this meeting?"

"This is true. Your life story holds no interest to me whatsoever. It's just that most women prefer a bit of chit-chat before the discussion of important information takes place. I'm pleased that you are not one of them. I've always believed it to be a waste of time." He crossed one leg over the other. "I leave for London on Sunday and thought I would stop by to speak to Miss Hunter before I depart. I have no doubt you'll aid me in such a request."

"I'm afraid that without her parents' permission, I cannot allow you to see her without prior notice, my lord," Agnes replied. "I do my best to maintain some sense of propriety. My students must understand what it means to be a lady of good moral standing and to experience the expectations for gentlemen callers." The last thing she wanted was to let this man anywhere near Emma. If it were up to her, she would have sent him packing. Such an odious man!

The viscount reached in his pocket and withdrew a letter. A single die dropped and rolled across the floor.

Agnes raised her brows. "My husband enjoyed playing games of chance."

"Did he now?" Lord Egerton asked.

"He did, and he won his fair share. Sometimes he even wagered an entire pound on a single roll. I acted as an attendant during some of the games he held for his friends."

"A whole pound?" Lord Egerton asked, his voice filled with amusement. "I would not even consider such negligible stakes." He handed her the letter.

"You mean you've wagered more?" Agnes asked as she took the letter, adding an air of wonderment to her tone.

The viscount swiped at the sleeve of his coat. "Hazard is a gentleman's game and is not for the fainthearted. I've played where the stakes reach the hundreds, if not thousands, of pounds. Fortunes have been won and lost, although I'm usually on the winning side." He leaned forward, his eyes glinting with greed. "Estates, Mrs. Rutley. I've won entire estates with the roll of a single die!"

"That's quite impressive, my lord," Agnes said in awe. She eyed the letter. "A moment, please."

Lord Egerton waved a hand at her. "Take your time."

Sliding a finger beneath the seal, she unfolded the letter and read over it. The contents gave the viscount permission not only to call on Emma but also to take her on an outing if he so chose, as long as a chaperone accompanied them.

"Well, this certainly simplifies matters," Agnes said as she refolded the letter. "Although you have permission to escort her out, I'm afraid that her studies must come first. Evenings are quite out of the question, for she must have her rest. I'm simply not certain when she will have time for more than a call."

"I've been invited to a party on Saturday," Lord Egerton said. "At the home of Lord Cooper."

Agnes's stomach clenched. Was that not the very event Emma was to attend with Lord St. John?

The viscount stood. "I'll be here at six to collect her," he said, rebuttoning his coat.

"And I'll arrange for a chaperone," Agnes said, also standing. Her initial thought had been to have Diana be Emma's chaperone, but now she was not so sure. Perhaps someone who was not so close to Emma would be more appropriate.

"There will be no need," Lord Egerton replied. "I've already made arrangements for a chaperone. Now before I go, I wish to see Miss Hunter."

It took all the self-discipline Agnes could muster to walk to the door and send Mrs. Shepherd in search of Emma. Once the poor girl learned she would be attending her second party with the viscount rather than the baron, she would certainly be upset. And Agnes despised seeing any of her girls distraught. Yet, it was a necessary evil.

"Can't you stop him?" the cook asked in hushed tones.

Agnes shook her head. "I don't want to stop him. Lord Egerton is a man who enjoys gambling. It's best to let him believe he's winning while I come up with a plan to get us—and more importantly Emma—out of this pickle."

"Miss Hunter will be here momentarily, my lord," Agnes said, returning to her place behind the desk.

Neither spoke as they waited, and it was not long before Emma entered the office. Her yellow dress looked so lovely on her with its white ribbons and lace. Out of all her students, Emma had an innocence about her that Agnes felt a need to protect.

Lord Egerton stood. "Ah, Miss Hunter. I'm quite pleased that I didn't have to wait too long. You'll learn rather quickly that I'm not a man with a great deal of patience."

Agnes clenched her fists at her side. Oh, how she wished to pummel this man!

Emma dropped into a curtsy. "Yes, my lord," she said in her soft voice. "I didn't expect you today."

The viscount frowned. "Yes, so I understand. But I've come with wonderful news. I received an invitation to a party on Saturday evening, and you will go as my guest."

"This Saturday?" Emma asked. "I'm sorry, but I will not be able to—"

"Emma," Agnes interrupted in a firm tone, "you should thank His Lordship for taking time out of his busy schedule to come here with a personal invitation."

"But—"

Agnes gave her an encouraging nod. "Thank him now, Emma."

"Thank you, my lord," Emma said with a quick bob, but Agnes did not miss the clenched jaw or the anxiety on her features. "I look forward to accompanying you to this party."

The way the viscount's gaze raked over poor Emma's body made Agnes's stomach churn. He even licked his lips like a man sitting down to a succulent roast! What a revolting, foul creature he was!

When Lord Egerton turned his attention to Agnes once more, she had to stop herself from taking a step back from the fire in his eyes. "It's apparent that her training here is not yet complete. A man does not want a wife who argues, but rather one who does his bidding without comment. Come January, I hope to see this repugnant behavior gone. I trust you'll see this happens, Mrs. Rutley."

"Your observations are astute, my lord," Agnes replied as she dug her nails into the palms of her hands to keep the smile on her lips. "Have no doubt that, come January, Emma will be ready for her new life. You have my word."

The viscount turned to Emma. "I'll be here on Saturday to collect you. I would like you to wear the dress you are wearing now."

Emma glanced down at the yellow day dress printed with white flowers. "Yes, my lord," she squeaked.

Agnes had seen the poor girl suffer enough. "May I see you out, my lord?"

"There's no need," Lord Egerton replied. "I know the way. Good day to you." After one last inspection of Emma, he left the room.

"Oh, Mrs. Rutley!" Emma cried when they heard the sound of the front door slamming shut. "What am I to do? Lord St. John invited me to go with him to that same party on Saturday. Now I must cancel and attend with the viscount. Do you believe he'll be upset with me?"

Placing a hand on the girl's shoulder, Agnes smiled. "Not at all. I'll send a letter this evening explaining that you have a previous engagement of which you were not aware when you accepted. Lord Egerton leaves for London on Sunday, so I don't see this problem arising again."

Emma threw her arms around Agnes. "It does not matter if he leaves for two weeks or two months. Either way, he'll return. Oh, Mrs. Rutley, I don't want to marry that man! But I have no choice, do I?"

Since she first opened the school, Agnes had taken great pride in being honest with all her girls, even when it hurt to do so. It was during those hurtful times when she enjoyed it least.

"No, I'm afraid that in this matter, you have no say at all."

CHAPTER 10

Despite all the bad luck she had been having as of late, Emma considered that at least some good had intervened. The very day Mrs. Rutley sent the letter to Andrew explaining that Emma could not attend the party with him, another arrived at the school not an hour later. In it, Andrew wrote that he had an important business meeting he had to attend and therefore regretted being unable to accompany her to the party. Although relief had flooded over her at how easily that problem had been worked out, worry over being forced to spend time with Lord Egerton took its place.

When Saturday arrived, that sense of dread had become outright panic, which she now was forced to hide as she sat beside the chaperone the viscount had appointed to her, a Miss Rebecca Elkins. The woman was five years Emma's elder with dark curly hair and a plump figure. Her deep-blue gown matched her eyes perfectly.

On the arm of Lord Egerton was not how she wanted to spend a Saturday evening. Or any evening, for that matter. So many fears filled her mind, making her hands feel cold and her thoughts muddled. How many people would be at this gathering? Would there be music? What a silly question. Of course, there would be. That led to her next concern. Would she be forced to dance with the viscount? Oh, how she wished she could have avoided this evening altogether!

At least Andrew would not be in attendance. She could not have endured them being in the same room where she would be unable to speak to him. For Lord Egerton would certainly not allow her to do so.

"Are you avoiding conversation with me, Miss Hunter?" Lord Egerton asked from the seat across from her. "You've not spoken but two words to me since we left the school."

"Not at all, my lord," Emma replied, her heart attempting to burst through her chest. Did he have the ability to hear her thoughts? "It's just that I'm looking forward to this evening." The lie burnt her tongue.

Lord Egerton chuckled. "Tonight will be a test of the training you've received and the type of woman you have become because of that training. Once we are wed—if you meet my standards, that is—you'll be allowed to attend other parties with me."

Emma swallowed hard. "Standards?" she asked, aghast. And she would be *allowed* to attend?

"But of course," he replied. "A man must have certain standards that his wife must meet. To fall short of them can result in making one's life miserable."

Your life, you mean, she thought, although she kept that thought to herself. He cared nothing about whether her life was miserable. As long as his was not, that was all that mattered.

She glanced at the carriage door. They were traveling at an even clip, but she considered leaping from the vehicle and running away. This was the man her parents wished her to marry? He was a madman! The fact he was far too old did not matter as much as how he frightened her out of her wits. What sort of punishments would he set upon her if she displeased him? She was too afraid to ask.

As the carriage slowed, she turned to find the viscount staring at her. She was surprised saliva was not dripping from his chin!

"The dress you're wearing," he said, "why did you choose it?"

Emma glanced down at the yellow dress. Had he forgotten? "Because you requested it of me, my lord."

The corner of his lip curled. "You're already trying to please me.

Do you see how simple it is? Continue doing so, and you'll find life quite pleasant once we're married."

Emma wished to scream, to cry, to wail! To tell this old man that Andrew would never allow such treatment of her. But she did not. Instead, she gave a tiny nod and allowed him to hand her from the carriage without comment. At least they would be in the company of others. He would not mistreat her in public. Or so she prayed.

The country estate was massive. The stable alone was the size of the building where the school resided. "I was unaware that you had friends here in Chatsworth," she said as a couple walked past them and up the step that led to the front door. "Is that how you received an invitation?"

The viscount turned a sneer on her. "I'll only say this once, Miss Hunter. Do not ask questions of me. As a matter of fact, don't ask me questions at all. My friends and acquaintances are my business and not yours. Now, come with me and don't speak again unless I request it."

He pushed out his elbow, and stifling a grimace, Emma put her arm through his. They walked toward the portico, Miss Elkins trailing behind them.

The foyer was a massive room with dual staircases lining opposite walls that led to an upper landing. Brass sconces hung from the walls and a crystal chandelier filled with dozens of candles glowed above them in the otherwise empty room.

"We're late," Lord Egerton growled. "No doubt because of that deuced Rutley woman. Let's see if we can join the party without anyone noticing."

Unlike the party Andrew had hosted, no orchestra played, which seemed to incense Lord Egerton. "Cooper's far too smart to pay for music. A dalcop if I've ever known one. What is a party without music? Ah, there he is. I want you and Miss Elkins to find a seat until I return for you." He turned toward her, clutching her arm. "And don't speak to any other men. If one approaches, ignore him or have Miss Elkins explain that you are not to speak to anyone. Is that clear?"

Emma gave an emphatic nod, her heart pounding so terribly that her chest ached. "Yes, my lord." Did her voice have a tone of panic in it?

Apparently, it did, for he smiled at her response. "Good. You're doing far better than I expected. Keep following my directions, and I'll see you receive a gift." And with that, he walked away.

Tendrils of anger seeped through the fear that had enveloped her. How dare he treat her like a dog in training! A gift indeed!

Unfortunately, the anger that rose was not enough to displace the fear completely. So, this was what her life would be like married to that man? A life of servitude. At least if she had become a maid, she would have received a wage!

A row of chairs sat against one wall, and Emma sat beside an older woman who appeared to be in her mid-seventies with Miss Elkins on her other side. This night had been meant for her and Andrew, not to be shared with Lord Egerton. Well, at least he was leaving tomorrow and not returning until January. That gave her a nice reprieve to allow time to focus on Andrew and their budding relationship.

Emma turned to Miss Elkins. "Have you been a chaperone long?"

"No," Miss Elkins replied in a clipped tone.

"Mrs. Rutley usually hires our chaperones, but I don't recall ever seeing you before."

"That's likely because I've never been to the school before this evening. Lord Egerton hired me to act as your chaperone."

Emma gave her a warm smile. "Oh, I knew that. I was just curious—"

"It's rude to be nosy," Miss Elkins snapped. "Now, I suggest we remain quiet, so we don't draw Lord Egerton's ire. I, for one, would rather not feel his wrath again."

Again? Emma thought. That meant Lord Egerton had employed Miss Elkins before tonight. Did that mean he had other women in the village with whom he had attended functions such as this? Perhaps another woman would catch his eye, and Emma would be set free of his hold over her. Surely, he could find a lady more to his liking in London while he was there. She could only hope it was so!

Her thoughts were interrupted when Miss Elkins leaned in closer and whispered, "Whether or not you agree with anything His Lordship says, don't argue with him. If he says the sky is green, compliment his wisdom. And you were wise to wear the dress he requested, for any disobedience leads to terrible consequences."

"I must admit that I'm a bit confused," Emma said, frowning. "How do you know so much about him? Have you been in his employ before?"

"I'm simply warning you, is all," Miss Elkins said. "Now, please, no more questions." Her voice had a strange strain to it. Was she afraid the viscount would take his anger out on her rather than Emma? But that made no sense. All she had to do was sit there and make sure no men harassed—or even spoke—to Emma.

They remained sitting there in silence while those around them enjoyed themselves. At least it was only a single night that she would be forced to contend with. Then she would be free to be with Andrew.

Emma gasped. A group of men across the ballroom roared with laughter. In the middle of the circle stood Andrew. And he was not alone.

A woman was on his arm, with hair the color of ash piled high upon her hair and dotted with glinting gems. She wore a gown of white muslin trimmed in gold and covered in gold-threaded lace. She had to be the most beautiful woman Emma had ever seen. Any man would hope to spend time in her company.

But Andrew was supposed to be at a business meeting. That had been his excuse for being unable to attend the party. Oh, what a fool she was! He had lived up to his moniker!

She forced herself to remain calm. Perhaps there was more to what she was seeing. If so, who was that woman? Was she a friend? A love interest? Just because she was currently in Andrew's company did not mean they were a couple. Perhaps she had something to do with the business he was conducting this evening.

No, that made no sense. Women did not conduct business. The more Emma tried to make excuses for Andrew, the sicker she felt.

Andrew's companion glanced over her shoulder, whispered something in his ear, and then left the room. Andrew said something to the men and, much to Emma's dismay, followed after the young lady.

Emma was afraid she knew all too well what was happening here. The other girls at the school had told dozens of stories about couples meeting at parties, only to slip away for secret kisses. It was a dangerous game for a young unmarried lady to play; if one were caught in such a precarious situation, her name would be ruined forever.

Yet had Andrew not said that Emma was the only woman he thought beautiful? The memory of what he had told her that day she had encountered him in the alleyway off Rake Street entered her mind. Were the rumors indeed true? Was Andrew a rake who used compliments about a woman's beauty as a means to woo her?

Well, there was only one way to learn the truth!

Emma rose from her chair.

"You're to remain seated until Lord Egerton returns," Miss Elkins hissed. "Did you not listen to my advice?"

"I..." Emma searched her mind for any excuse. "I must find the retiring room. But I see no reason for you to follow me. I promise not to sneak away with any gentlemen."

Except Andrew, she amended silently.

Miss Elkins pursed her lips. "Very well but don't be long."

After promising she would hurry, Emma made her way toward the exit. To her left, she noticed Lord Egerton speaking to a woman perhaps twenty years his younger. Good, at least he was occupied. Maybe he would become interested in her and set Emma free.

Once in the corridor, Emma went to the first closed door and listened for any sounds of life, but there was only silence. She moved on to the next door, and it, too, lacked any indication anyone was inside the room. A footman stood at attention in the foyer, but of Andrew and the woman there was no sign.

Smiling at the footman, Emma headed down the opposite corridor. The first door was ajar, and whispers wafted into the corridor. Pressing an eye to the tiny opening, she covered her mouth to stifle a gasp. The woman had her arms wrapped around Andrew's neck!

"Now, Lord St. John," she was saying in dulcet tones, "it's about time you kissed me."

Much to Emma's horror, he leaned down and did as the woman bade.

Pain erupted in Emma's chest, as if the entire world had collapsed upon her, and she could not stop the choked sob that emitted from her lips.

"Emma!" Andrew said as he pushed away the young woman. "Wait! I can explain."

She had no desire to listen to any of his excuses! All she wanted was to get away. She turned and walked right into the solid mass of Lord Egerton. The blood in her head began to pound as she stared up into his cold, dark eyes.

He glared down at her and hissed, "What are you doing here?"

<hr>

Andrew, Lord St. John, better known as the Baron of Rake Street, wanted nothing more than the night to end. The party had begun not an hour earlier, but unless Miss Morton had a sudden urge to leave, he had no choice but to remain. This night had been meant to be spent with Emma, not another woman, but he had made his own bed. Now he was paying.

After all the wooing, after all the lies he had told and the games he had played, Andrew had looked forward to a fresh new start. It felt strange that he now found himself wanting to be the baron Emma believed him to be. Never had the urge come over him to become a better man, a man of integrity and honor, until he began seeing himself through Emma's eyes.

Yet the past had suddenly returned to haunt him—all in a single day. No, within a single hour! Miss Morton, Mr. Finch, Lady Flemming, all had made him see that he had made more enemies over the past months than he had made friends. For every wrong, there was a right, a way to make amends, and he hoped that tonight he could begin by quelling the anger of Miss Hestia Morton.

They had spoken briefly at the beginning of the party, and then Andrew had excused himself to join Lord Walcott and several other men in a heated conversation about gaming.

"Although Walcott denies it," Lord Crigons was saying, a spindly man with a beak of a nose and silver flecking his otherwise dark curly hair, "I've now heard from two sources that he's been seen frequenting a gaming hell." He turned to the earl. "So? Are the rumors true? Has Lord Walcott, the most respected man in all of Chatsworth, been engaging in such nefarious behavior?"

The earl seemed to be taking the ribbing in stride. "Very well," he said with an exaggerated sigh, "I'll admit that the rumors are true. Can a gentleman not engage in a game of chance from time to time? Or should I remain a bore like the rest of you, spending my time speaking of exploits in hunting that happened decades ago?"

The others burst out in laughter in response.

Andrew glanced around the room, and his gaze fell on Miss Morton, who was speaking to two young ladies. He prayed they would continue whatever gossip they were sharing the entire night and keep his annoying companion otherwise engaged.

"And what sort of business occupies your days, St. John?"

Andrew swallowed hard as he considered the best lie he could tell, for the truth would be far too embarrassing.

Lord Walcott, however, came to his rescue. "St. John has become involved with agreements far too valuable to share with the likes of you," he said with a chuckle. "In truth, he has an exceptional head for business, which is why I've asked him to join me in a venture that should make us a great deal of money."

"Oh, do tell!" Lord Wellington said. He was as wide as he was tall with a pudgy, youthful face, despite the fact he was ten years older than Andrew. "We are all friends here. What sort of scheme has Walcott gotten you into?"

The worries of the evening lifted, and Andrew laughed. "I'll tell you gentlemen two things," he said, leaning in closer. "The first I cannot share, for Walcott and I wish to keep what we are working on secret. The second is... well that, too, is for only the two of us to know!"

The men roared with laughter.

Lord Crigons raised his glass and said, "To our newest friend, Andrew St. John. A man with a quick mind and tongue!"

"Here, here!" agreed the others.

Andrew nearly jumped in surprise at the sudden appearance of Miss Morton at his side. "It seems you are well-liked, my lord," she whispered, her breath hot on his ear.

"It would appear that way," Andrew said. "And are you enjoying yourself? I'm finding this all quite boring if I'm to be honest. I've already seen several people leave. What is a party without lively music?" He hoped she would recommend leaving as well.

Instead, she looked behind her and then leaned in closer. "Across the foyer is a library. Meet me there in five minutes." Before he could respond, she hurried away.

Andrew frowned. Why would she want to meet him there? He snorted inwardly. Trusting her was not anything he was willing to do. Not now. Being caught alone with an unmarried young lady would not bode well for either of them. He had no doubt she had some sort of scheme in mind. She was far more devious than he had first believed, and that lack of foresight could see him pay much more than any night of gaming.

He sighed. Charming Miss Morton had proven to be more work than he had intended. Perhaps they could come to an agreement of sorts—he would return what she had given him, including the monetary value of the jewelry, and she would be willing to end this madness. He was weary of being at her beck and call.

"If you'll excuse me," he muttered before turning and leaving the ballroom. The footman standing in the foyer did not even glance in his direction as he hurried to the opposite corridor and entered the library. The room was filled with dark-stained oak bookcases built into the walls, all filled with leather-bound tomes. Several candles sat in a holder on a table beside a set of leather chairs.

"Miss Morton," Andrew said as he approached the young lady, "I don't believe it's prudent for us to be alone together. If anyone were to stumble upon us, we would be the subject of a great deal of gossip."

"One would think so," she replied, her eyes twinkling. "Although, I do wonder how it would compare to the shame of stealing from a woman with tales of starving orphans."

Andrew forced a nervous chuckle. "If you're referring to what I shared with you, I can assure you—"

"Oh, do stop!" she snapped. "Miss Trudeau has pointed out several flaws in your tale."

"Miss Trudeau?" Andrew asked, searching his mind for any mention of this person.

Miss Morton pursed her lips, her eyes blazing with annoyance. "My chaperone," she replied. "She accompanied us when we spent time together. Surely you have not forgotten her?"

"No, of course not," Andrew said. "But perhaps Miss Trudeau is misinformed."

"My friend, Miss Betty Chancellor," Miss Morton continued as if Andrew had not spoken, "confessed you not only kissed her, but you also convinced her to give you three months of her allowance!"

A lie formed on Andrew's tongue, but he swallowed it back. Perhaps it was time to tell the truth. Emma had been bold enough to do so. Therefore, why could he not also be as brave?

"Your friends are correct," he said, heaving a heavy sigh. "There are no orphans, or at least none of which I'm involved with. I know my word holds little value to you at the moment, but I swear that your money, including the value of the jewelry you gave me, will be returned to you soon."

Rather than the burst of anger that he had expected, Miss Morton instead took his hand in hers. "My lord, when a woman has been tricked as I have, she should be angry. She should rant and rave about how she was used. Yet, that is not how I feel."

"Truly?" Andrew asked, taken aback by this response.

"Truly," came her reply.

A sense of relief washed over him. "Then you'll allow me to repay you, and you'll keep this between us?" This was almost too good to be true!

"Indeed, you will repay me," she replied, a tiny smile playing on her lips. "And it is true that I am not angry about your trickery, for unlike you, I'm not one to tell falsehoods."

Humiliation roared through him. He was a liar, and she had every right to remind him of it.

"But I must admit that I'm a bit jealous."

"Jealous?" he asked in utter confusion. "Why would you be jealous? And of whom?"

"Of my friend Miss Chancellor, for she said the kiss you gave her was quite powerful, one she remembers with fondness to this day." She gave him a small pout and batted her eyelashes at him. "I would not mind receiving such a kiss. Though the ones you have given me have been nice enough, I wish for one like Betty received. If you do this for me now, I'll never speak a word to anyone of your deception. Refuse, and I'll inform Father this night all you did. Then again, perhaps I should allow you to refuse, for then you'll be forced to marry me."

Andrew's heart leapt into his throat. Marry Miss Morton? He had no desire whatsoever of marrying her—or any other woman.

A sudden image of Emma appeared in his mind. Kissing Miss Morton was akin to betrayal, despite the fact he and Emma were not even courting. Yet, if doing so kept Miss Morton from revealing what he had done, he had no other choice.

"Now, my lord," Miss Morton said, her eyelids fluttering, "it's about time you kissed me."

With guilt engulfing his heart, he lowered his head and pressed his lips to hers. His eyes opened wide when she returned a kiss of such force that he had to brace himself or stumble.

When the kiss ended, a nearby sob made him turn, and pain gripped his heart.

"Emma!" he shouted, pushing Miss Morton away. "Wait, I can explain!"

With lips pursed in a thin line and rage in her eyes, Emma turned and disappeared from sight.

As Andrew turned to follow, Miss Morton grabbed his arm and forestalled him. "Now I can tell Miss Chancellor that my kiss was far better than hers."

He jerked his arm from her grasp and hurried out the library door. A man with silver hair had hold of Emma's arm. Emma had a look of terror on her face.

"How dare you!" the man was saying.

Andrew pushed his way between the pair, anger pounding behind his ears. Then his eyes widened when he recognized the man from the gaming hell.

The older man glared at Andrew. "Do you know her?"

Andrew looked at Emma, who gave him the slightest shake of her head. Why would she hide the fact that they knew one another? Unless this was the man she spoke of, the one who had an interest in her.

"No," Andrew replied. "I was simply curious who had been spying on me. A gentleman expects at least a modicum of privacy."

The man snorted. "It appears her training has not included that eavesdropping is considered bad form." He gripped Emma's arm once more. "We're leaving. I've had enough embarrassment for one evening."

"Excuse me," Andrew said when Emma winced in pain. "I believe your grip may be too strong. It appears you are hurting her."

This made the man halt and turn back around. Andrew counted silently to himself. If the man did not release her by the count of ten, Andrew would force him to do so with his fist.

Both glared at one another, and when Andrew arrived at the count of eight, the older man released Emma from his grasp. Narrowing his eyes at Andrew, he said, "I know you. You're the boy who lost against me at hazard."

Andrew forced his fists to his side. As much as he wished to pummel this man at the moment, Emma's look of stark terror and her adamant shake of her head forestalled him.

"I am," he replied.

"Allow me to give you a bit of advice, boy," the older man growled. "As her betrothed, this girl is my property. Her father and I have a contract, and I'll not have anyone tell me how to handle that which belongs to me! Do I make myself clear?" He did not wait for Andrew to respond. "Come. We'll find that half-wit of a chaperone and leave this place before you humiliate me further."

Andrew stood in bewilderment. Signed contract? Emma had not mentioned that fact.

The feel of a hand on his back made him turn to find Miss Morton smiling up at him. "It appears the young lady is already spoken for," she said. "But I'm not. Perhaps we can come up with an arrangement of sorts, one of which we both can benefit." She leaned in close and lowered her voice. "My parents will be away next weekend."

Andrew barely heard what the woman was saying as he marched

after Emma. In the foyer, he watched as she and the older man walked through the front door, another woman following close behind.

Likely the chaperone, Andrew thought. She looked vaguely familiar, but he could not place where or when he had seen her before. Shrugging, he returned to the ballroom. Perhaps she simply reminded him of someone he knew.

As he grabbed a glass from the tray of a passing footman, he considered what to do. Emma had lied to him about her reasons for not being able to attend the party with him. Of course, he was no better, for he had lied to her for the very same reason—they both had others pulling at their strings.

Yet it was her look of heartache that worried him now. Heartache and fear. What would he have felt if he had found her kissing another man? Likely irate beyond belief.

Then as if by magic, Andrew remembered who the young woman was and where he had seen her before. She was the very woman he had seen with the older man that night at the gaming hell.

"That is not his daughter but rather his mistress." Andrew repeated the words Lord Walcott had said under his breath before gulping down another glass of brandy. Was Emma aware of who she was? And how could that scoundrel allow the woman he meant to marry to be subject to having his mistress as her chaperone?

Andrew paused, a sudden realization making his heart skip a beat. Lord Walcott's words came to mind. *"That is not his daughter but rather his mistress."* Now, Andrew understood the man's intentions!

Hurrying outside, Andrew glanced around in hopes that he would catch Emma before she left, but she was long gone. He worried the old man would attempt to do more than kiss her but dismissed that notion. The viscount was most certainly upset, which meant he was likely rushing to the school to berate Mrs. Rutley. Though, he would probably also have harsh words for Emma.

"Please let her remain safe," he said as he returned to the party. There was nothing he could do about it now, but soon, he would put an end to the treachery that was sure to come.

CHAPTER 11

Lord Egerton breathed angrily through his nostrils. Besides that, the only other sound Emma could hear besides the movement of the carriage was the blood thumping behind her eardrums. Keeping her gaze on the floor, she prayed they would arrive at the school without delay.

Emma's mind and heart were a swirl of emotions. She was sick about what she had seen in the library. Andrew kissing another woman should not have surprised her after all she had heard about him, but she had trusted him, had believed him when he said that he wanted to change.

In all honesty, Emma should have realized that the rumors were true. Yet somehow, she believed she could look past them, that he had not lied to her. What a fool she was for believing she had the ability to make a man change his ways! Especially in nothing more than a few weeks!

Amid that anger and sickness resided fear, a deep terror that kept her from even glancing at Lord Egerton. Miss Elkins, who sat in silence beside her, had warned her not to stoke the man's temper. But Emma had paid her no heed.

She rubbed the tender place on her arm where Lord Egerton had grabbed her. Who knew what the viscount would have done if Andrew had not intervened?

The carriage slowed and came to a stop, and Emma was surprised at how quickly they had arrived at the school. Granted, she had hoped they would make haste, but surely, they had much farther to travel. She moved aside the curtain and found not the school but rather a field beside them.

"Where are we?" she asked without thinking.

"Be silent!" the viscount spat. "You've upset me enough for one evening. Your father will hear of your disregard for my instructions, I promise you that!"

Emma shrank back. How could anyone make her feel smaller than her actual height? "There's no need to inform him, my lord," she said. "It's clear I've upset you, and I don't meet your expectations. Surely, there is another woman, a lady perhaps, who is more appropriate to become your wife."

Lord Egerton ignored her outburst as he threw open the door. Did he mean to hurt her?

"Come with me," he commanded. "And don't make me wait."

"Will you be joining me?" she whispered to Miss Elkins, who simply looked away without comment. Emma tried to control her breathing. "You're a chaperone. It's your duty..." Emma's words trailed off as realization hit her. Miss Elkins was not a chaperone. If not, then who was she?

"If I must ask you again," the viscount barked, "there will be trouble to pay!"

Doing her best to summon her courage, Emma stepped from the carriage. With a firm hand, he grasped her by the arm and led her away from the vehicle. Through a haze of fear, she tried to pull away, but his grip was too strong.

"That man you were spying upon," he said as he came to a stop beside a ditch at the edge of the field, "what was the reason?"

"I-I was searching for the retiring room," Emma whispered as she turned her head away. "And I walked in on them... kissing."

"Yet you appeared as if what you had seen hurt you in some way. As if he betrayed you." Lord Egerton grabbed her chin and forced her to look at him. "Do not lie to me, girl. Why did him kissing that woman cause you pain?"

Doing her best to control her breathing, she replied with the first excuse that came to mind. "I'm acquainted with the woman he was with. Her mother hosted a party I attended once. I held her in very high regard, for I believed she was a woman of integrity. The man she was with is not her fiancé. How could a woman act against the wishes of the man she is to marry?"

For a moment, Emma thought Lord Egerton would not believe her excuse, but he finally sighed and released her. "You're correct in your judgment of women such as she. They are repulsive, to say the least." When he trailed a hand up her arm, she could not keep from shivering. "Still, I requested that you remain seated, and you disobeyed me. As I said, your father will hear of this."

"Would you not be happier to find another woman more worthy to be your wife?" Emma asked again. Perhaps if she made the recommendation enough times, he would see the value of her suggestion.

He stepped forward, his face mere inches from hers. "I've already made an agreement with your father, Miss Hunter." He ran a finger down her cheek, and it took every ounce of will to keep from pulling away. "Now, allow me to kiss you, for I've been hoping to indulge myself all evening."

Running would do her no good, nor would anyone come if she were to scream. Fighting down the bile that rose in her throat, she closed her eyes and allowed his cold, unfeeling lips to brush hers. "There, that was not so bad, now was it?"

If she had been alone, she would have been sick. But she shook her head, nonetheless.

"Let's get you back to the school," he said, smiling at her for the first time. It was not a kind smile like she received from Andrew. There was a malevolence to it that made cold sweat run down her back.

When they returned to the carriage, Emma sat beside Miss Elkins. Was that a look of pity the woman gave her? Disgust?

Emma glanced in the chaperone's direction—or whatever role the woman played. Miss Elkins looked away. At least the baron would not attempt to kiss her again, even if this woman was not a chaperone.

When they finally arrived at the school, Lord Egerton walked Emma to the door. "I'll return in just over two months," he said. "Your family will collect you, and together, we'll return to my estate and be wed."

Emma nodded as the world spun around her.

Lord Egerton smirked and then returned to his carriage. Emma had never wanted to be away from any man as much as she did the viscount at this moment! Once the vehicle had pulled away, she wiped her mouth with the back of her glove. What a disgusting rogue that man was!

Opening the front door, Emma entered the foyer to find Diana descending the staircase. "Emma?" she asked. "What's wrong? You look upset."

Emma could do nothing to stop the tears from coming—tears that expressed the anger for what she had witnessed. For the fear she had endured at the hand of the man with whom she would be forced to spend the rest of her life. Oh, how she despised feeling so weak!

Diana wrapped her arms around her. "Did he hurt you?"

Emma nodded, for both men had hurt her in their way. "That woman was no chaperone," she said, wiping tears from her cheeks as Mrs. Rutley entered the foyer. "The man who I wished to kiss, kissed another. And the man I despise, the one I'm meant to marry, kissed me when I did not want him to! I wish now that I had run away that day! My life is over."

Emma's entire world was crumbling down around her like an old castle falling to ruins, and there was nothing she, or anyone else, could do about it.

Mrs. Rutley turned to Diana. "Tell Mrs. Shepherd to prepare a tray for us. Then I'd like you to join us in my office."

"Yes, Mrs. Rutley," Diana murmured before hurrying away to do the headmistress's bidding.

"Now, come and tell me everything that happened. Leave out not a single detail."

It took nearly half an hour for Emma to tell her story. Mrs. Shepherd had remained after bringing the tea, and with each detail, she gave a firm huff of anger.

"Miss Elkins warned me that Lord Egerton has a temper. If I would have listened and remained in my seat, he would not have had reason to grab me as he did. I'm sorry for not following his orders."

Mrs. Shepherd slammed a fist against a nearby table, her face purple with rage. "No man hurts any woman I care about!" she shouted. "He'll learn soon enough that I can—"

"That is quite enough, Mrs. Shepherd," Mrs. Rutley snapped. "You are excused. Thank you."

Emma wondered at this strange behavior. Never had she heard Mrs. Rutley raise her voice at anyone, let alone the cook, for they had been close friends for a very long time. And with the headmistress's pursed lips and glaring eyes, Emma made no comment.

"Now," Mrs. Rutley said once the door was closed, "what transpired tonight was not your fault. Do you understand me? There is never a reason for any man to use violence against a woman. Never."

Emma considered her headmistress's words. "I understand. But what am I to do?" Emma asked. "He says that Father has already signed away my hand in marriage. Come January, I'm to leave with him forever."

Diana gave Emma's hand a squeeze. "She'll come up with a plan. Won't you, Mrs. Rutley?"

"Do you think I should run away?" Emma asked.

"That will do nothing to solve your problems," Mrs. Rutley replied. "Your father still has not responded to my first letter. I'm surprised at the delay. Do you know if he is away?"

Emma shook her head. "I don't know, but... wait, when mother last wrote, she said something about him traveling to the home of my uncle, but she did not say for how long." Emma let her gaze fall to Mrs. Rutley's side, where her fist remained clenched.

The headmistress shook her head. "There is not much I can do at the moment. For now, I'll write to your father again and ask for confirmation that what Lord Egerton has said, concerning this contract for your hand, is true. Until we hear from him, you'll enjoy your time here with your friends."

Emma stood. "What if Lord Egerton returns, wishing to see me again before my parents reply? What will happen then?"

"I'm afraid he'll simply find you unavailable," Mrs. Rutley replied. "Don't worry, Emma. He'll not harm you again, not if I have anything to do with it."

Although everything inside Emma told her that Mrs. Rutley would be unable to keep such a promise, judging by the fierceness in the headmistress's eyes, Emma found she believed her.

CHAPTER 12

Even after four days, Emma lamented what she had witnessed at the party. Having Lord Egerton gone was a relief, to be sure, but seeing Andrew kissing another woman continued to haunt her dreams—both waking and sleeping.

Sitting in her bedroom after dinner, she turned over the letter from Andrew in her hand. It had arrived several hours earlier, but she simply could not seem to get herself to read it.

"It would be best to open it," Louisa Dunston said. "I believe I speak for everyone when I say not knowing what it contains will only make matters worse."

Louisa was the nosiest of her circle of friends, but Emma had no doubt that her intentions were pure. And she was right. Emma could either spend eternity wondering or simply open the letter and learn its contents.

Emma glanced around the room. All the girls who had made the pledge had come to support her—minus Julia and Mrs. Rutley, of course. Oh, how she loved each and every one of them!

Ruth leaned against the closed door and let out a deep sigh. "I'm sorry this happened, but I did try to warn you."

"I know you did," Emma replied. "Still, this is the second letter he's sent. Perhaps he regrets his actions."

Jenny tugged on her braid, wearing a deep frown. "Mother caught Father kissing another woman once. When she confronted him about it later, it emerged that he had hit his head earlier in the day and was confused. Perhaps something similar occurred."

Unity Ancell rolled her eyes, which was not at all surprising. The secret she had shared that day beneath the oak tree had been about her mother having an affair. If any of them knew about the ways of those who chose to step out on their marriage, she would. "There's only one way to learn what that letter says, Emma. Open and read it."

With a sigh, Emma nodded. With hands that reminded her of her great-aunt Penelope, she unfolded the piece of parchment and began reading it aloud.

Dear Emma,

Words cannot express how sorry I am for what transpired Saturday evening. I'll not lie and say that what you saw was not what you believed it to be.

Ruth snorted. "And why would he deny it?"

The others gave Ruth a firm "*Shh!*" and Emma continued.

I do have a reasonable explanation for having to kiss that woman and assure you that it had nothing to do with love. Or even lust, for that matter. I would rather not attempt to explain in writing why that incident occurred but would prefer to tell you in person. Just know that I had no choice in the matter.

Again, as I stated in my last letter, I wish to call on you. If you so agree, please respond yes to my request.

Sincerely,

Andrew St. John

. . .

Emma refolded the letter and handed it to Diana, feeling more confused than ever. "I'm uncertain what to do," she said, sighing heavily. "He's apologized and says that kissing that woman was done against his will."

Ruth threw up her hands. "I cannot believe you would even consider believing such nonsense!" she snapped. And with that, she marched out of the room, followed closely by Theodosia, who gave Emma a sympathetic smile as she left.

"Is that how you all feel?" Emma asked.

"I think you should speak to him," Jenny replied. "Then you can know for sure what happened." She stood. "Let me know what you decide."

Unity patted Emma's arm as she followed Jenny out of the room.

Emma turned to Diana. "Andrew once said that everything about me is perfect, even my height, and I believed him." She gave a tiny laugh that had not a drop of mirth. "I chose to ignore the rumors about him, but now I wonder if he said that only to woo me." She sighed. "And the woman he kissed? She's far more beautiful than I could ever hope to be. Perhaps she's caught his eye."

Diana gave a sniff. "That's preposterous. It was more likely he was inebriated on wine and fancied a kiss."

Emma frowned. "If that were the case, would he not want to kiss me? Instead, he chose *her*."

"I imagine it's because he admires you enough to not steal your kisses. Either way, you must trust me. Whoever this woman is, she cannot compare to you in any way."

"What do you believe I should do, then?" Emma asked.

Diana pursed her lips in thought. "I'd write and explain how hurt you are by what he did and that you don't wish to see him, at least not yet. It does not matter his reasons for such beastly behavior. I say it's best he learns now that such actions have consequences."

"You're right," Emma said firmly. "I'm going to write him this instant. At least, I'll have more time to think on the matter."

Leaving the bedroom, Emma made her way downstairs, meaning to go to Mrs. Rutley's office. Although Diana had her own paper and ink and would have been happy to allow Emma to use what she wanted, Emma had burdened her friend enough.

Midway down the staircase, however, Emma stopped. In the foyer was a man of perhaps sixty speaking to Mrs. Rutley.

"Thank you, my lord," she was saying. "We'll speak more on this later."

The gentleman dipped his head and walked out. Mrs. Rutley closed the door and remained standing there, her hand on the back of the door.

Mrs. Rutley glanced at Emma as she walked up to her. "When I was a girl not much younger than you, rumors abounded that there was a man who was kidnapping women in the village where I lived. It caused me to worry every time I left the house. I see that same look on you now. Is that same rumor making its rounds again?"

Emma could not help but laugh. "No. I'm sure you know that I received another letter from Lord St. John. He's asked permission to call, so he can explain what I saw at the party."

"And what have you decided?" Mrs. Rutley asked as they walked toward her office.

"I'll tell him that I need time to think," Emma replied. "He claims he had a very good excuse for kissing that woman, but what sort of excuse could he possibly have? One does not simply kiss someone without cause. I admit that I'm unsure if I should believe him."

Mrs. Rutley walked around her desk and sat in her chair. Emma took one of the seats across from her.

"Emma, you have every right to feel hurt by what you saw. I cannot command you to feel a certain way. Nor can I say whether you should take Lord St. John at his word. What I can say is that it is never wise to walk away from your problems, for doing so will not make them vanish. Therefore, if you wish to wait to speak to him, do so. But at some point, you should allow him the opportunity to explain. It's when you have all the facts that you can make an informed decision."

"But how will I know if he's speaking truthfully? And how can I be certain that he does not do it again?"

Mrs. Rutley pulled a blank piece of parchment from a drawer and placed it on the desktop. "You cannot know the future," she said.

"That is what makes life so mysterious. All worry about tomorrow is in vain, for we have no idea what it will bring. We can wish, hope, and dream, but what it brings is never certain. All you can do is decide to trust." The headmistress rose from her seat. "Now, you may use my desk to write your response if you'd like."

"Thank you," Emma said. "And Mrs. Rutley? I've one more question if I may. You said I should not worry about tomorrow, for we don't know what the future holds. How, then, can you tell me that matters with Lord Egerton will be all right? That no harm will come to me again? How can you be so certain?"

Mrs. Rutley stood in the doorway, her back to Emma. For the space of ten breaths, she remained quiet. Would she respond?

"What I know does not matter," Mrs. Rutley finally said. "Now, write your letter." And without another word, she left the room.

Emma took a seat in the headmistress's chair. She picked up the quill and stared at it.

Sometimes, she thought in frustration, *Mrs. Rutley makes little sense!*

With a sigh, she considered what she would say in her letter. Once she had it finalized in her mind, she dipped the nib into the ink and began to write.

After she completed it, she returned the quill to its holder and waited for the ink to dry. Tomorrow, when Andrew received her letter, she would wait for his response, for it would prove how pure his intentions toward her were.

Friday morning, Andrew alighted from the carriage, thankful his head did not ache. Although he had refrained from entering the gaming hell over the past week, he had indulged in far too much brandy the night before. Emma had sent him a letter, stating that she needed time to consider what she had witnessed, and he could not blame her. What she had seen had embarrassed him, so it was no wonder that it had angered her.

Patting his breast pocket, Andrew felt a sense of achievement. How often did he make it through an entire week and still had money in his pocket? Not often enough. But he did enjoy the pride he felt in such a wondrous accomplishment. And he did not doubt Emma was the reason for it. Now he worried he had ruined anything he could have had with her.

"Give it time," he murmured as he glanced up at Foxly Manor. Lord Walcott had arranged a meeting between them to discuss business; the first step of many that would see Andrew's estate put to rights.

He grasped the ledger that held the accountant's summary of his entire estate, per Lord Walcott's request, and rang the bell.

The door opened to a stiff, middle-aged butler with a balding pate surrounded by a ring of thin, graying hair. "Lord St. John," the man said with a bow. "If you will follow me, His Lordship is waiting in the parlor."

The foyer was tastefully decorated with a dark oak table polished to a gleam and two matching side tables, each holding a white vase etched with yellow flowers. A single painting depicting several men on horseback chasing after a pack of hounds who were in turn chasing after a wide-eyed fox, hung from the wall beneath a staircase that followed the wall on the right side of the room.

Andrew followed the butler to the parlor.

"Lord St. John, my lord," he announced.

"Ah, yes," Lord Walcott called. "Well, let him in, Deacon."

The butler moved aside, and Andrew entered the room. It, too, had an elegance to its décor. The walls were papered with feathery bronze fern leaves dotted with tiny red rose buds. Red and bronze fabric covered the two chairs and couch as well as the square-patterned rug that lay between them.

"Deacon," Lord Walcott said to the butler, "have a tea tray sent up."

"Yes, my lord," Deacon replied before leaving Andrew and Lord Walcott alone.

"Welcome to my home, St. John," the earl said, indicating one of the two chairs. "You look well-rested."

Andrew chuckled. "Likely because I've refrained from entering Rake Street," he replied. "I find myself with a full wallet for the first time in a long while." He held up the ledger. "The documents you requested."

"Ah, very good." Lord Walcott took the book from him. "I'll have a quick look."

As he watched the earl flip through the pages, Andrew braced himself for the horrible news that it was too late to save his estate, and his only option was to sell everything outright and begin again anew. Although he had not a head for business, even he recognized failure when he saw it.

After what seemed like hours, Lord Walcott closed the ledger and set it on the low table between them. As expected, he was frowning. "Your situation is quite horrid."

Andrew snorted. "I'm aware of that. But can it be saved? Or will I be forced to sell everything?"

Lord Walcott readjusted himself in the chair. "All is not lost, St. John," he said with a small smile. "You're not completely destitute. What you lack is money."

"Is that not what I've been saying?" Andrew asked with a derisive laugh.

The door opened, and Deacon entered carrying a tray.

"I'll serve, Deacon," the earl said. "Thank you."

The butler bowed and left the room again.

"You misunderstand me," Lord Walcott replied as he poured a cup of tea for Andrew and handed it to him. "You see, without funds flowing into your coffers on a monthly basis, your debts can only increase, causing your value to plummet." His brows knitted. "I am curious about something, however. You own quite a bit of land that sits empty. Why is no one farming it? Or renting it for grazing? You could even build cottages on some of the lots and fill them with tenants who will pay you rent."

"I don't know," Andrew replied. "Father handled all the business affairs, but he never included me in any of it. The tutors I had were excellent, but by the time I inherited everything, I felt overwhelmed and unsure how to proceed." Andrew cast his gaze to the ground.

"The estate was already in trouble when I received it." An image of

Emma came to mind. "I've only made matters worse with my gambling."

With a shake of his head, Andrew felt the familiar frustration rise. "But what does it matter? One must have animals for a farm, and as you have said, I'm far too poor to purchase any." Lord Walcott barked a laugh, and Andrew leaped from his seat. "I don't appreciate being mocked, Walcott. If that's why you brought me here, perhaps I should leave."

Lord Walcott raised a hand. "I'm not mocking you," he replied. "Please, sit. I simply find this situation a bit ironic. It reminds me of a fable I once heard."

Andrew returned to his seat, but if Lord Walcott laughed again, or if he said anything that came close to insulting, he would leave and never speak to the man again!

"You see," the earl continued, "you have land with no animals. I've been given the opportunity to purchase three dozen heifers, but I have no land suitable for them to graze on. Each of us has a problem and will need the other to overcome it."

Andrew smiled. "I see it now," he said. "So, what will happen next?"

"The summary of your estate includes a small farm with an empty cottage. I propose that I rent that land and cottage from you at a price upon which we can agree. I'll then find a tenant knowledgeable in caring for cattle and pay him a small wage."

"Business is this simple?" Andrew asked with a laugh. "I've always believed it was far more complicated."

"It can be simple if both parties in an agreement wish it to work. Although this can be a good start, it won't be enough to fund the running of your estate. You'll likely need to sell some of the parcels of land you own so you have the funds to improve those you retain."

"Improve how?" Andrew asked. "Adding cottages and such?"

Lord Walcott nodded. "And to renovate the inn you own in the village."

Andrew frowned. "What inn? There was no mention of an inn in that summary."

The earl reached for the ledger, opened it to a certain page, and read aloud. "'The property on Drury Lane has been abandoned for two decades but can readily be put back to use.'" He glanced up. "Have you no idea which building this is?"

"Is it that old inn that's been vacant for years? I had no idea Father owned it. Why would he allow it to sit empty?"

"Perhaps he believed it too costly to run," Lord Walcott offered with a shrug. "But his reasons don't matter. What does, is that you have a means to gain a substantial income. With your permission, I'd like to have a man look at it, one who knows about buildings. He can inspect the property and estimate how much it will cost to have it put back in working order again."

"Yes, I'd like that. Thank you."

They discussed the possibilities of resurrecting the inn, each making and dismissing ideas.

After some time, Lord Walcott took a sip of his tea and grimaced. "It's grown cold," he said with a chuckle. "How quickly time passes when one is focused on the matter at hand."

Indeed, more than an hour had passed since Andrew had arrived. Although he was far from returning his estate to its former glory, for the first time in his life, he felt hopeful. He would not have to resort to his old ways. That realization made him straighten is back. He could become the man he truly wished to be—a man with integrity!

"I don't know how to thank you, Walcott," he said once the discussion concluded.

"Just be wise in your decisions is all I ask. Otherwise, you owe me nothing except the agreements we make."

"Now if I can only make things right with Emma," Andrew said, "all will be well." He clamped his mouth shut. Drat his wagging tongue!

The earl raised his brows. "So, a young lady has caught your eye, has she?" he said with a chuckle. "I presume that some sort of issue has arisen."

Andrew debated whether revealing what had occurred was prudent. After all, he wanted to prove to Lord Walcott that he had changed his ways. "Let's just say she caught me in a situation I would have preferred not to have been in the first place. I've written to her twice, expressing my regret for what occurred and requesting to speak with her to explain."

"And what was her response?"

"That she needs time to consider," Andrew replied, shaking his head. "I fear the longer we're apart, the worse the damage will be."

The earl rose, and Andrew followed suit. "Let me ask you this. Do you care for this young lady?"

Andrew pursed his lips in thought. "I do care for her. What I mean is, I don't want to see her hurt, but we've only been acquainted a short time. I know very little about her to say I have any strong romantic feelings for her, but I respect her a great deal and enjoy her company."

Lord Walcott rubbed his chin. "Let me put it another way. Do you believe this woman is worth pursuing?"

Andrew nodded. "I do."

"Then allow me to be blunt. Why is she worth pursuing? Is her dowry that great?"

For a moment, Andrew's heart leaped into his throat. Lord Walcott knew him far too well to fool. "When you told me about your wife and how you cared nothing for the dowry that came with her upon your marriage, I must admit..." He sighed. "I thought you were a fool."

The earl threw his head back and laughed. "You're not the first, I assure you."

"After spending several afternoons with her, however, I found I didn't care about the monetary gain I would receive in marriage to her. I hope you don't think me weak, but I find her fascinating. She's from a family without rank, her father is a baronet, but she has the confidence of a giant. I find that I admire that. And she says that she sees it in me."

That unfamiliar sense of pride washed over him as he said those words, for they were the truth.

"Trust me, my friend," Lord Walcott said, clasping Andrew on the shoulder, "you're not weak. You've come to recognize true riches, and that makes you wise."

"So, what do you believe I should do?" Andrew asked. "I wish to see her, but thus far she's refused me."

"Then don't call on her," the earl replied. "Instead, call on Mrs. Rutley. I'm sure that will give you an excuse to inquire after Miss Hunter."

"That's a brilliant idea," Andrew said. "Thank you."

"Now, I say we meet again next Friday at the same time," Lord Walcott said as he walked Andrew to the door. "I'll have a better idea of how we should proceed."

Thanking him again, Andrew exited the manor. A sense of hope filled him, not only for his estate, but for Emma as well.

As he traveled home, an odd thought came to mind. He could not recall mentioning Emma's surname, nor the fact that she attended the school. How had the earl known? Was he checking on Andrew behind his back?

No, that made no sense. Andrew had to have named her at some point and simply forgot about it.

With a sigh, Andrew settled back on the bench and began thinking of Emma. And that was the easiest task he had done all day.

CHAPTER 13

Early Saturday morning, Andrew found himself standing in the foyer of Mrs. Rutley's School for Young Women, facing the extremely suspicious countenance of the school's cook. Flour covered Mrs. Shepherd's apron as she rested her hands on her hips, her eyes narrowed. "So, you're telling me that you're here to speak to Mrs. Rutley, are you?" she asked.

"I am," Andrew replied, finding this woman far more intimidating than even Jenkins at the gaming hell.

A flurry of voices made him turn to see more than a dozen young ladies descending the stairs.

"Goodbye, Mrs. Shepherd," one of them called out as the group headed toward the front door. Several gave him odd looks. A red-haired young woman even gave him a downright nasty glare! He was uncertain what exactly was taught at this school, but clearly none of the girls would be trifled with.

"Well, my lord," Mrs. Shepherd said once the last of the girls were gone, "Mrs. Rutley's not here, and she didn't mention any meeting with you or anyone else."

A sense of desperation washed over Andrew. "Mrs. Shepherd, you seem a reasonable woman." Her frown told him that his assumption was wrong, but he forged ahead, nonetheless. He would go to battle if he had to if it meant seeing Emma. "You're correct. Mrs. Rutley and I scheduled no meeting. The truth is that I'm here to speak to Miss Hunter. I've upset her and wish to apologize, but she has refused to see me."

Mrs. Shepherd's demeanor changed not at all. Clearly, he had not thought this far enough ahead. If he had not been so foolhardy, he would have set up a time to call, using whatever excuse he could to see it happen. Now, however, he had ruined any chance of seeing Emma.

"I'm sorry to have bothered you," he said, hanging his head in defeat. "Please inform Miss Hunter that I called."

As he turned to leave, a familiar voice called out to him.

"Wait," Emma said, descending the staircase, her friend Miss Kendricks at her side. "All is well, Mrs. Shepherd. He may remain."

The cook shook her head in wonderment. "But weren't you going out with the others?"

Emma turned to her friend. "You may go if you would like. I'll follow later. After Andrew and I have spoken."

"I'll stay if you don't mind," Miss Kendricks replied. "You'll need a chaperone, and I've nothing I need to purchase in the village."

"Girls and their love interests," Mrs. Shepherd said beneath her breath. "All right, you can see her since Miss Diana's agreed to chaperone."

Emma gave Mrs. Shepherd a small smile. "We'll likely be in the drawing room. But may we go for a stroll if we so choose?"

The cook's lips compressed for several moments before she replied, "I suppose so, but don't go out o' sight of the house. If I can't see you, it means you're getting into some sort of mischief. And we don't want that now, do we?"

Although Andrew was certain the words were directed at Emma, the cook's eyes remained on him.

"I'll make sure we maintain perfect propriety, Mrs. Shepherd," he said, offering her one of his infamous smiles.

And as before, she did not return it. Perhaps his charm had been diluted.

With a grunt, Mrs. Shepherd turned and marched past the stairs toward where the kitchen was likely located. She was a hard nut to crack! One would have believed she was hired on to guard the girls rather than cook for them.

"Thank you for agreeing to hear me out," Andrew said.

"I've not agreed to listen to what you have to say, my lord," she snapped. "I'm merely standing here in your presence and nothing more."

"As long as you're here, I'll at least have my opportunity to say my piece."

Emma glanced at her friend, who nodded. "Very well," she said finally. "Let's go outside where we can have some semblance of privacy."

A distant snort told Andrew what Emma meant by these words. After his last encounter with the cook, he would not have been surprised in the least if she was indeed listening in on their conversation. That snort did sound familiar.

"The stable should provide what we need, and we'll still be within sight of the school."

They walked at a snail's pace across the gravel path that led to the stable, which allowed Andrew a moment to gather his thoughts. He had so much he wished to say, but if he said too much, he would only make matters worse.

As if they could possibly get any worse!

"I thought you wished to speak to me," Emma said with a sniff. "If you think I'll be initiating this conversation, you're sorely mistaken. Perhaps you did not mean to come today." She jutted out her chin. "If you would rather leave, you may. Diana and I have other plans we can see to instead."

"It's not that I didn't want to come," Andrew replied. "For I did, so I could explain that I was blackmailed into kissing Miss Morton. I had no choice."

Emma gave a derisive snort and shook her head. From behind them, Miss Kendricks laughed but quickly covered it with a cough.

"You apparently don't realize the exorbitant number of rumors I've heard about you," Emma said, coming to a stop halfway to the stable.

"I so wanted to believe they were fabrications, but after what I saw, I now understand that they were irrefutably true."

Andrew went to respond, but she held up a hand. He clamped his mouth shut.

"You've given me your explanation, and now I must have the opportunity to respond. The truth is, I now question everything you have said, everything you have done." She turned and resumed the steady stroll toward the stable. "Do you truly believe I'm beautiful? If so, why would you wish to kiss another woman? Or perhaps you do believe so, but you're unable to resist the temptation. There is much I don't know, but the majority of my confusion circles around one concern. Did you not cancel our plans because you had a meeting you had to attend? That's what your letter stated. Or was that a lie so you could take someone else in my place?"

Andrew drew in a deep breath and slowly released it. "At the expense of embarrassing myself and angering you, I'll tell you every-thing I can about the woman with whom you saw me. Her name is Miss Hestia Morton, and two months ago, I called on her..."

He went on to explain about the lie he had told concerning the war orphans, the money, and jewelry he had received from her, then ended with her threat to reveal the truth to her father.

"I feared what Lord Morton would do, so I agreed to the kiss. I realize that all this seems improbable, but it's the absolute truth. I want you to know that I'll never do anything like it again."

Emma studied him for several moments, and Andrew wondered if she would demand he leave. She had every right, every reason to do so. If the tables had been turned and it was he who had stumbled upon her kissing another man, he would have been just as angry if not more so. That did not mean he could not hope she would forgive him.

"As outrageous as that story sounds," she whispered, taking his hand in hers, "I believe you. I don't know if I'm just a fool or if you deserve to be heard, but I do believe you. But I must ask myself, will you hurt me again?"

Guilt washed over him. He had never set out to hurt her, nor would he do so again. "I swear to you that since we first met, I've changed. I'll not confess how, but know this. I give you my word that what you saw will never happen again."

As the words left his lips, he wondered at such a promise. He had told Lord Walcott that it was far too early to know what he felt for this woman, but here he was, making vows to her as if they were courting. Yet doing so felt right. He somehow knew that Emma deserved such a promise.

Emma gave his hand a gentle squeeze. "Then we'll speak of it no more," she said, smiling as she released his hand.

Andrew cleared his throat. "I have another matter about which we must speak, something that has bothered me greatly this past week. That older gentleman you were with, I've seen him before at the gaming hell. That woman with him was no chaperone. I believe she's his mistress."

She dropped her gaze. "Yes, I gathered as much."

"When he grabbed you, I wanted to strike him but did not. I make one more promise to you this day. Never again will that man ever hurt you if its within my power. If he does, I'll make him pay."

The smile Emma gave him had a sad tinge to it. "I very much appreciate your offer of protection, for Lord Egerton has hurt me in more ways than you can imagine. No, he has not taken my virtue." A blush crept onto her cheeks. "But he did hurt me." She glanced past him. "Let's move to the garden. It appears Mrs. Shepherd has brought out some food for us."

Pushing down the anger that rose inside at the images of this Lord Egerton hurting Emma, Andrew glanced over his shoulder to find the cook carrying a basket in one hand and a blanket draped over the other.

"That sounds lovely," he replied, offering her his arm. "And you can tell me all that happened to you at the party."

How could he care for this lovely young woman in such a short period of time? Perhaps because she was so different from the other women he had encountered over the years. Or was it she believed in him even when he struggled to look at his own reflection.

No, the answer was simple. She made him a better man. For that, he adored her and would make good on his vows to keep her safe.

But would that promise be like all his others—given and never honored?

Andrew had spread out the blanket beneath a large tree with boughs large enough to provide shade. Although it was nearing November, the light breeze did not carry the biting chill it had the previous year but, instead, cooled the unseasonably warm air.

Emma waved away the selection of cheese and fruit as she considered where to begin.

"When Mrs. Rutley requested my presence in her office," she said as she wrapped the fabric of her skirt around a finger, "I didn't realize Lord Egerton was there. He mentioned a party and demanded that I attend with him. Of course, when I learned it was the same one you had invited me to, I so wanted to decline the earl's invitation and go with you. But Mrs. Rutley refused to give permission and thus her reason for her letter to you."

She went on to explain about the party and its aftermath, finishing with Lord Egerton nearly dragging her out of the house and the pain it had caused her, both physically and emotionally. The more she spoke, the redder Andrew's face became.

"I asked Miss Elkins to intervene on my behalf, but she ignored me. That was when I realized she was more than just a simple chaperone, and my future was grim, indeed. If the man I'm supposed to marry is willing to bring his mistress on an outing to act as my chaperone, what will he be willing to do once we are wed?"

Emma shook her head. "On our last outing, we swore never to lie to one another, yet here we are explaining ourselves again. But I never want to lie again, especially to you."

"Nor do I," Andrew replied. "I know that what occurred last week was hurtful, but I've one more question to ask. He claimed he has the right to your hand. Is that true?"

"I don't know for certain," Emma said. "Mrs. Rutley wrote to Father to learn the truth. We're still awaiting a reply, though I do not know when that will be."

"Well, I for one don't care," Andrew said in a firm tone. "Whether he does or not, I would like to speak to your father about this Lord Egerton. Surely I can make an agreement with him that will keep that man away forever."

"That would be wonderful," Emma exclaimed. "With the size of your estate and the lands you own, Father will surely see you as a worthy suitor!"

Oddly, he looked away, a grimace on his face, which contradicted his next words.

"We'll marry."

"I beg your pardon?" Emma asked with a gasp. Her thoughts began to swirl, and her heart thudded. Had she heard him correctly? How could he be proposing when they had yet to court?

Not that she minded, of course, but it was so sudden!

Andrew stood and offered a hand. Emma took it and allowed him to help her up.

"We'll marry, Miss Emma Hunter. I'll make an offer for your hand. One your father will have no other choice but to accept. My family's name and title are one of the oldest in England." He grasped her hands. "I'm far younger than Egerton, and I can make you very happy. I know I can."

Emma's mind raced. Andrew was handsome, had a good heart, and was titled. But marriage? She enjoyed his company, true, but did she love him? In fact, she hardly knew him.

"How can we possibly marry?" she asked. "My father knows nothing of our secret courtship. And there's also the matter of love. We're friends, maybe even a bit more than friends. I do admire you, but you must understand that what I feel for you has not been fully realized."

"But if we aren't betrothed, you'll be forced to marry Lord Egerton, and I know you don't want that. So, either you marry me or him. It's madness, yes, but I think until our wedding day, we can learn more about one another. I, too, wish to grow closer and..." He lowered his voice to a whisper. "And learn to understand my own feelings for you."

Emma worried her bottom lip. "We will have to keep this secret," she said. "Diana can be trusted, but no one else can know."

"Agreed," Andrew replied.

"Then, when my father's reply returns..." Her voice trailed off as the reality of what could happen blanketed her. "What if it's true? What if Lord Egerton has the right to my hand? What will we do then?"

His smile was like sunshine on a cloudy day as he grasped her by the hands. "It won't matter. If Egerton insists on recompense for breaking the betrothal, I'll pay him off. Whatever it takes!"

For a brief moment, Emma thought there was a flicker of guilt in his eyes, as if he had just made a promise he would be unable keep. But that was nonsense. He was far too wealthy for her to worry about his ability to pay.

"Then I accept your proposal," Emma said.

Yes, he was rumored to be a rake, but she found envisioning a life with him more than pleasant. There was goodness in him that many overlooked because they refused to take notice. Well, she would not be one of those people.

"I'll be the perfect husband, just you wait and see. One you can trust to provide for you. No more gambling, no more late nights drinking. You've made me very happy, Miss Emma Hunter, and as I said before, I'll never lie to you again."

Guilt tore at her soul. She had to reveal the truth about her father's lack of wealth. "There's one more thing you should know," she said, but when she saw the eagerness in his eyes, she could not bring herself to spoil such a special moment. She had to tell him that truth before they married, but it could wait for the time being. "I cannot wait until our next outing."

Andrew laughed. "Nor can I," he said.

The sound of someone clearing their throat made Emma turn. Mrs. Shepherd was standing on the veranda, her arms crossed over her chest and a wooden spoon in one hand.

"I hope Mrs. Rutley answers the door the next time I call," Andrew said, dropping Emma's hands. "I don't think Mrs. Shepherd likes me very much. And I admit she frightens me."

Emma laughed. "Trust me, she is always this way. Have I ever told you about the first time I met her?"

Despite the cook's steady glare, they shared in several stories that made both of them laugh. Not only did they learn a great deal about one another, but Emma also felt a new hope with each story they told. Gone were the threats of a marriage she did not want to a man who treated her badly. Instead, a new future dawned before her with someone for whom she had come to care. And Emma was certain nothing would ever change it.

CHAPTER 14

Although Emma was elated that she was now engaged—engaged! She could hardly believe it! Being forced to keep such wonderful news to herself was exasperating. Two weeks had passed since that wonderful day when mishaps were forgiven, and new promises were made. In that time, she had seen Andrew only once, yet their conversation of their happy future together had sustained her.

Today, Mrs. Gouldsmith was giving a lesson in the proper way to take a stroll with a young man. At times, Emma wondered if the tutor had ever encountered a man, gentleman or otherwise. How difficult could it be to merely walk?

"There are many reasons a lady might take a stroll," Mrs. Gouldsmith was saying as they passed the stable. "Yet there is one that I believe stands far above the others. You see, men can be prone to bouts of anger. Not necessarily due to an annoyance with a woman in his life, but for any variety of reasons. It does a woman well to take a stroll when those moments arise, for it gives the man the opportunity to cool alone, so to speak."

As Mrs. Gouldsmith continued her lecture, Jenny leaned in and whispered, "How is it that Mrs. Gouldsmith keeps her position here?

Her views on married life are far different from those of Mrs. Rutley. The way she speaks, one would think marriage is the same as enduring torture in a dungeon."

Emma's laugh was far louder than she had hoped, which drew a scornful eye from the tutor.

"And what do you find so amusing, Miss Hunter?" Mrs. Gouldsmith asked, her eyebrows disappearing beneath her bonnet.

"Nothing, Mrs. Gouldsmith," Emma murmured. "My apologies."

"What you find humorous will not serve you well once you're married to—"

"Lord Egerton," Abigail Swanson said in that overly sweet tone that always made the hairs on the nape of Emma's neck stand on end. "That's his name, you know, her fiancé. And he's old enough to be her grandfather. Do you think your children will be born already grown?"

Her two constant companions, tawny-haired Margaret Tranter and plump Lydia Gilstrap, laughed at this. Neither girl ever seemed to think for herself.

Tiny strands of Abigail's bright red hair peeked out from the edges of her bonnet. It was not the lovely shade Ruth possessed, but rather a tone that matched her sharp, fiery tongue. Oh, how Emma wished she could tell this *gobermouch* about Andrew!

"Abigail, you sound jealous," Louisa said in a tone that matched Abigail's. "Is it because Emma has found a suitor who is at least of noble blood, whereas your father scours the taverns in hopes he'll find a man desperate enough to marry you?"

A chorus of laughs filled the air but came to an abrupt stop when Mrs. Gouldsmith let out a shriek. "Enough with this rebellion! We'll continue our stroll in silence so you may consider how your words can embarrass your good standing. I've no idea what has come over you girls as of late, but whatever it is, it must stop!" The older woman pivoted on the spot in a huff and resumed the stroll—or rather a quick walk.

"Thank you," Emma whispered to Louisa.

If only she had the ability to speak her mind as her friends did. Yet every time she found herself in situations such as those with Abigail, it was as if her tongue tied itself in knots. It was not until much later that an appropriate retort came to mind, and by then, too much time had passed to bother.

The autumn temperature had dropped over the past week, and Emma drew her wrap in tighter.

Jenny leaned closer and whispered, "Father says that when autumn weather is late, it means that we'll have heavy snow. Is there anything more beautiful than a snowy landscape?"

"I cannot think of any," Emma whispered back. "Whatever is to happen, I wish it would happen soon. All this cold without snow is a waste of time."

Mrs. Gouldsmith led the students to the school, blessedly without further lecture on the importance of taking in fresh air or how to place one's hand properly on the arm of a gentleman caller. Emma could think of better ways to spend an afternoon! One with Andrew came to mind.

Once they returned indoors, they removed their wraps, and the tutor dismissed them. "And please remember that we'll be reading a selection in Latin when we meet again for our next lesson."

Emma and Diana headed to their bedroom, Emma speaking of her upcoming outing with Andrew.

"He's refused to tell you where you'll be going?" Diana asked, shock in her tone.

Emma nodded. "He promised it would be a wonderful surprise and nothing more."

"Surely he's mentioned what clothing you should don or some other sort of clue."

"Only that I'm to wear something appropriate for the outdoors," Emma replied. "Which could mean any number of places."

Diana sighed dreamily. "He's very romantic, isn't he? I do hope to find someone like him one day. Knowing my luck, I'll be forced to marry a bore."

Emma clicked her tongue. "Don't say such a thing. Is there not someone near your home who you wouldn't mind marrying if you could choose?"

Diana glanced at the closed door and then leaned over the edge of the bed where Emma was sitting. "The blacksmith's son," she said with a laugh. "I've not seen him since coming here, but he was oh, so hand-some! And the muscles on his arms were this big!" She used both hands to form a large circle. Then she sighed. "By the time I return home, he'll likely be married. Besides, Father would never allow such a match. Well, it does not matter. I'd rather become a spinster anyway."

She said the last part as though she had meant it. Frowning, Emma went to respond, but Diana laughed and added, "I'm only teasing, of course. You know that I wish to marry for love."

Emma understood all too well. Her mind turned to Andrew as it was often apt to do. "I find it odd that I'm happy Andrew will marry me, yet sad I cannot share the news with anyone. But it's the right choice for the time being. Although, I know she would not do so on purpose, Louisa would have every girl here discussing it. She just cannot help herself."

Diana patted Emma's hand. "They'll learn soon enough. For now, keep it to yourself. Now, we should go, or we'll be late for our next lesson."

Emma found it difficult to keep her mind on her studies. So many questions filled her mind that there was no room for Latin. Questions such as: Where was Andrew planning to take her this time? When would her father send his reply to the letter Mrs. Rutley sent him? And what would Lord Egerton do when he learned that Emma had accepted a proposal from another man?

It was all so much to consider, but Emma had no doubt that, no matter what, Andrew would make it all right in the end.

The morning Andrew was to collect her for their outing, Emma had awoken earlier than usual. Her sleep had been fitful, the excitement for the day waking her often. Despite her lack of sleep, however, she was not the least bit tired.

With Diana's help, she had taken extra care preparing herself for the outing, choosing a white day dress with yellow and purple flowers. Beneath it, she donned woolen stockings to keep her legs warm, and she wore a wool-lined pelisse.

Diana offered Emma the sapphire ring and a necklace, once again refusing to take no for an answer.

"They're meant to be worn, Emma. I've already chosen this." She fingered the cameo on its black ribbon. "If you don't wear it, it will only sit in my jewelry box, feeling unloved and useless. Don't make my poor necklace and ring feel that way!"

Emma had given in reluctantly, which was how she came to be sitting across from Andrew in his carriage wearing jewelry for the second time she could never have afforded.

Unfortunately, Andrew had been rather quiet these first ten minutes since collecting her and Diana, a tiny smile twitching at his lips. She had made several attempts to learn where he was taking them, but no matter how hard she tried, he refused to reveal their destination.

Therefore, Emma decided to change tactics. "You know, I suddenly recall that Diana and I are meant to join our friends for tea. Perhaps it would be best that we turn back at once." She paused and batted her eyelashes at him. "Of course, I may reconsider if I knew where we were going."

Andrew grinned at her. "If I told you, then there'd be no surprise, now would there? But if you insist, I'll reveal the surprise now."

"No, wait!" Emma said. "Don't tell me. It's just that I can be a bit impatient, is all. And why have you chosen to remain as silent as a monk? Is something worrying you?"

"I've not a single worry," Andrew said as he leaned back onto the bench. "I've been meeting with Lord Walcott. We've made several business agreements concerning a collection of farms that will benefit the both of us quite well."

"Then what has taken your thoughts hostage that you're not joining in conversation?" Emma asked. Learning that his thoughts had been on business and not her made her feel a bit sad.

"They have been on how pleasant it is watching you suffer, not knowing where we are going."

Emma burst out laughing, and soon, they fell into light conversation until the vehicle came to a stop.

As she alighted from the carriage, Emma studied her surroundings.

"I see a field, two cottages in the distance, and a small forest," she said, frowning. Was this the wonderful surprise he had in mind? The view was lovely, but it could have been any view in any part of England. But she would not hurt his feelings by saying so aloud. "Are we to have a picnic?"

Andrew smiled. "We'll be taking a rather lengthy stroll." He glanced at his empty arm. "It appears you have no interest."

Emma crossed her arms. "I simply want to know," she teased.

Heaving a dramatic sigh, Andrew turned to the driver and said, "Hodge, will you be so kind as to return Miss Hunter and her companion to the school? It appears they have no desire to remain."

"Yes, my lord."

Emma quickly placed her hand on Andrew's arm. "You're terrible," she said as they began to walk, Diana following behind at a discreet distance. "I'll ask no more questions, even though it pains me greatly."

Their stroll, which would have been better described as a trek, took them down a narrow path that led to the mouth of a forest. Beneath those enormous trees, Emma had never felt smaller in all her life. The sun trickled through the dense canopy, and the ground was littered with pine needles and leaves long dead.

"Did you know that a ghost resides in these woods?" Andrew asked. "Each year on a certain day..." He paused and pursed his lips in thought. "Come to think of it, I believe that day may be today. Regardless, he appears every year. Let's hope we don't encounter him."

Emma was far too old to believe in ghosts or any other such nonsense, but that did not stop her from starting at the crunch of every leaf or the rustle of an overhanging bough. The eerie surroundings intensified her apprehension, and she caught herself searching for any signs of a disembodied spirit, despite her skepticism.

"This ghost," she said as she peered into a dark place beside a large bush, "whose is it?"

"A prince who once lived here and became lost," Andrew replied.

Emma laughed outright. "A prince? Princes don't live in forests. Am I to believe that he lived in a hut or a tree?"

"Of course not," Andrew said as he stepped across a fallen log covered in moss. "He lived in a castle." He offered his hand first to

Emma and then Diana to help them cross safely. "You see, legend says that the prince was out walking through these woods when a sudden blizzard hit. For hours, he wandered through the dense woods, searching for a way to return home to his princess, a woman he fiercely loved.

"Yet as the snow increased, visibility decreased, and he somehow turned himself about and headed away from his castle rather than toward it. His corpse was found days later, tears he had wept for his bride frozen on his cheeks. They say that he still wanders these woods in search of his princess to this very day."

Emma gave a dreamy sigh. It was a beautiful tale, indeed, but it was only a tale. Castles were simply not built in forests such as these. And what would a prince be doing walking without an escort of a dozen guards? Perhaps a long-dead prince had gotten lost in the woods somewhere, but legends had a strange way of twisting truth.

As they neared the crest of a hill, the trees thinned, allowing rays of the sun to filter through the overhanging branches. Andrew had put forth a great deal of effort for this outing, but she was not accustomed to such excursions. At least she had worn her sturdier shoes.

"Lord St. John," she said, stopping to place her hands on her hips and catch her breath, "how many more miles must we walk?"

She awaited the laugh she was sure was to come. When it did not, she opened her mouth to apologize.

"Look," he said from a place just above her.

Blowing out her breath, she took his hand and allowed him to help her climb the remaining distance. When she reached the top of the hill, her jaw fell open. Below them was the forest and sitting amidst the trees was indeed a castle, or rather what remained of one. Smaller than most, its gray stone walls were covered in patches of dark-green moss. Many of the windows were missing, as was most of the roof. The tops of two of the four corner towers had crumbled into ruins, leaving behind piles of rubble where they once had stood.

"I've never seen anything so beautiful," Emma said breathily, and she could hear Diana echo the sentiment. "Does this belong to you?"

"No, but I wish it did. When I was young, my friends and I would come here in search of the ghostly prince from the story."

Emma laughed. "And did you ever find him?"

Andrew shook his head. "No, unfortunately not. Come. I'd like to show you the grounds."

Taking hold of his arm with one hand, Emma took Diana's hand with her other, and they followed Andrew down the steep embankment that led to the castle. A flutter of wings echoed through the forest as a murder of ravens erupted from one of the two remaining towers, their angry squawks expressing what they thought of the humans' intrusion.

Emma's shoe slipped on a moss-covered rock, and Andrew grasped her by the waist to keep her from falling. For a moment, her breath caught and time stopped.

"You should watch your step," he said huskily. "The path can be treacherous."

With his hands holding her so intimately, Emma could only nod. She could have remained there forever. Then she remembered Diana and took a step back. Having a chaperone was proving to be much more important the more time she spent with Andrew.

The portcullis had long been removed, allowing them to enter a large courtyard hidden within the stone walls. There were signs that others had been there before them—small fire circles, a torn piece of cloth, a cracked clay jug. Spots of wild grass, broken stone, and other natural debris also littered the floor.

"Are there any rooms remaining that are safe to enter?" Emma asked, eager to explore. "Which areas have you enjoyed seeing when you were younger?"

"I enjoyed exploring all of it," Andrew replied with a grin, looking very much the young boy he had mentioned. "And yes, there's one passage we can take that I would consider the safest. Follow me."

He walked to an opening that led to what had once been a long corridor. The outer wall had long since fallen, allowing in the light of the sun. At the end of the corridor was a tight staircase with narrow stone steps that spiraled upward. Where it led, remained to be seen.

"Be careful," Andrew said, glancing down at Emma and Diana from an upper step. "It's very easy to lose your footing. I'll go first to make sure the way is still passable. It's been some time since I've been here."

Emma looked up at him with admiration. How brave he was! Never had she thought him so alluring. She waited for him to declare the way safe before placing her hands on the wall on either side of her, her arms bent at the elbow. Several steps up, she looked under her arm to see how Diana was faring.

Poor Diana was pale with fear, and her eyes were fixed on the next step.

"Are you all right?" Emma asked.

"Yes," Diana mumbled, apparently her attention on nothing but placing her foot on the next step.

"If you would like to remain at the bottom, you may."

Diana looked up at Emma. "You wouldn't mind?"

Emma smiled at her friend. "Of course not. And I promise to be on my best behavior."

With a grateful smile, Diana inched her way back down the few steps, sighing with relief when she reached the bottom. "I'll be waiting in the courtyard."

Nodding, Emma continued her climb. The way was indeed quite steep, and she could not blame Diana for not wanting to scale it. Even she, Emma, who did not mind high places, felt a bit nervous in such a narrow space.

Partway up was an opening, and she found Andrew waiting for her. Inside were several pieces of rotted furniture, including an end table that appeared to be held together by dust.

"Here, this room," Andrew said as he placed a hand on a heavy wooden door, one of the few that remained, as far as she had seen. With a grunt, he forced the door open, the heavy hinges grinding with displeasure at being woken from their long sleep.

Emma followed him into the room and gasped at what remained of a large oak bed with four corner posts. A wardrobe lay on its side, its doors and contents long gone, and a rotted rug lay on the floor. Despite the cobwebs that covered the furniture, despite the decay, Emma imagined what the room had been like in all its glory.

"Is this the room that belonged to the prince and princess?" she asked. "Surely such a bed was for them!"

"I've always believed so," Andrew replied. "It's magnificent, is it not? The room, I mean."

"Indeed," she replied. "It all seems so... familiar somehow." She placed a hand on the stone mantel. "Although the fireplace sits cold and empty, I can imagine a roaring fire with dozens of logs within it." She went to the wardrobe and peered inside and then moved to the bed. There was something special in the midst of ruin, and Emma could feel it. "Love built this place," she said, unable to keep the awe from her voice.

The sun shifted, and shafts of light flowed through the only remaining window she had seen thus far, and she gasped. "It's stained glass!" she said, hurrying over to stand in its colorful rays. Within it was the image of a knight.

"Emma! You're glowing," Andrew said as he joined her. "I must say you've never looked more beautiful."

With her heart fluttering, Emma reached out and took hold of Andrew's hand. "I must admit I thought the tale of the prince was nothing but legend, but now I'm not so sure. To think that the princess likely stood here, fearing for her husband as she waited for him to return from the storm that raged outside." The thought made her sigh. "I'm by no means a princess, but I believe I understand her pain. For I wished that one day, my prince would come to heal my worries, to take away my pain." She looked up at his strong jawline, his noble cheekbones, his broad chest, and her heart filled to overflowing. "But unlike her, my prince did come."

CHAPTER 15

The damp air in the ancient castle was not what made Andrew shiver. No, that reaction came from the words Emma spoke. Once again, he questioned how a man could know a woman for such a short time and yet feel so deeply for her. Still, he had no answer to that burning question.

Regardless, the moment was perfect for him to somehow convey his feelings for her. The fact he struggled with this was strange for he had spoken honeyed words to many women. Yet this time, he meant them. Perhaps that was why they were more difficult to form.

"I've no royal blood," he said, smiling down at Emma, "but I've often thought of that story and the fate of the prince. The suffering he had been forced to endure being lost in such a terrible storm had to have devastated him. I've always believed it was the cold, or perhaps the hunger and thirst, that had caused him pain, but today I know differently." He took her hand and brought it to his lips. "Now I have a much better understanding for his plight, for like him, I, too, was lost in a storm—one of deceit and desperation that blinded me and made me unable to find my way."

A surge of an emotion he had never felt rushed through his body, and it took him a moment to recognize it. "Then I met you. I'm amazed at how quickly you've cleared the storm from my life. And unlike the prince before me, I've not failed, for I've found my princess."

He cradled her head in his hand as he lowered his lips to hers. Unlike the kiss they shared in the alleyway, this one would be in his memory forever. Her lips were soft and supple, and she met his eagerness with an urgency of her own. He had never tasted lips so sweet, and her small gasps of air made him hold her tighter. He would have kissed her like this all day if he could, but he resisted out of respect for Miss Kendricks, who waited for them downstairs.

"That was beautiful," Emma whispered as she gazed up at him, her lovely blue eyes bright.

He cleared his throat and pulled away, fearful that he would take things further than he wanted. This would be done right; he would make sure of it. "Perhaps we should look around a bit before we leave."

They spent more than an hour exploring not only the abandoned bedchambers but the remaining areas of the castle that still held on to life. The last room they entered was a grand dining hall. All that remained were the long wooden table that had collapsed long ago and a few broken bowls scattered across the floor.

"It's a shame that it has fallen into such a state of disrepair," Andrew said as he looked around the room. "Soon the remaining walls will collapse to join the rest of the rubble." He bent down to turn over a cracked wooden bowl, and a beetle scurried past his foot. "We should leave soon before the hour grows too late."

Emma was peering beneath the far end of the broken table. Curious as to what had caught her attention, Andrew joined her.

"Look," she said, pointing to where one end of the table touched the floor.

Andrew squatted and peered into the dark shadows. His eyes widened upon seeing two silver chalices. As often as he came here, how could he have missed them?

"Do you think they belonged to the prince and princess?" Emma asked.

Andrew licked his lips. They had to be worth a small fortune, perhaps two or even three hundred pounds, despite their tarnished and bent state. With a grunt, he attempted to lift the table's end, but it was far too heavy. That was likely why no one had ever come across such a treasure. He glanced around for anything that would help him free the goblets.

Taking a long plank of wood, he propped one end on a rock and slid the edge beneath the table. Using all his might, he pressed down on the wood, and the table lifted. Emma reached underneath and grabbed the chalices, and he lowered the table back to the floor.

The chalices were heavy! Once he sold them, he could invest the money in the business ventures he and Lord Walcott had planned. His estate would be put to rights far sooner than expected!

"What would you like to do with them?" Emma asked.

Andrew studied the wondrous find. Would taking them be considered theft? Their owners had long since perished, so likely not. And if they were going to be put to good use, surely there was no harm in selling them and using the money—

He paused. The castle belonged to someone, and that someone was not him. Had he not been doing all he could to change his ways? If that was true, how could he, in good conscience, keep them for himself? No, he was not a thief. Not any longer. Emma had shown him who he truly was, and he would never disappoint her again.

He took the goblets from her and smiled. "I think the best things for these," he said, walking over to the fireplace and placing them upon the mantel, "is to leave them with their owners. One day, the prince will return, and he and his princess will be able to raise their cups in celebration for their great reunion. I, for one, am unwilling to deny them that pleasure."

The look of approval Emma gave him was worth far more to him than any money he would have received from stolen chalices. Even the birds cheered his decision, and a deer had stopped to honor their departure.

Once they joined Diana in the courtyard, the trio made its way back to the carriage.

"Andrew," Emma said as she walked beside him, "what do you think of love?"

That was a question he had not been prepared to hear. The old

Andrew would have recited a line of prose or made a wild claim of how he had once possessed it but lost it. "I'm unsure," he answered honestly. "My friend, Lord Walcott, has experienced it. Therefore, if you are asking if it exists, I believe it does. What about you? What do you think?"

"Oh, I'm certain it exists. I also have a friend who found love, and it was beautiful bearing witness to its blooming. I've never seen Julia so happy."

If love was measured by how happy a person was, then perhaps that was what Andrew was feeling at this very moment. But surely there was more to it than mere happiness.

Emma glanced up at him. "It's my hope to one day experience what she did."

Andrew swallowed hard, uncertain how to respond. How could he be sure that what he felt was love and not contentment disguised as love? Perhaps he would ask Lord Walcott later when they met to discuss business.

Yet he could not simply leave her wondering about him. "I, too, hope to find love," he replied as they approached the carriage. He gave a relieved sigh when she smiled, and her cheeks reddened. He had said the right thing. "We should get you back to the school before it gets dark. I do hate these shorter days. They make the time I could be spending with you far too short."

They spent the return journey discussing the castle. By the time they reached Courtly Manor, he found that he wanted to remain in her presence forever. But alas, he could not. Not yet.

As they stood beside the carriage, Emma said, "Will you call next Sunday?"

"That's my intention. Unless Lord Walcott schedules a meeting." Then he frowned when the door opened, and a man exited the school. "That's strange. What's he doing here?"

"I've seen him here before," Emma said. "Mrs. Rutley has met with him, but I've no idea what they've discussed. Is he the same earl with whom you're doing business?"

Andrew nodded. "I'll send a card in a few days to inform you of my plans."

With a quick goodbye, Emma and Diana entered the school.

Andrew walked over to where Lord Walcott was gathering the reins of his horse. "Good afternoon," he called. "What are you doing here?"

"Making inquiries into my niece's education. I trust your outing went well."

"It did," Andrew said. "But I'd love to hear your thoughts on a few matters if you don't mind."

"Unfortunately, I don't have time today," the earl replied with a grunt as he mounted his horse. "Call over on Wednesday at three. We can talk then. I understand that the infamous Baron of Rake Street is still absent from the gaming tables. Is this true?"

A sense of satisfaction washed over Andrew. "It is. I no longer wish to risk that which I cannot afford to lose."

"That's wonderful news," Lord Walcott said with a large smile. "Well, I'll see you on Wednesday."

"Wednesday it is."

Lord Walcott rode away, and Andrew returned to the carriage. Soon, he was on his way home. Not only had he forsaken games of chance, but he had also given up lying and false attempts of wooing, as well. Now, he had to figure out how one went about considering the notion of love.

In the past, such a riddle would have sent him spiraling out of control. However, he had weathered the storm and found his princess. All he had to do was make certain he could afford to buy her hand.

***

Andrew arrived at Foxly Manor at exactly three in the afternoon on Wednesday. As he and Lord Walcott sat in the parlor sipping brandy, the earl spoke of the plan he had devised to aid Andrew.

"Once the property is sold," he was saying, "you can begin the work on the inn. I assume you spoke with the builders yesterday, correct?"

Andrew nodded. "We reached a reasonable agreement. They will begin construction when the funds are ready." He had been surprised at the cost of materials and labor, but once the inn began bringing in clients, the cost would be well worth the profits.

For two hours, they discussed contracts, mulled over various ideas Lord Walcott had devised, and agreed to more than one investment. In the past, such talks would have embarrassed Andrew greatly, for he lacked the will—and the knowledge—to participate. Now however, he listened to every suggestion, every idea, and asked questions of his own.

"Your understanding of numbers is far better than you believe," the earl said. "All great men of business know their numbers."

"But is that not what accountants are for? To work the numbers so we don't have to?"

"Well yes, but you must be aware of the outgoing expenses and the income your investments bring. You never want the former to be higher than the latter. Consider your accountant as the man who checks your calculations, for even I have made mistakes that would have cost me dearly if my bookkeeper had not found them first. Once you have a firm grasp on all aspects of running a business, or investing in one, you'll find your work far easier."

"Then you truly believe my estate will not go bankrupt?" Andrew asked. "I feared that by January, I would have no choice but to sell everything."

"With the changes you've made and the path you're now on, I believe all will be well. But having a plan only works if one remains steadfast to the correct way. Deviate even the slightest and one may find himself lost."

"Like the prince," Andrew mumbled, drawing a raised eyebrow from Lord Walcott. "I'll explain about that later. Unless we've completed our discussion already."

The earl leaned forward and placed his glass on the table. "There is one more thing. I'm sure I informed you at Lord Cooper's party that he and I have come to a trade agreement. Don't take offense, St. John, but I had to see that you were up to the task. It's one thing to lend you aid in the financial sense and quite another to bring you in as an equal partner."

"No offense taken," Andrew replied. "I cannot blame you for your misgivings. You must understand that for a long time, I was far from truthful with everyone. I found myself struggling to keep straight which lie I had told to whom, pretending that I was someone I was not. I believed that I could make my fortune at the gaming tables, not the office. But I can assure you that those ways are behind me. My word is far stronger than it ever has been."

"Your actions as of late have shown me as much," Lord Walcott replied, smiling like a father proud of his son, something Andrew had never experienced and found he rather enjoyed. "Now, I'd like you to come to my office."

Andrew followed him to the room that held a highly polished desk and a pair of dark-stained chairs. On the desk lay a large, rolled piece of parchment tied with twine.

"Are you familiar with Cornwall?" the earl asked as he undid the string.

"Father and I traveled there once when I was eight, but I've not been there since."

"I've done a bit of research and found that there are areas in that county that have seen a great increase in population due to the discovery of several veins of copper." He unrolled the paper to reveal a map. "Right here"—he pointed to a place on the paper—"are several villages that have seen an influx of residents. Now, I believe that as more copper is discovered, the more these villages will grow."

"Are you saying we should somehow make improvements in those villages?" Andrew asked. "You would like me to invest there, as well?"

"When the time comes, yes," the earl replied as he re-rolled the map. "Not only will you invest, but perhaps you'll even consider moving nearby to oversee the businesses we place there."

Andrew went to nod in agreement but then stopped. "And you would remain here to oversee what already is in place?" he demanded. "That doesn't seem fair. Forgive me for sounding ungrateful, but I don't think I like those terms. I'll have far more responsibility, and I'm not sure I'm ready—"

Much to Andrew's surprise, Lord Walcott barked a laugh. "You're wise to think as you do," he said, clapping Andrew on the back. "Trust me. When the time comes, you'll think differently."

The earl had been kind thus far. Perhaps he, Andrew, had spoken out of turn. And far harsher than he had intended. "My apologies for my tone, my friend. I would hate for you to think I don't trust you."

"Good." The earl took a seat in the chair behind his desk. "Now, when I saw you at the school on Sunday, you mentioned something about needing advice on a matter. Did you wish to discuss it now?"

Andrew sighed and sat in one of the chairs in front of the desk. "I've mentioned Miss Hunter to you, correct?" When Lord Walcott nodded, Andrew continued, "During our outing, she asked me what I thought of the notion of love."

"And what did you say?"

"Honestly? I was unsure how to respond, so I simply said I was willing to give it a try and left it at that. Do you think I'm weak for even considering the idea of love? Or should such thoughts be left to women?"

Lord Walcott smiled, clasping his hands on the desktop. "St. John, you'll soon learn that men who refuse to speak of such matters are the ones who are weak. Those who are willing to confront their emotions are truly the brave ones. I'm not saying you should walk around reciting sentimental poetry or singing sonnets." This made them both chuckle. "But I think you get my meaning."

"I suppose it's no different from refusing to admit that my estate was in trouble. I ignored my problems, continued to make the same mistakes, and refused to accept the truth."

"Then you have your answer," Lord Walcott said with a shrug. "The more you confront and learn from your feelings, the better equipped you'll be to make decisions in the future."

Andrew frowned. "Are you certain? The solution you offer sounds far too simple. Surely there's more to it than that."

"It's complicated in its simplicity," Lord Walcott said, rising from his chair. "In fact, love can be quite complex."

Andrew rubbed his temples. "And now I'm left more confused than ever. Is there no other advice you can give me?"

"Perhaps I can offer you this. Seek it, and you'll find it. Now, let's meet again on Monday at three."

Seek it and you'll find it? What kind of nonsense was that? Not wanting to appear half-witted, Andrew simply thanked his friend and returned to his carriage.

What had Lord Walcott meant about love being simple yet complex? Was it some sort of riddle one had to solve in order to understand whether he was in love? Had Emma already solved it? If so, she was far wiser than he.

When he arrived home, he walked into the foyer to find his mother standing in front of one of the large vases, murmuring words he was unable to hear.

When she turned, she wore a worried expression. "I'm so glad you're home."

"What's wrong?" he asked. "You appear as if you've seen a ghost."

"Several men called here earlier asking for you. Andrew, they frightened me."

"Men? What men? Can you describe them?"

She frowned in thought. "There were three of them, but the only one I remember well had a scar over one eye." She ran a finger from just above her eyebrow, over her lid, and down past her cheek.

Fear gripped Andrew, for he knew exactly who they were and their reason for coming to his home. They had come from London to collect the money he owed.

His mother must have seen the recognition in his eyes, for she asked, "Who are they?"

He had sworn to never lie again, and he would keep his promise. Once he took care of the debt he owed, she would never have to know the details.

"They work for a gentleman with whom I had a disagreement. What did you tell them?"

"That you were not in, and I was uncertain when you would return." His mother's brows knitted with concern. "Andrew, they were far worse than what you are telling me. I'm certain of it."

Andrew forced a smile and headed up the stairs. "You worry too much. If they come again, which I doubt they will, inquire where they are staying so I can call on them."

"And if they ask where you are?"

"Tell them I'm out most of the time, which is true," he replied without turning to look at her. "And that's why you've asked them to leave an address."

Once he reached his rooms, he closed the door and leaned against it. The amount of his debt was far greater than he could possibly manage, but those men were not the types to care about a man's situation. It was hard telling what they would do to see he paid his debts, but what they chose would likely be unpleasant, to say the least. He had been so certain the men from London would not find him here, but he should have known better. The locations of his holdings were common knowledge, and their lot did not give up searching for money owed to their masters.

His head ached, and his stomach was knotted in worry. His life was finally righting itself, but his past had come back to haunt him once again. And if he did not find a way to settle his debts soon, he would have no choice but to run. Far away.

CHAPTER 16

Chatsworth was bustling early Saturday morning as Emma and the other students from the school went into the village for their weekly outing. Carriages and carts lined the streets, riders on horseback, young children, and delivery men with heavy burlap sacks flung over their backs weaving between them. Liveried servants hurried about—stepping off the footpaths to allow their betters unimpeded passage—likely off to complete whatever errands assigned to them for their masters.

The signs above the various shops lobbed to and fro whenever the wind gusted, and a man went running after his hat as it tumbled down the street. Autumn had indeed arrived with a vengeance, and Emma now wished that she had donned her fur-lined pelisse rather than the wrap she had chosen.

"Theodosia and I wish to see if the millinery has any new hats," Unity said. "If any of you would like to join us, you may."

Ruth pursed her lips in thought. "I was hoping to purchase a new brooch. But I'll meet you there once I've finished." She hurried away, her hand on her bonnet to hold it in place.

"And what do you have planned?" Louisa asked, wisps of blonde hair flitting around her face. "Jenny and I were considering going to Welby Park for a stroll in search of eligible bachelors."

"In this wind?" Emma asked.

Louisa shrugged. "And why not? Are gentlemen afraid of the wind?"

Jenny held up a handkerchief upon which she had embroidered a blue rose. "My sister advised me to drop this when a handsome gentleman passes by. When he picks it up for me, he's then obligated to call on me."

Emma smiled. Although she adored Jenny, the young woman's sister had filled her head with the most absurd ideas about men and women. Even Ruth—who had said on more than one occasion that society's idea of morals and values were far too stringent for anyone's good— had threatened Jenny with bodily harm if she ever attempted any of her sister's suggestions before marriage.

Diana shook her head. "Emma and I were hoping to visit Mistral's to see what new novels they've received. Perhaps we can meet you later."

"And Jenny," Emma said, taking her friend by the hand, "please be careful. Not all men are gentlemen."

"Oh, you've no need to worry," Jenny said. "I'm far too wise to fall for their tricks. My sister has taught me everything I need to know."

"Yes, I'm quite aware of what your sister has taught you," Emma said flatly. "Just take care is all." She reluctantly released Jenny's hand. The girl would get herself in all sorts of trouble if she was not more prudent in the advice she chose to follow.

As Jenny and Louisa walked away, Emma sighed. "Why must she make me worry about her all the time?"

Diana snaked her arm through Emma's. "For the very reason I worry about you. Or why Mrs. Rutley worries about all of us. Because we care about what happens to each other."

As they made their way to the bookseller's, Emma was grateful that the wind had lessened. "I thought you only purchased books from The Temple of the Muses in Larkston," she said, glancing at Diana. "The bookseller here offers nowhere near the selection."

The previous night as they discussed their plans for the day, Emma had not missed the frantic note to her friend's tone when she mentioned the bookseller's shop. Before Emma was able to question Diana, however, several of the other students joined them in their room, so she chose not to press the matter.

Now that they were on their way to the village, Emma hoped to learn the truth.

"I'm not going there to purchase a book," Diana said as they passed by the cobbler's shop without so much as a glance at the window. Mr. Hill never changed the display of shoes. "I heard a rumor that a certain gentleman frequents the place, a Lord Barrington. And do you know what people call him?"

Emma shook her head.

"The Marquess of Magic!"

"Magic?" Emma said so loudly that an older woman passing them clicked her tongue and shot her a glare. She lowered her voice. "What do you mean 'magic'? Surely he's not involved in witchcraft?"

Diana shrugged. "I don't know for certain, but the rumors also say that although he's nearly thirty, he appears far younger. Hence, the moniker of magic. I just find it so fascinating."

Emma sighed. What had come over her friends as of late? Jenny took her sister's word as gospel, and Diana had a strange interest in a man who spent his time dabbling in the dark arts! "Well I, for one, have never heard of him. But is it true what they say? Does he indeed appear much younger than his age?"

"I don't know," Diana said. "I've never seen him. From what I've learned, he spends the majority of his time in London, but he's only recently returned to Chatsworth. My source tells me that he frequents the bookseller every Saturday soon after they open. I would like to go and see for myself if the rumors are true.

"Who is this source?" Emma asked skeptically.

"Why, Mrs. Shepherd. You know as well as I that she's acquainted with just about everyone in the village. I overheard her gossiping about the marquess with the man who does the deliveries for Mr. Daniels." She frowned. "Though I'm unsure why she was so excited he had returned. You don't think she's got aspirations for him, do you? No, that makes no sense. She mentioned that there are all sorts of rumors floating around the village about him."

Before Emma could inquire into what sort of rumors, they came to a stop in front of the tiny bookseller's shop. *England's Greatest Bookstore* was etched in the glass.

Diana pulled on Emma's arm. "Let's go inside."

Tall bookcases that touched the ceiling ran along the walls to the right and left of the entryway. Two long shelves half the height of the others ran down the middle of the shop. Emma had never seen so many books in one place in all her life. She had always wanted to see what the proprietor had to offer, but without the funds to purchase even a single book, perusing the titles seemed a waste of her time.

A thin man with round spectacles sitting on a long, straight nose approached them. "Good morning, ladies," he said with a toothy smile. "If you're in search of magazines depicting the latest fashions, you'll not be disappointed. I've even been able to procure several from France if one wishes to read them."

"We would like to browse first," Diana replied. "But thank you for the recommendation."

"Well, if you need any help with a selection, all you must do is ask. I've read quite a few of the titles here. Although, I doubt you would be interested in books on warfare." He grinned, as if what he had said was an attempt at humor.

Diana gave him a smile. "Not likely. But if I happen to change my mind, I'll be sure to request your expert opinion."

Emma followed Diana down one of the aisles, staring at the variety of tomes that filled the shelves—dark brown or black leather, deep shades of greens and blues, most with gilt or silver typography.

"They're all so beautiful," Emma breathed, daring to reach out and touch the spine of one. "They're all works of art simply sitting on the shelves."

Diana did not seem impressed. "Father has quite a collection already, but I think they're more for decoration than for enjoyment of the writing within. I've never seen him read any of them."

They moved down each aisle, but they encountered no other patrons. Diana heaved a sigh. "Perhaps Mrs. Shepherd heard wrong. Or we missed him."

"Maybe we're here too early," Emma said in an attempt to cheer up her friend. "I don't mind staying here for a while to see if he comes." The tiny bell above the door tinkled, but their view was blocked by one of the center cases.

Diana shook her head. "I couldn't ask that of you. Let's just go. We can try again next week."

"If that's what you wish to do," Emma replied.

They turned to walk back to the front of the shop when a man entered the aisle. He was tall with broad shoulders and short, wavy blond hair. He held himself in a regal manner that Emma would have thought interesting if she and Andrew were not already betrothed. Yet she found his choice in apparel peculiar, for he was covered from head to toe in black.

"Ladies," he murmured, giving them a quick bow before stepping aside to allow them to pass.

"Is it he?" Emma whispered, glancing over her shoulder.

"I'm not sure," Diana replied. "But he is handsome, is he not?"

Emma stifled a laugh. A deep blush covered her friend's face, and she was pushing back the tiny hairs that peeked from beneath her bonnet.

The gentleman had stopped at the end of the aisle and was flipping through a book he took from the shelf.

"I wonder why he hasn't removed his gloves," Diana said in a whisper. "It's quite warm in here."

Emma nodded. "Perhaps the rumors are true. I mean, look at his clothing. Even his shirt is black! Only a practitioner of witchcraft would wear nothing but black. For a man nearly thirty, he does appear closer to twenty."

Before Diana could respond, the man approached and stopped in front of them. "My apologies, but I could not help but overhear part of your whispered conversation. Were you by chance speaking about me?"

Diana's face had gone a deep crimson. "Oh, no!" she blurted. "I would never do such a thing... Forgive me, I don't know your name."

"I'm the Marquess of Barrington," he replied bow.

"It's a pleasure to make your acquaintance, my lord. I'm Miss Diana Kendricks, and this is my friend Miss Emma Hunter." Diana's voice had a strange huskiness to it.

They offered him a polite smile and gave a quick bob as they touched their skirts. There was not enough room to perform a proper curtsy.

"The pleasure is all mine," the marquess replied. "Now tell me, Miss Kendricks, what would have two young ladies such as yourself whispering about me?"

Diana pursed her lips. "About you, my lord? Of course not." She reached for the closest book and pulled it off the shelf. "We were just discussing the merits of this book."

Emma caught sight of the title, and her eyes widened. She attempted to gain Diana's attention, but to no avail.

"And what did you decide?" Lord Barrington asked in an amused tone. "I would love to hear your opinion on such an important topic."

Diana's face was filled with pride. "I was just saying that it will provide us with a great deal of knowledge on such a fascinating subject. As a matter of fact, we plan to discuss it at length later today."

The marquess placed a gloved hand on his chin. "I see. So, you are not the only person to put into practice what she reads?"

Emma tried to pinch Diana on the back of the arm, but her friend ignored her.

"Of course," Diana replied with a lift of her chin. "Why read in a particular field if one does not plan to implement that knowledge in some way?"

"That's a pity, Miss Kendricks," Lord Barrington said with a shake of his head. "I thought a lovely looking lady such as yourself would keep away from such scandalous topics." He ran a gloved finger across the front cover and read aloud the title. "Ancient Mating Rituals of Early Man?"

Diana paled considerably before shoving the book back onto the shelf with the others. The marquess gave a light chuckle and returned to his browsing at the opposite end of the aisle.

Emma followed Diana from the shop, nearly running to keep up with her.

When they were several doors away, Diana came to a sudden stop and whirled around. "Oh, Emma!" she lamented. "I can never see that man again, not after embarrassing myself to such a degree! I'm ruined!

Out of all the books I could have chosen, why did it have to be that one? Surely just picking up such a book is a stoning offense!"

Emma took her friend's hand. "It was an honest mistake. No one will chastise you for it. Only you and I know about it besides the marquess, and I see no reason for him to mention that encounter to anyone."

Diana removed a handkerchief from her reticule and dabbed at her eyes. "Are you certain?"

"Quite certain," Emma replied. "You're beautiful, and the way he smiled at you confirmed he took notice of that fact. The book itself makes no difference whatsoever. I would say he found the situation more humorous than shameful. Don't worry. He'll look your way again."

"Oh, thank you," Diana said, hugging Emma.

"I'd not listen to love advice from the likes of her. She knows nothing about the subject."

Emma turned and frowned as Abigail Swanson walked up to them, her constant companion, Margaret Tranter, smirking at her side. For a moment, she wished the wind that had slowed considerably was strong enough to carry them away to another school.

"After all," Abigail continued, "look at who's willing to marry her— a doddering old grandfather." She shrugged. "I suppose that even she must marry someone."

For far too long, Emma had allowed Abigail to treat her badly. Oh, but what she would not give to put a stop to it!

Then she smiled. Had Andrew not said that she was far more confident than she believed? If he said so, then it had to be true! Especially after he had promised to never lie to her again. Yes, it was time that she stood her ground once and for all.

"I was just thinking," she said, turning to Diana as if Abigail were not there. "As often as Abigail mentions Lord Egerton and his age, I cannot help but wonder if she hopes to steal him from me." She turned to face the other two women. "Tell me, Abigail. Do you lust after him? If you'd like, I can ask if he has a friend who may be willing to call on you. Or perhaps I can introduce you to the viscount himself. He might to take you on as a mistress. After all, he did mention that it's very important to him that his wife meet certain standards, and I have this feeling that you will not measure up."

"What...? I... How dare you!"

"How dare I?" Emma asked sweetly. "It's my understanding that women who spend so much time teasing and spreading lies about others is because they're jealous."

"Jealous?" Abigail demanded. "Why would I be jealous of anyone? Especially you?"

Margaret laughed as she brushed at a wisp of tawny hair from her cheek. "What she says is true, Abigail. You do spend a great deal of time discussing Lord Egerton. I must admit that now I'm beginning to wonder myself."

Emma was stunned. So, the girl *could* think for herself after all!

"I've heard enough of this," Abigail snapped, putting her nose in the air and marching away on a cloud of indignation. Margaret hurried after her, but not before smiling and winking at Emma.

Diana doubled over with laughter. "That was brilliant! What's brought on this sudden change?"

Never had Emma felt so proud, so fierce! For the first time in her life, she had stood up for herself, and it gave her such a sense of satisfaction that she never wanted to return to the meek child she had been up until this moment.

And Emma knew who had brought about this change in her. She grinned. "My prince," she replied, putting her arm through Diana's. "I've found mine. Now it's time we discuss finding yours."

———

By the time Emma and Diana returned to the school that afternoon, Diana was once again smiling. Emma was pleased she had been able to help her friend. After all, Diana had come to her aid so often, it was the least she could do.

As they entered the foyer, they found Mrs. Shepherd scolding Jenny before sending her to her room.

"She's a lovely girl," the cook said with a sigh, "but as thick as custard. Did either of you hear about her antics in the village today?"

Emma shook her head.

"Dropping her handkerchief to catch a man's eye!" Mrs. Shepherd said, her voice filled with incredulity. "There's a right way to perform such actions, but using it for the chance to bend over to give him a good look at your wares is going all too far. She'll be the death of me yet, I tell you." She blew out a heavy breath. "Well, it don't matter. I've set her straight. Now, Miss Emma, Mrs. Rutley wants to speak to you."

"Is she in her office?"

The cook shook her head. "The garden." When Emma glanced at Diana, Mrs. Shepherd added, "You're to go alone."

"I'll see you in our room," Diana whispered, giving Emma a sympathetic look.

Nodding, Emma walked to the door that led to the veranda behind the house. She followed the path until she caught sight of Mrs. Rutley, standing at the back of the gardens staring out over the vast field beyond the property of the school.

"You wished to speak to me?" Emma asked.

"How was your outing today?"

"Enjoyable," Emma replied. "I didn't make any purchases, of course, but that does not matter."

Mrs. Rutley turned toward her. "Why does it not matter?"

The question caught Emma by surprise. "Father never has enough money for trivialities, and what he sends me is far too small to purchase more than a scone or a new ribbon for my hair. I don't fault him, for I know he would send more if he could. I've learned that I don't need material things to make me happy." Then she noticed that the headmistress held two letters. Had her father finally sent his reply?

Mrs. Rutley made no reply as she turned her attention once more to the field. With each passing second, Emma's curiosity—as well as her concern—rose.

Finally, the headmistress spoke. "Over these past weeks, I've seen you smile more than you ever have. It's as if you've become a different woman. Mrs. Gouldsmith says you speak up more often than you once did, and your studies have improved tremendously."

Emma nodded. "I feel more self-assured," she replied. "I find that I no longer care what others think of my height or the fact that my family lacks wealth. Neither truly matter, do they?"

"I would say they have little bearing on a person's worth," Mrs. Rutley agreed. "Sadly, however, we live in a world that claims they do. A man's coffers oftentimes determine how he is viewed by society. And those who judge him by such standards decide whether they should embrace or push him away." She sighed and looked down at the letters in her hand. "I received these today. The first is from Lady St. John. She's invited us to dine with her and the baron the Friday after next."

"How wonderful!" Emma said. Then she frowned. Why was the headmistress not as pleased about this as she? "Do you wish to refuse?"

"I would love nothing more than for us to attend." Mrs. Rutley pursed her lips. "But you see, two weeks may be too late. The second letter is from your father."

"What does he say?" Emma asked as fear gripped her heart. Did she truly want to know the letter's contents? "Does Lord Egerton have the right to my hand?"

Mrs. Rutley turned toward her. "I don't know, for I've not yet opened it. Your answer to my next question will determine when I do."

Emma nodded. "I swear that I'll be truthful whatever you ask."

"Has Lord St. John been the cause of your smiles as of late?"

Emma drew in a deep breath and slowly released it. Did she dare tell the headmistress that he had proposed to her? Or what she truly was beginning to feel for him? "I would say that he is indeed why I've been happier. He's helped me realize that I'm more worthy than I once believed, and I think I've helped him, as well. When I first met him, he was unshaven, and his breath reeked of alcohol. Despite that, I felt drawn to him. He's become a better man, and I've come to care for him very much. I don't think it's love, of course, but I do admire him."

Mrs. Rutley pursed her lips in thought. "I've seen a great deal of change in him, and I've no doubt that you're the cause. But if I open this letter and your worst fears are confirmed, I cannot, in good faith, go against your father's wishes."

Emma's heart clenched, and she dropped her gaze. "I understand."

"Although..." the headmistress said thoughtfully. "If Mrs. Shepherd had been the one to collect the letter on my behalf and forgot to give it to me until, say, after we dine at Redborrow Estate, we would not know its contents now, would we?"

Joy bubbled up inside Emma. "I suppose not."

"Have you considered what you'll do if your father confirms the claim Lord Egerton has made?"

"Andrew and I have discussed it."

"I'm listening."

Emma wrung her hands. "He wants to marry me, and he's willing to compensate Lord Egerton if the need arises. From what I understand, Lord Egerton has offered Father a generous sum, which is how he convinced Father to consider him as a suitor. If that is true, Andrew's wealth and title and his offer to pay damages to Lord Egerton should be enough."

Mrs. Rutley frowned. "These matters are not as simple as you seem to believe them to be, Emma. The viscount could demand an exorbitant amount to avoid scandal. Does Lord St. John have the funds to make such an offer?"

Emma nodded. "He's quite wealthy. I've seen his lands and all the estates he owns. Even in London, he owns nearly a dozen properties and has plans to purchase more in the near future. I can assure you that money is not an issue."

Mrs. Rutley placed a hand on Emma's arm. "There is nothing wrong with hoping for the best, but you should also prepare for the worst. We'll have a better understanding two weeks from now. You may return to the school."

"Will you remain here?" Emma asked.

"I shall. I've many things to consider. Go inside and enjoy the remainder of your day."

Emma walked to the manor. Once she reached her room and Diana, she relayed all that she and the headmistress had discussed. They spoke at length about what the unopened letter could contain, and by the time they changed for dinner, Emma was certain of one thing—it did not matter what her father said. Andrew had the wealth to buy out any contract.

And that gave her a sense of peace she had not felt for a very long time.

CHAPTER 17

In the ten days that followed the outing to the castle, Andrew had seen Emma only once. His days were filled with meetings in an attempt to put his estate in order. Lord Walcott continued to deem the task "simple yet complicated," which only confused Andrew more.

Once he sold a particular plot of land, he would have enough not only to pay the servants their wages, but he also would be able to hire replacements for those who had left. Although he was proud of the progress he had made, a worry about the three men from London tugged at his mind.

He should have kept away from that gaming hell. How many terrible stories had he heard about what happened to those unable or unwilling to pay their debts? Too many. Yet, if he could put off the men finding him, perhaps he would have time to gather the funds to begin making payments. With what he assumed would be outlandish interest, he was sure, but at least his limbs would remain intact. And his life.

"For a gentleman about to welcome guests, you appear quite unhappy," his mother said, breaking him from his thoughts. "What's bothering you, my son?"

"Nothing at all," he said, smiling. "I was just thinking about a proposal Walcott made recently."

"I suggest you think about that later. A certain young lady will be arriving very soon, one of whom I believe you've grown quite fond."

He gave her a quick nod just as the new butler, Trout, entered the parlor. "Mrs. Rutley and Miss Hunter," he announced in formal tones.

"Send them in," Andrew said, rising from his seat.

As the two women entered the room, Andrew's gaze went immediately to Emma. She wore a pale blue dress with white ruffles on its hem and sleeves. In the past, he would have taken note of the gems in her ring or if she was wearing gold at her wrist. Now however, he found he no longer cared that her father could afford such trinkets. Emma was worth far more than any extravagant jewelry she owned.

As his mother engaged in small talk, Andrew studied Emma. Perhaps it was about time he told her the truth—that he was not rich, at least not for an aristocrat. Would she be willing to give up the life to which she was accustomed and live more conservatively?

"Andrew," his mother hissed, "Miss Hunter is addressing you."

Andrew smiled. "My apologies. I'm afraid my mind wandered. What did you say?"

"I just wanted to thank you for inviting us to your home." Emma turned a smile on Andrew's mother. "And thank you, my lady. It really is very good to see you again."

"I thought an evening amongst friends was necessary," his mother said.

The door opened, and Trout announced dinner.

Andrew stood. "May I escort you to the dining room, Miss Hunter?"

"Yes, of course," she replied, a lovely blush coloring her cheeks as she placed a hand on his arm.

Once everyone was seated—Andrew at the head, his mother to his right, and Emma to his left beside Mrs. Rutley—Andrew smiled and said, "Winter will soon be upon us. I've heard several people predict that we may endure quite a bit of snow soon. It's been a long time since we've had a good snow storm."

"Let's hope whatever comes melts quickly," Mrs. Rutley said. "The last time we saw a heavy snow, the roads were impassable for over a week, and even then, the mud it created made passage by carriage difficult."

As they ate, Andrew could not help but watch Emma. For some reason, she seemed distressed. From their first encounter in the alleyway to tonight, so much had happened over the past months. December would be upon them in ten days, and for many, the Season would begin soon after. Would she be one of those who traveled to London early? She had said that her father planned to have her go in January.

Or perhaps her distress came from a desire to make a good impression on his mother. She had no reason for concern, of course. His mother seemed to enjoy Emma's company, so she should not be concerned about that. And once they announced their engagement formally, she would also not need to concern herself with the Season. At least not as a debutante.

"I've decided that I'll holiday near Dover next summer," his mother was saying. "It's been far too long since I've left Chatsworth."

Seeing an opportunity to include Emma in the conversation, Andrew said, "I imagine that Emma's father can recommend a fine hotel, Mother. Perhaps even one of his own."

"He owns hotels?" his mother asked, her brows raised in surprise.

"Of course he does," Andrew said. His mother was not one for rudeness, so why was she choosing to be so now? "Emma... forgive me, Miss Hunter, did you not say that your father owned hotels near Dover?"

"He sold them last month," Emma said. "I'm sorry, but I'm not allowed to say why, for he swore me to secrecy."

What reason could the man have for selling in such a hurry? Andrew glanced at Mrs. Rutley, who was frowning. Perhaps the headmistress knew of her promise not to divulge the information. Well, he would not put her in a precarious situation by demanding she reveal to him that which she should not.

"Miss Hunter," his mother said, "have you been enjoying your outings with my son?"

Thank goodness for his mother! She could put to rights any conversation that had gone astray.

Emma laughed. "I have, my lady. His Lordship has been very kind in showing me the many properties he owns around Chatsworth. He has so many that I'm surprised the village is not named after your family."

Panic washed over Andrew. Now his mother was frowning. If Emma learned the truth, she would surely run away!

"Did you hear that there are those who are predicting snow this winter?" he asked. "I've heard many saying that we'll see so much that the roads may become impassable."

His mother's frown deepened. "We've already discussed this topic, Andrew. Or have you forgotten?"

"Well, no," Andrew replied, doing his best to ignore Emma's puzzled look. "It's just that I find it rather fascinating. Would you care to share with us more about your account of the storm from several years ago Mrs. Rutley?"

"Andrew," his mother said, her brows knitted so tightly together they nearly touched, "you were here during the last storm. I'm sure Mrs. Rutley's experience was very much like yours."

Another lie had returned to haunt him. Andrew prayed that Mrs. Rutley would ignore his mother's interruption and simply answer his question. At least then he would have time to think.

To his relief, she did just that.

"I don't mind, for it was a very exciting time, I'll admit. I recall the first morning. We woke to snow so deep that it was up past the gardener's thighs. None of the girls could go outside, not with skirts..."

Grabbing his glass of wine, Andrew took a healthy gulp. He had sworn off telling lies, leaving him to endure awkward moments like that which had just occurred. He could not continue to live this way!

Luckily, his mother was able to keep the conversation to more general topics as he considered his next steps. By the time the footmen were clearing away the last dishes, he had reached a decision.

He had to tell Emma the truth about his financial situation *tonight*. The question was, when would be the appropriate time?

Emma had hoped the evening would act as a reprieve from her qualms, a cushion to protect her thoughts from worries over what was contained in her father's letter. Instead, dining at Redborrow Estate had proven to be dreadful. How could Andrew have proposed her father's hotels? Hotels he did not own!

Now had come the day of reckoning. Would Andrew despise her once he learned she was poor? Or would he toss her aside like a dented mug? Were his feelings for her strong enough to overcome such a tremendous lie?

Unable to consume another bite, she set her fork on her plate. Her mind battled between her worries over the fate of their relationship and Andrew's insistence of hearing Mrs. Rutley speak of the weather five years earlier. He had been acting strange all evening, and she was curious to know why. She prayed this had not all been a test to make her confess!

"Now, Miss Hunter," Lady St. John said, "I understand that you've been sworn to secrecy concerning your father's enterprises, but is he in good health?"

Emma's heart thudded in her chest. Every eye in the room was upon her, judging her, measuring her. Even the footmen seemed to be holding their breath, awaiting her reply. She imagined the baroness calling on the local reverend to condemn Emma for the terrible person she was.

Gripping the edge of the table, she spoke the first words that came to mind. "Father also believes we'll soon see a great deal of snow."

Lady St. John shook her head, and Mrs. Rutley frowned again.

Her chest tightening, Emma wished someone would say something, anything! She looked to Andrew, pleading with her eyes to save her from this moment of embarrassment in which she found herself.

Somehow, he understood. "Shall we withdraw to the parlor?" he asked as he pushed back his chair. "I find conversation flows much more freely there. Trout, will you see coffee brought to us there?"

As they made their way down the corridor, Mrs. Rutley said, "My lady, you made mention of a vase in the foyer. I would very much like to see it now if you don't mind."

Lady St. John furrowed her brow. "A vase? What vase? I don't recall..." A look of understanding crossed her features, and she smiled. "Oh, yes, *that* vase. Of course, I'll take you there now. I think you'll appreciate..."

Emma watched the two women walk away. Had they all gone mad? Discussion of long-past weather. Vases Emma could not recall being mentioned. Yes, they were all quite out of their minds.

"We'll wait for them in the parlor," Andrew said, leading her into the room.

Emma sat on the couch, her hands in her lap. "You appear troubled," she said as Andrew sat across from her. "Are you well?"

"Oh, yes, quite well," he replied with a laugh that sounded forced. "In fact, I've never felt better in all my life." His voice squeaked in the midst of that statement.

Something was not right, Emma was certain of it, but how would she broach the subject if he refused to admit his concerns?

Do I truly wish to hear what bothers him? she wondered. What if she was the cause of his current state of misgivings?

"And you?" he asked. "You seem worried about something. Is there anything I can do to help?"

"Oh, no, not at all. I'm well."

They sat in silence for several moments, Emma twisting her fingers together as she looked everywhere but at Andrew.

"The evening's been wonderful..."

"I hope you've enjoyed..."

They gave nervous laughs, and Andrew said, "Please, you first."

"I was saying that I've never had a better evening." Yet another lie! How had telling falsehoods become so easy?

Andrew sighed. "Emma, will you tell me why your father sold the hotels? I know he asked you not to tell anyone, but I find it odd that he sold them in such a short period of time."

"I'm sorry, but I cannot," she said, staring at her writhing fingers. She had to change the subject and soon! "I had not meant to offend your mother by mentioning your holdings. I merely wanted to express how much I admire your success."

"Mother's a bit old-fashioned," Andrew replied. "She holds to the idea that discussing one's finances is uncouth."

"My father's the same," Emma murmured.

For the first time since they met, Emma wished to be away from Andrew. Not for any wrong he had done but rather for her own failings. To sit across from him and tell lie after lie made her feel like hiding in a hole and never emerging again.

"Emma, I must tell you something. Something that's been troubling me as of late."

She nodded. "I have something I must confess to you, as well, about my father and... another matter."

The room fell silent. Emma continued to stare at her hands. Looking at Andrew was arduous. Would he hate her once he learned the truth?

"About my properties here in Chatsworth—"

"It's getting late," Mrs. Rutley said as she entered the room, making Emma start and Andrew leap from his seat. "My lord, I would like to thank you again for inviting us to your lovely home."

A sense of remorse washed over Emma. She had not been able to confess the truth, and she had been ready for the first time since they had met! Now she would have to wait until the opportunity arose again. The question was, would she have the courage again when that time came?

"You are most welcome," Andrew said, giving Mrs. Rutley a bow. "I do hope we can do this again soon."

Mrs. Rutley smiled. "I'm sure we shall. Come now, Emma. We really must be on our way."

The return journey was quiet, the only noises the creaking of the carriage wheels and the clopping of the horses' hooves. Emma stared out the window, her thoughts now balanced between what Andrew wished to tell her and the letter from her father that awaited her at the school.

"Mrs. Rutley," she said as she turned to face the headmistress, "when I mentioned that Andrew wished he could afford to pursue my hand in marriage, you said it would not be that simple. What did you mean?"

"Let's wait until we see what your father has to say. There's no point in worrying before we learn the truth."

Emma always found Mrs. Rutley's views on the future fascinating, for she always spoke as if there was never a need for concern over what had yet to happen. That was all well and good, but with a letter that would determine what fate awaited her, it was difficult to adhere to such an auspicious perspective.

The sun was just disappearing behind the horizon as the carriage came to a stop in front of the school. After alighting from the vehicle, Emma followed Mrs. Rutley to her office, her mouth dry and her heart threatening to choke off her breath. She sent up a fervent prayer for good news.

Mrs. Rutley picked up the letter. "Would you like to read it yourself, or would you prefer I read it first?"

"You, please," Emma managed to squeak. What she wanted to say was that the headmistress could throw it into the fire.

Mrs. Rutley murmured as she read the contents of the letter to herself, but Emma caught, *My travels to see my brother took far longer than expected and thus has delayed my response.*

Then she came to one particular part and read it aloud.

As to your inquiry concerning Lord Egerton and my daughter. The viscount, indeed, holds the right to her hand, which I gave him in writing. Therefore, as we draw closer to Emma finishing her schooling, I don't believe it will be prudent for her to speak nor to have any other suitors.

The room began to spin, but Emma forced it to a standstill. "It doesn't matter," she said firmly. "Andrew will offer more. Lord Egerton will have to agree, for Andrew will make him an offer he cannot refuse!"

The headmistress took Emma's hands in hers. "Emma, I'm afraid Lord St. John will not be able to do that."

Emma frowned. "I've never argued with you, Mrs. Rutley, for I've never seen cause to do so. But this time, I must. You don't know the amount of wealth—"

"The St. John estate is nearly bankrupt," Mrs. Rutley interrupted. "He's gambled away his father's fortune. Gambled and drank."

"No!" Emma shouted. "That cannot be. Who told you such horrible lies? If Abigail has started more rumors just to hurt me—"

"Miss Swanson is not the source of this information. I learned it from Lady St. John herself. Do you remember the carriage that collected me some time back?"

Emma nodded.

"She sent for me because she was concerned about the condition of the estate. I hoped I would not have to tell you this, but now I have no choice."

"Then, he's lost everything?" Emma whispered. Her heart trembled as much as her body when the headmistress gave a grave nod. "That means he'll be unable to pay off the viscount. He told me he had changed his ways, yet that was a lie. He's told so many. I'm not sure I can believe anything he says."

"Oh, he's changed his ways," Mrs. Rutley said. "And I've no doubt that you're the reason. I understand that he's been working hard to correct his past mistakes."

Hurt, confusion, and rage engulfed Emma. "You knew all this and never told me?" she demanded. "Now I see why you arranged for him and me to meet. It was a favor to his mother!"

"If you wish to call it that, then yes, it was a favor."

"I trusted you! When the others spoke poorly of Andrew, I told them you would never allow anyone to hurt me. That you were the wisest woman I know. That you would never put me in a position where I would be hurt. But you betrayed me!" Tears now streamed down her face, and she did nothing to stop them. She had a right to those tears!

"You misunderstand our intentions," Mrs. Rutley said. "His mother and I thought the two of you would be good for one another. And we were correct in that assumption."

"Well, you were wrong!" Emma snapped. "Both of you! You did all this to help a friend, caring nothing for my heart. I'll not be able to see him again, will I?"

Mrs. Rutley shook her head. "I'm afraid not."

"And Lord Egerton will return one day to marry me and take me away with him." Never had she felt such anger, such bitterness—such betrayal!—in all her life. "Why would you do this to me, knowing Andrew and I could never be together? Is your loyalty to his mother so great that you're willing to step on me to give her what she wants?"

"Because I'm a firm believer in hope," Mrs. Rutley replied, seemingly unfazed in the face of Emma's rage. "Hope that situations change, that what we plan works out differently. Everyone needs that kind of hope in their lives, especially you."

"Hope?" Emma demanded. "Hope will not fill Andrew's coffers! Hope will not save me from the marriage I'll be forced to endure! I once thanked you for not allowing me to run away, but now I despise you for stopping me!"

And with that, she turned on her heels and marched out the door, not caring that she had disrespected the woman she once held in great esteem.

"Please, don't leave, Emma," Mrs. Rutley called.

Emma ignored her.

By the time she reached her room, she slammed the door and threw herself on her bed and sobbed into her pillow. Not meeting Andrew at all would have been far better than the agony of losing him!

"Emma?" Diana hurried to her side. "Emma, what's wrong?"

"Everything!" Emma said, her voice muffled. "My life's now over, and my fate's been sealed. And there's not a thing I, nor Andrew, can do about it!"

CHAPTER 18

There was no weight heavier than a guilty conscience, or so Andrew had come to learn. It had been nearly two weeks since the dinner with Mrs. Rutley and Emma. He had made several attempts to call, but each time he'd been refused. Oh, the excuses were reasonable, most expressing the need to concentrate on her studies, but something was terribly wrong, he was certain of it.

Then a thought occurred to him. What if Emma had confirmed that this Lord Egerton did indeed hold the right to her hand? He had promised to find a way to buy out the viscount's offer, but like every other promise he had made, it was a lie. And lies festered like untreated wounds until the person either died or lost a limb.

The bitter cold wind made him draw his overcoat tighter, and he ducked his head for added warmth. The tip of his nose burned, as did his ears, and thoughts of a glass of brandy—or ten—were appealing. How easy it had been to return to drowning his sorrows in alcohol, despite the weeks of abstinence. Without Emma nearby, his motivation and resolve waned. She was the strength he needed to stay on the straight and narrow.

In his pocket were his flask and nearly two hundred pounds, an amount far too low to tempt Lord Egerton. But perhaps a few games of hazard would see him earn enough to make the man's mouth water.

He paused in the doorway of a closed shop to remove the flask, took a healthy swallow, and continued his trek to Rake Street. The light murmurs of people behind him made him quicken his step. No doubt rumors about him had begun anew.

He's a liar and a cheat, they were likely whispering behind their hands.

He destroyed everything his father had spent years building!

What can he offer anyone, let alone a bride? Nothing!

If they were indeed making such comments about him, he could not refute them for they were true. All of them. He had made Emma a promise, and now she would suffer because of it.

Well, luck would be on his side this Friday evening. The dice would finally fall in his favor, he could feel it. He had not gambled in nearly a month, and Lord Walcott had been approving. But these were desperate times that called for one last chance.

As he turned into the alleyway that led to the gaming hall, a man's voice called out to him. "Lord St. John, is that you?"

Andrew turned. "Yes?"

His blood ran cold as three men approached him. They wore simple trousers and rugged coats that did nothing to hide their muscular bulk. One wore a distinct scar over one eye. So, his luck had not changed after all.

"We've been looking for you for some time, my lord," the man with the scar snarled, using his title more as a curse than a show of deference.

Andrew glanced around him for any sign of escape, but the scarred man's companions blocked his way.

"Now, there ain't no use in running, so don't bother tryin'."

Andrew forced a laugh. "Running? I've no plans to run. In fact, I'd like to inquire about making payments."

"Payments?" the leader said with a laugh that made the hairs on the nape of Andrew's neck stand upright. "You missed that chance months ago. Now it's time to pay." He grasped Andrew by the collar and threw him against the wall. "Now, where's the money?"

"What? Do you honestly believe that I'd carry around twelve thousand pounds on my person?" Andrew replied, forcing calm into his tone. He could not allow this man to see any signs of weakness. "In fact—"

The blow to his midsection made him double over in pain, leaving him breathless.

The scarred man chuckled. "I'd say that was worth... what? A farthing?"

"Nah," one of his companions said. "I'd say at least a ha'penny. I've felt the force of your blows." The trio roared with laughter.

"What's your name, sir?" Andrew managed to gasp.

"Name's Locket. Ewen Locket."

Andrew forced himself to straighten his back. "Well, Locket, might I beg of your good graces and allow me to pay you what I can now?"

Locket jerked his head at one of the others. "Go inside and get the boss."

"The boss?" Andrew asked.

"Yeah," Locket replied. "The man you didn't pay back. Lucky for him, he arrived here this morning." So, he would finally meet the mysterious benefactor who had backed his debts. Whenever Andrew had inquired in the past, he was told it was none of his concern. Apparently, that had changed. Whether that was a good thing or bad remained to be seen.

Andrew glanced past his captors for any signs of aid, but with the darkening alleyway and the empty streets, his cries for help would go unnoticed. Or ignored. Few cared to lend aid anywhere near the gaming hell.

"I'm a baron," Andrew said. "If you kill me, the *ton* will seek vengeance on you."

"Don't worry 'bout me," Locket said, patting Andrew on the cheek. "We'd just kill you here where no one'll take any notice. Do you think your life'd be the first I've taken as payment for debts owed? I know how to do my job well enough that no one'll know who did it."

Behind Andrew came the sound of footsteps, but he was unable to turn to see who approached.

"So, this is Andrew St. John, is it? The boy who thinks he can steal from me?"

"I didn't steal anything from you," Andrew said. "I borrowed—" He stood, stunned when Locket spun him about, and he came to stare into the face of the very man Emma was meant to marry. This was whom he owed money? The odds were so great that if he had placed a bet with his guess, he would have owed more money than existed in the whole country. In the entire world!

"You're in a great deal of trouble, boy," Lord Egerton growled as he came to stand in front of Andrew, his hands on his hips and a scowl on his face.

Andrew tried to take a step back, only to collide with one of the massive men who had cornered him. "I know I owe you a large sum of money, but I'm willing to make payments."

"I'm listening," Lord Egerton said.

"What do you say to monthly payments?" Andrew asked. "With interest, of course."

The viscount barked a laugh as he gripped Andrew by the shoulder. "Of course, there will be interest! But why should I allow you to make payments? I was kind enough to extend credit to you at my London establishment, trusting you to repay me in full. Yet upon losing it all, you disappeared. What name did you give? Oh yes, Andrew Hedgeworth."

"I apologize for my deceitful behavior," Andrew said. "So, do you agree? And if so, what will be the terms?"

One of Locket's companions sneered. "I wouldn't let 'im off that easy, my lord."

Lord Egerton shot the man a glare and waved him away. "I don't need your council, Crummit." He returned his gaze to Andrew. "Six hundred a month for the next two years."

Andrew calculated the total in his head and nodded. That was far better terms than he had expected.

"I expect each payment on the first of each month beginning in January. Let's just say that it's a good way to start off the New Year." He grasped Andrew by the collar. "But if you're late, even by a day, you'll be charged a fee."

"What sort of fee?"

Lord Egerton drew back his fist and shoved it into Andrew's stomach, making him double over with a grunt, all the breath driven from him for the second time.

"Now that I've finally found you, I can resume other meaningful pursuits."

The viscount nodded, and one of the men struck Andrew again. If this continued, he'd be left with broken ribs and no breath in his lungs! Even his eyes watered from the pain.

"My generosity can only go so far," Lord Egerton said. "Let's just say that's for the interest you already owed me. And this is for my distress."

Pain erupted in Andrew's jaw and blackness enveloped him. When he woke again, it was to the sound of a familiar voice and a hand shaking him.

"St. John? St. John, what happened?"

Lord Walcott helped him to a sitting position.

Andrew rubbed his aching jaw before responding. "Well, Walcott, I'm afraid that all my wrongs have finally caught up with me. It's over. My life is forfeit." He could do nothing to quell the tone of defeat in his voice.

With a sigh, the earl placed a hand under Andrew's arm to help him stand. "Nothing's over," he said as he brushed dirt from Andrew's coat. "There's always hope. Come, let's get you out of here."

A fire crackled in the hearth as Andrew placed a cool cloth against his aching head. His left eye and cheek throbbed, and he was certain at least one rib was broken.

"Here," Lord Walcott said, handing him a glass of whiskey. "Drink this. It'll help with the pain."

"Thank you." Andrew took a sip and grimaced, the burning in his throat matching his humiliation.

The earl took a seat across from him. "Now, explain what occurred in the alleyway."

"You're well aware of how much I used to gamble," Andrew said with a sigh.

Lord Walcott nodded. "I am."

Andrew shifted in his chair, grunting in pain from the movement. "Five months ago, I went to London under the pretense of meeting a client to discuss the signing of contracts." He shook his head. "I don't even remember what lie I told about what agreement we were making. The true reason I went was I had heard about a gaming hell that offered generous credit to those who needed it. And trust me, I most certainly needed it."

"Generous?" Lord Walcott said with a snort. "You know as well as I that places such as that may be generous in extending credit, but they are far from charitable when it comes to collecting."

"Trust me, I know quite well," Andrew said.

At least the men kept me from the gaming tables, he thought with a wry chuckle as he gingerly touched his eye. *I kept my promise to Emma, albeit in a roundabout fashion.*

Aloud, he continued, "I took a thousand pounds, every farthing I had. When that was exhausted, I asked for credit. I'm telling you, Walcott, that old man, the one you said likely made a pact with Lucifer? As it turns out, he's the man who owns that establishment. He and his men were the ones who did this to me as a reminder of what happens if I don't pay my debts."

He paused to take a sip of the whiskey. "But that's not all," he continued once the burning in his throat had dissipated. "He's also the man who signed the contract for Emma's hand in marriage."

The earl stood and walked over to the table that held the liquor decanters. "I assume you'll be unable to persuade this man to end his betrothal with Miss Hunter because you already owe him a great deal of money. And now you're afraid she will be doubly hurt. Am I correct?"

Andrew nodded. Then a thought came to mind, and he frowned. "How did you know I planned to do this? I never mentioned it."

This was not the first time Lord Walcott had mentioned what Andrew had not yet revealed. Where had he come across such knowledge?

The earl returned with two glasses. He handed Andrew one and then sat, sighing deeply. "It's not by chance that we were both at the gaming hell the first day we spoke. There are those who've been concerned about you and asked for my help."

"Who?" Andrew shook his head. "Mother."

Lord Walcott leaned his forearms on his knees. "Yes. And Mrs. Rutley from the school. I've been able to combine what you've told me with what they've shared. It wasn't difficult to fill in the missing pieces. You've wasted your life over these last few years, but there's always hope."

Rage boiled in Andrew. "I'm glad that my failures have caused everyone I know to conspire against me."

"Your mother cares about you, St. John. She saw the destruction you've caused and had no choice but to request my aid."

Andrew snorted. "She cares only for the estate. I'm nothing but a disappointment to her."

"Don't speak about your mother in such a heinous way!" Lord Walcott snapped, making Andrew jump in surprise. "She cares for you. Have you any idea how much it pains her to see her own son destroy everything around him—including himself? That she's been forced to listen to rumors she knew were true? It was because of that pain, of her will to see you succeed, that she sought out Mrs. Rutley who, in turn, came to me."

"How are you and Mrs. Rutley acquainted?"

"That does not matter," the earl said. "What does is your livelihood. Do you have the funds to make the payments you've promised?"

"You know very well I don't. The only way I can is to sell off all the excess properties."

"But if you do that, you'll have no land left for grazing or for the various crops produced on them," Lord Walcott said. "Not to mention the cottages that you can build and rent. All those were to be sources of income. If they are gone, what will you do then?"

"Well, I refuse to sell Redborrow Estate, for it would only crush Mother. I'll sell what properties I can and pray the inn will make up for the lost income. But none of that helps me with Emma. Egerton will marry her, and there's nothing I can do to stop him."

He threw back his head and gulped the rest of the whiskey. If there were only a way!

Then an idea occurred to him. "You've seen the changes I've made as of late, correct?"

"I have."

"Perhaps you can loan me the money. I can pay off Egerton for Emma's hand. We can draw up whatever contracts you wish, and I'll pay you back monthly and with interest. Would you be willing to do this for me?"

With a sigh Lord Walcott said, "I see no reason why Egerton would wish to give up a woman as wealthy as Miss Hunter." Andrew frowned as the man continued, "Let's presume he would consider compensation and agree to not cause a scandal. He knows you lack the funds it would take to meet his demands. It would not be prudent to even consider this option." The earl set his glass on his knee. "Regardless, I don't have those kinds of funds readily available. And even if I did, I don't like the idea of involving myself with a man I'd prefer to have nothing to do with. He's far too dangerous."

"But you won't have to deal with him," Andrew said. "I'm sure you have the means to gather what I need. Then you'll give me the money, and I'll see it given to him. Your name never has to be mentioned."

Andrew knew he was being presumptuous, but he fought to keep the impending hopeless from settling upon him. He felt horrible for putting Lord Walcott in this position, but he was at the end of his tether.

The earl shook his head. "Then you would be in my debt, and that is not the best place for friends to be. I've seen too many friendships ruined by deals such as this."

"You speak of our friendship ending? Well, I'll tell you now that if you don't help me, I may not be around to be your friend. Please, Walcott, don't make me beg. Surely there is some way you can help me."

"I'm sorry," Lord Walcott replied as he stared into his glass. "I cannot."

Andrew stood and tossed the cloth on the table. "All that talk about me changing my ways," he snarled. "Of me becoming an honorable man whose word is good. What of this hope you keep speaking about? I don't see that being of any help to me now. How many times did you tell me about the happiness you found with Mary? Not in her dowry but in the love the two of you shared. That is what I feel for Emma. I've made great strides to become a better man, but things I've done, my old ways, have come back to threaten us—Emma and me."

Lord Walcott continued to stare into his glass and said nothing, which only incensed Andrew further.

He barked a rueful laugh. "Tell my mother and Mrs. Rutley that you've completed your work for them. I've learned a very important lesson."

"And that is?" The earl finally looked up at Andrew.

"That one can believe in the idea of friendship and love, but only I can save myself. Goodbye, Walcott."

Andrew barely noticed the chill in the air as he made his way down the street. Lord Walcott had filled his mind with impossible ideas. The feelings he had for Emma would not save her. Or him.

Yet perhaps her father would prove to be a reasonable man. He was wealthy, and few wealthy men refused to at least consider a generous offer.

Before he could approach Sir Henry, however, Andrew had to speak to Emma. For if her father could not help, Andrew would have no other choice but to run far away.

And he planned to take Emma with him if he did.

CHAPTER 19

The gardens outside Emma's window had transformed from summer to winter in the matter of weeks. The once deep green leaves of the trees lay discarded and discolored on the grass. Flowerbeds once filled with their glorious displays now lay dormant and plain. The bright-blue sky now billowed with dark-gray clouds. The season had finally made its change.

In Emma's hand was a letter, delivered five minutes earlier. Andrew wished to meet her in Chatsworth at an abandoned inn. As it was Saturday, meeting him would not be an issue, for all the students would be taking their weekly excursion into the village. The question was whether she dared. After all, he had lied to her concerning his financial situation.

Yet had she not also humiliated herself through her own lies? Her father had no wealth. All he owned was a parcel of land that he farmed. And what difference did any of that make now? Even if she revealed that truth to him, fate had played a horrible trick on them. It had decided her future no matter if he forgave her deception or not. Therefore, why torment herself—or him—by agreeing to meet him?

Through all the confusion and heartache, she knew why. She cared for Andrew. A bond had formed between them, and not seeing him these past weeks had made her feel fractured. It was as if a part of her had been taken away.

January was approaching far more quickly than she could have imagined. Things would change, and the realization she might never see him again did not sit well with her. Perhaps she should go, at least to say goodbye.

"Have you decided?" Diana asked as she sat down beside her.

Emma glanced down at the letter and gave a tiny nod. "I should at least say goodbye. It will likely cause us both a great deal of pain, far more than what I'm feeling now, but it must be done. I cannot leave this thread untied or I may unravel."

Diana smiled. "Perhaps he has a plan. There is always a chance that everything will come together as it should."

"That's kind of you to say, but I don't think it's possible." Emma walked over to her wardrobe and removed her winter coat. "Do you know what I find odd about all this?" she asked, absently running a hand over the soft wool lining. "The very subject of both our lies—our financial situations—is what will keep us apart."

Diana helped her don the coat. "I agree. That is a bit odd."

Emma let out a choked laugh. "In all the old tales, such as that of the lost prince, wealth does not matter. Love is what propelled the heroes. What guided and saved them. But now I understand that such ideas are for fools. Women like me, used by parents who seek to gain acceptance by those who look down on them, our fates are sealed. Believing in the fairy tale love of those stories is childish, for it does not happen in reality."

With a sigh, she followed Emma out of the room. When they reached the top of the staircase, a familiar voice made her come to a sudden stop. Her heart attempted to leap from her chest, and she placed a finger to her lips.

Diana nodded, and they peered over the railing.

Lord Egerton was speaking to Mrs. Rutley in the foyer, but Emma could not make out their words. For a moment, she considered sneaking down a few steps, but the viscount was facing the staircase and would likely catch her movements. The last thing she wanted was to see him today! Or any other day, for that matter.

Frowning, Emma pulled back. What was he doing here? Her father was not due to arrive until January, and that was still a month away.

When she heard the sound of the front door closing, Emma hurried down the stairs. Mrs. Rutley had remained at the door, her countenance solemn.

Since Emma's terrible outburst, she and Mrs. Rutley had spoken no more than a few words to one another. Gone was the mother and daughter rapport, replaced by the strict headmistress and student relationship.

"What did Lord Egerton want?" Emma asked.

Mrs. Rutley turned with a start. "It appears that matters have changed. His Lordship has completed whatever matters of business he had and no longer wishes to wait until January to marry. I'm sorry, Emma, but your parents will come to collect you next Saturday."

It was as if the floor beneath Emma had suddenly disappeared, and she had to grasp Diana's arm to keep from collapsing. "This cannot be!" she said. "I've one more month!"

"I'm sorry," the headmistress said. "But I'm afraid it's so."

Emma could not help but give a derisive snort. "It's exactly as you said, Mrs. Rutley. I cannot change my fate, can I?"

"I'm afraid not."

Pushing away Diana's arm, Emma opened the door and stepped out onto the portico, Diana at her side. The back of the viscount's carriage was just disappearing down the drive.

"I wish there was something I could do," Diana said as they made their way in the direction the carriage had taken. "You would think with all the money my father has that I could help in some way..." She stopped. "Wait. My jewelry. We can sell it. Or we can offer it to Lord Egerton. Perhaps if we give him enough money, he'll be willing to release you from the contract."

"That's very kind of you," Emma said, "but I cannot take your money. Or your jewelry. Even if I chose to do so, it would likely not be enough, but I appreciate the gesture all the same. You're a very good friend."

"But I don't mind."

Emma shook her head. "It would do no good, anyway, Diana. Lord

Egerton sees me as nothing more than an object to be possessed. I doubt he'll give up so easily."

When they reached the main road, Emma realized she would have to share this horrible news with Andrew. It had been bad enough when she was merely going to tell him goodbye, but now it was somehow worse. Perhaps because any chance for rescue had been stolen from her.

For a moment, her mind returned to the day her parents had brought Lord Egerton to Courtly Manor to tell her the terrible news. She had packed her bags that day, ready to flee. But she got no farther than the great oak tree in front of the house before she was stopped. The members of the Sisterhood had gathered to assure her that they would always support her no matter what happened.

Emma never doubted anything they said that day, but she also knew their support of her could only go so far. None of her friends had the power or wealth to help her escape her future. And Mrs. Rutley had only filled her with false hope.

Despite the harsh weather, Emma and Diana walked all the way to the village. Chatsworth was once again a scurry of people, most hunched over and peering through the collars of their overcoats in search of a way to get out of the chill wind that had risen. On most days such as this, Emma would have gone to Mrs. Weatherby's Tea House for a cup of hot chocolate and a warm scone. How many Saturdays had she spent sitting in one of the tables by the window to watch the braver souls dash from door to door?

Today she had more important matters to see to. Today would likely be the last chance she would have to bid him farewell.

When they reached the abandoned inn, two men blocked the doorway.

"If ye think a 'ammer's the best tool, then yer a fool, Tinsdale," one of the men was saying, his cap sitting on large ears that were bright red from the cold. "It's gotta be the saw 'cause that's what makes the wood."

Tinsdale snorted. "And what do you know about trees, huh? I seen you get scared just standing on top of a cart!"

Emma politely cleared her throat, making both men jump.

"Ladies," Tinsdale said, removing his hat to reveal an unruly crop of dark hair as he bowed.

"We're here to speak to Lord St. John. Is he here?"

"Sure, miss," Tinsdale said, his brows knitted. "Jus' go in an' walk to the far end. That's where they're puttin' the clerk's counter. Behind there is a door to another room. He oughta be in there."

Inside, dust filled the air as several craftsmen plied their trades. Two men carrying a long piece of timber walked past, making Emma dance around them. At the far end was the door mentioned by the man out front.

With a quick glance at Diana, Emma pushed through the door and stopped to look around. A long, flat board lay across a pair of sawhorses, creating a makeshift table. She recognized Andrew immediately, despite the fact he had his back to her.

"Andrew?" she said, walking up to him. "We must talk. I have something very important to tell you." Andrew turned, and Emma could not help but gasp. "Faith! What happened?"

An ugly bruise circled his left eye, making him look like a one-eyed raccoon. She hurried up and touched it, and he pulled back with a wince.

"Much has happened these last few days," he said. "I know you've been avoiding me because of the letter you received about Lord Egerton."

Emma could not stop the heat of shame from burning her cheeks. "That's part of it, certainly. But I've also not been completely honest with you about some of what I've told you. It's about time I told you the truth, too."

"That's fine," Andrew replied as if her lying to him had made no difference. "But first I need you to listen, for I've devised a way to save us both."

Besides the muffled sounds of the men working in the other room, all was quiet. Andrew had sent away the others, leaving only him and Emma and Diana.

"All right," Emma said impatiently. "Tell me your plan." If he had a way to rescue them, she was willing to listen.

"Before I do, I must explain something important. When we first met at the party, I lied about searching for you. The truth is, I was on the hunt for a wealthy woman who could help me get out of debt. Then I overheard you and Miss Kendricks discussing your father's finances and believed I had found a way to save my estate from bankruptcy."

He could have struck her across the head with a piece of timber, and she would not have been as stunned as she was now. "I see," she managed to say.

Once he learned all she had said that day was further from the truth than England was from the Americas, what would he do then? Surely, he would see no reason to save her from Lord Egerton.

"But that day at the waterfall," he continued, "I came to realize several truths. One was your reaction to our surroundings that day. After showing you all those properties, after doing all I could to influence you with what I owned, it was the waterfall that impressed you. I must admit that *you* impressed *me* that day, far more than you can imagine."

"But—"

"But that was not all," Andrew interrupted. "You also saw me as this gentleman who possessed a great deal of confidence. I'm here to say that everything I pointed out to you, all I said, was pure bluster. I was attempting to cover the many lies I had already told. But I've told one important truth, Emma. I *will* protect you from Egerton. I cannot do so by offering some grand amount of money, for I have none. My estate is nearly bankrupt and has been for some time now." He dropped his gaze. "I'm a baron, that much is true, but I'm also an imposter. Some may say I'm a swindler, and they would be right. That's the truth about who I am."

Emma's heart warmed at his confession. It certainly helped that she had known this beforehand, but it was good to hear it from him.

"I know that once your father sees my financial situation, he'll turn away in disdain," Andrew said. "But I've good news. I've been making several investments, including this inn, and in time, I'll be able to pay off the debts I owe." He gave a light chuckle. "I suppose that does not help us now, but it's at least a start. I was thinking that perhaps your father, in his mercy, will consider your happiness and the prestige of my title. I don't know the size of your dowry, but it should be substantial. Perhaps then I can prove that I'm worthy of your hand and save you from Egerton." He ran a hand through his hair. "Do you think any of this is possible?"

"We once made a promise to no longer lie to one another," Emma said. "But I've not honored that promise any more than you have. The night you heard me speaking to Diana about my father's wealth..." She swallowed hard. How could she say the words?

But he's revealed the truth, she chastised herself. *It's about time you were honest with him. Show a bit of backbone!*

"What I said," she continued, "was not what you believed it to be. I was describing my life not as it truly was but rather what I believed it would have been if I had come from a wealthy family. The truth is... my father is poor. We've no grand estate, no fine horses except the aging pair used to pull the carriage. Every day is a challenge, and what Father does own hangs in the balance, which is why he and Lord Egerton made the agreement for my hand. He quite literally bought the betrothal. I can only apologize for allowing you to believe what I said was true. But I knew if you learned the truth, you would not want me anymore."

Emma held her breath as she awaited his response. Would he cast her aside now? Would he decide she was not worth fighting for? She could bring nothing to a marriage. She had no true dowry except a few quilts and a trunk filled with her grandmother's soup tureen and a handful of matching teacups.

Rather than pushing her away, however, he gathered her in his arms. She pressed her cheek against his chest as he held her, the sound of his heartbeat soothing her soul.

Andrew gave a laugh that made him sound mad. "Have you realized, as I have, that we're both as poor as church mice? Fate has a very strange sense of humor." He shook his head. "My reasons for pursuing you were dubious. No, they were downright wretched. But I've come to learn that rich or poor makes little difference if I have you. That's all I'll ever need."

Emma wanted to sob, not in despair but rather with joy. But she had yet to reveal her reason for coming to see him. "Andrew, there's more. Lord Egerton has returned from London early. Next week, Father's coming to collect me. We'll be returning home to prepare for an early wedding." She reached up and lightly touched the purple and green bruise on face. "My heart breaks, for I'm to marry a man I despise rather than the man I love."

The revelation of that truth made her heart sing even as it tumbled to the ground. How could she not have seen it before? He had won her heart from the moment he first kissed her as payment for a nonexistent toll.

His eyes were tender as he looked down at her. "You have no idea how happy that makes me, for I love you, too. How strange that in this moment, when all seems lost and fate roars at us like an angry storm, I realize that I need you in my life. For you make me a better man, Emma. Without you, I'm lost."

Their lips met in a wonderful kiss, and Emma relished every moment of it. It was as if their surroundings disappeared—the room, Diana, the inn, Chatsworth, their troubles—all of it was nonexistent. All they had were one another and the urgency of that kiss. If her heart were a bird, she doubted it could have flown any higher.

When the kiss ended, Andrew took her hands in his. "I want nothing more in this world than to be with you, but I have another confession to make. Several months ago, I went to London for the chief purpose of entering a particular gaming hell..."

Emma listened as he talked about the money he had lost and how he had been extended credit. It was when he mentioned the name of the man to whom he owed the money that she took a step back.

"Lord Egerton?" she asked, her jaw dropping. "Oh, Andrew, what will we do now? Surely our story has turned into a tragedy!"

"No. There's still hope. We can leave today. Together."

"Leave? And go where?"

"Far away where no one will know us. We'll marry, of course, and I can ask Walcott to watch over Redborrow Estate while we're gone. I've been able to put away enough money and make several agreements that will see a steady income. I can use this to pay my debt to Egerton. Once my debt to him has been paid, we may return. Or we can live elsewhere if you'd rather. As long as you're with me, I don't care where we live."

Emma considered what he proposed. To leave this very day and never return was tempting.

"Andrew, running away will solve nothing. We cannot wed without Father's permission, and I cannot in good conscience desert my family, no matter how much I love you."

He kissed her hand. "Let's not call it running away. Instead, let's say we're leaving."

She gave him a sad smile. "They're the same. I don't know if I can, Andrew. I'm sorry."

"But don't you see?" Andrew asked as he dropped her hands and pointed at his face. "Walcott refuses to help, and if I'm unable to pay that debt, the men who did this will do it again. Or worse. Running will save us both. Otherwise, I'll be without money, and you'll have to marry that man. Please, go with me."

The thought of Andrew being hurt again tore at Emma's heart. As did the thought of him leaving without her. Running away would only put off the inevitable, for eventually, Lord Egerton would find them.

It was with a heavy heart that she replied, "I'm sorry, but I can't join you." Oh, how she wished there was another solution!

"Why not?" he asked in a sharp tone. "Is that what you want? To be forced to marry Egerton?"

"It's the last thing I want! Mrs. Rutley says that those who run away quickly learn that their problems follow them. Do you prefer a life of running? And when those men find you again, what then? What if they take your life the next time rather than leaving you bruised?"

"Then you will remain here?" Andrew spat. "You will allow me to leave here today and never see you again?"

She held strong in the face of his rage. "You know full well that I don't want that!" she said with equal vehemence. "What I want is for my prince to push ahead and face the storm. Not run away from it!!"

Andrew snorted. "You speak as if we're them, but we're not. This is not a fairy tale, Emma. This is real life. I'm a baron with no money, close to losing everything I have, and you're a woman who has been sold like a slave. That is the truth of our lives!"

Emma took a calming breath. "I'm quite aware of what's at stake here. Do you not think that this crushes my heart? That the idea of Father coming for me in a week does not make me feel ill?"

Andrew pinched the bridge of his nose. "That's why you must come with me. I don't understand why you're refusing!" He took her hands once more. "Emma, I love you, and although we have no castle to return to, we can leave together. Is that not the purpose of legends, such as the one about the lost prince? That in the end, loves find each other?"

"We did find one another," Emma replied. "But this storm is much too strong. It pains me to say it, but I cannot leave with you."

This time when he released her hands, he tossed them away from him. "Then we have no choice. I'm sorry, but I must go. I cannot remain here to learn that you've married another."

He grabbed his overcoat and threw it over his shoulders. For the first time, she noticed a bulging saddlebag and a portmanteau. Had this been his plan all along, to run away?

"But it's not supposed to end like this!" she cried. "Please, don't leave. Wait another week."

He paused at the door. "Why? So we can hurt more when you leave? No, I'll not do that to either of us."

The door banged closed behind him, and Emma sobbed into Diana's shoulder.

Everything was over. Her fate was sealed. And as Mrs. Rutley had said, Emma could do nothing about it.

CHAPTER 20

It was time to leave Chatsworth. Andrew had informed his mother of his decision the previous day, although he had told her he was going away for business. There was no need to worry her with the truth.

Despite his disappointment with Lord Walcott for refusing to lend him money, Andrew had sent a request to his friend asking him to act on his behalf in his absence. His destination was unclear, but Andrew was sure of one thing. If all else failed, his plan had been to meet with Emma one last time and convince her to elope. Doing so would alleviate both problems. Her father would then have no choice but to accept the marriage, and the viscount would no longer want anything to do with her after their wedding night.

That was how he found himself waiting for her amidst the chaos of the remodeling of the inn. What he had not expected was her confession. Or for her to refuse him. Of the two, the latter was far worse.

Hearing her cry out to him as he walked away filled him with guilt. But if she refused to join him, he had no choice but to go alone.

Setting the portmanteau on the footpath, he pulled up the collar of his overcoat. The colder temperatures sent many hurrying into shops, where they could find relative warmth. He was glad for the reprieve from the prying eyes of those who hoped to see him fail.

The fault was his. After all, he had not done anything to prove them wrong. Instead, he had continued with his asinine behavior. He had no one to blame but himself.

Taking a right, he entered an alleyway that led to where he stabled his horse. Once he collected the animal, he would be gone.

At the stables, however, he ran into an unexpected surprise.

"Walcott? What are you doing here?"

Wearing a triple-downed blue greatcoat, the earl appeared taller than usual. "I received your message and went searching for you at Redborrow Estate. Your mother informed me that you were coming to Chatsworth to check the progress of the inn before you went away. I recognized your mount and decided to wait for you here."

The young stable hand walked up to them. "Want me to secure them bags, my lord?"

Andrew nodded, and the boy carried the bags away, lifting them with a grunt.

"You still haven't answered my question, Walcott. Why are you here? I thought I was quite clear in the letter I sent you. My ledgers will be delivered next week, and you may take whatever percentage of my income that you deem necessary as a form of payment for your services."

"But you forgot to mention your reason for leaving," Lord Walcott replied. "Oh, I know you said it was business, but we both know that's not true. You're running away."

Andrew shook his head. "I'm leaving for reasons of my own. Why do you care?" Upon seeing his friend's raised brow, he added, "Very well, I'm running away."

"I see that. But why?"

"Because there's no other solution!" Andrew replied with a harsh kick against the stable door. He knew he was acting like a petulant child, but that was how he felt at the moment!

The earl seemed to ignore Andrew's behavior. "I'm on my way to the school to speak to Mrs. Rutley. Perhaps there's a way to save both you and Miss Hunter from all this."

Andrew laughed outright. "Mrs. Rutley?" He took the reins from the stable boy. "The woman who conspired with my mother and brought you into their gossip circle? She cannot help me, nor can you or anyone else. Just do as I ask. Mind my estate and see that Mother is taken care of. This is my burden, and I'll deal with it." He placed a booted foot in the stirrup and hoisted himself onto the saddle.

"I wish you would stay, St. John. If you leave, your problems will only follow you. And the problems you have may turn deadly."

"You sound like Miss Hunter," Andrew snapped. "Do you think I don't know how serious my problems are? Plus, what choice do I have? She returns home next week. Time's run out for both of us. Goodbye, Walcott."

"Promise me you'll consider one more thing. You care for Miss Hunter, do you not?"

Andrew sighed. "I do, which is why—"

"Then remain and find a way to save her."

He had racked his brain for hours, even losing sleep, and still no solution came to mind. Except to go where no one could find him. Every other option had been exhausted.

"I must be on my way before it gets too late."

"I'll be at Foxly Manor all week if you change your mind," Lord Walcott said. "Trust me when I say we can find a way."

With a nod, Andrew heeled the horse's flanks, and the animal took off at a light canter. The street was nearly empty as he headed to the road that led out of the village. Emma and Lord Walcott both had asked him to stay. Did they believe that some magical solution would suddenly appear?

No, he had found a solution of his own. Granted, he had hoped Emma would join him, but he understood her reluctance. He could not agree with her choice, but he did understand.

Yet as the village disappeared behind him, he could not stop the sense of regret that filled him. Emma was still there, and she was hurting as much as he.

Agnes Rutley turned the crude knife in her hand, a weapon she had owned since she was a young child. Sitting at her desk and awaiting a response from Lord Walcott, she allowed her thoughts to return to when she had last used the knife. She was fourteen at the time.

Her home had been the streets of London from the age of eight because, like so many other children at that time, her mother had left her at a shop and never returned. That particular day, she had used quick hands to slip the fragrant soap in a secret pocket she had sewn into the waist of her burlap dress.

"Caught you!" the shopkeeper had growled as he grabbed her by the arm. "I'm sick of urchins like you thinking you can steal from me."

Fear had enveloped her as the shopkeeper dragged her toward the back of the shop.

"I'm gonna beat you senseless!"

To her surprise, a man in a double-breasted coat and silver hair blocked the way. "Enough," he said. "Release the girl."

The shopkeeper gave the man a glare. "She's a thief, sir. I've got every right to beat her."

"Do so, and I'll beat you." The man had yet to raise his voice, but he may as well have, given the strength of the threat behind it. "So? What will it be?"

With a snort, the shopkeeper pushed Agnes toward the man. He wrapped a protective arm around her, which she found strangely comforting.

"Take her. She's one of them urchins always up to no good with no hope at life, anyway."

The shopkeeper's words stung her heart, but he could not have been more right. Most of the girls she knew had turned to prostitution, something she would never agree to. The boys sneaked into country homes and stole whatever they could. Hope had no place in the life of someone like Agnes Fitzimmons.

Her silver-haired defender did not agree. "There's always hope." He pulled out a few coins and handed them to the shopkeeper. "For the soap. Hardly an object worth striking a lady."

The shopkeeper had snorted, but he was not given the chance to say more. The silver-haired man grasped Agnes by the arm and led her outside into the cold.

"I know what your type wants," Agnes said as she pulled her arm from the man's grip and pulled a small pen knife from her pocket. "But you can't buy me for your needs. Go home to your wife for that." She crossed her arms to protect herself from the cold wind, although she hoped he would take it for steadfastness.

"My wife passed away some years ago," he said with a sigh. "Sadly, she could not handle the death of our daughter, a girl who looked very much like you. Now, put away the knife before someone gets hurt. I, for one, would prefer to keep my blood inside me."

Agnes noticed the tiny wrinkles around his eyes and could not help but allow her guard to drop. Perhaps she was a fool for trusting him, but he had saved her from a good walloping. She lowered the knife but didn't put it away.

"What's your name, child?"

She glanced around the nearly empty street. Would she be willing to do what this man wanted? An empty stomach and cold bones made her consider it. "Agnes Fitzimmons," she replied.

"Well, Agnes, my name is Mr. Porter. Thomas Porter. I've seen you about these last few weeks. You look very cold, and I imagine it's been a while since you've had a proper meal." He smiled, and for some reason, Agnes felt no fear. "I'm in need of a ward, someone to help ease my loneliness and perhaps bring laughter to an empty home. What do you say? Will you take on that position?"

"A ward?" she asked. "You mean you'll give me a bed and food to eat?"

Mr. Porter nodded. "You'll also learn to read and write and how to comport yourself in proper society. More importantly, you'll feel wanted."

This was too good to be true. And when something was too good to be true, it wasn't true. "And what do you get in return? 'Cause you ain't bedding me no matter what promises you make. I'd rather starve than to live that way."

"That's very noble," he said with a smile. "But I've only one requirement. That one day, you'll help others when you can. Other than that, there's nothing you must do to repay me."

A carriage pulled up, and the driver leaped down to open the door.

"I suspect that your mind is as quick as your hands. Let's see that both are used for good rather than a life of thievery. The choice is yours, Agnes Fitzimmons. Remain here without a roof over your head and food in your belly. Or go home with me and live a better life. You never know, perhaps you'll even become a fine lady someday."

He climbed into the carriage.

"Me, a lady?" Agnes snorted. "Like that'll ever happen. I've been in the streets nearly all my life. You heard the shopkeeper. There's no hope for girls like me."

Mr. Porter laughed. "Oh, Agnes, there's always hope, even for someone like you. One day, you'll understand what I mean." He motioned to her hand. "If it makes you feel better, keep the knife. I don't think you'll hurt me, but even so, I saw your hands. They're much too quick for me to stop you. I'd advise you to always keep it close. One never knows when she must defend herself."

Agnes dropped her gaze. Could what this man said be true? Was there truly hope for the likes of someone like her? All she could do was trust. So, she stepped into the carriage.

With a sigh, she returned to the present and opened the desk drawer. Inside was an assortment of items, including a wooden top. She set the knife inside the drawer and closed it once again.

"You ask me why I'm willing to do this," she said to Henry, Lord Walcott, who sat across from her. "It's because there is always hope. That's why."

Henry blew out a heavy breath. "Agnes, when you and Helen came to me, asking me to befriend the boy, I did. When you asked me to instruct him, I did. But what you ask of me now is too great a risk." He stood, and Agnes did the same. "What will happen if Miss Hunter's parents arrive early? Or any others, for that matter? I know you said the girls will be gone most of the day, but with the current conditions, any may decide to return early. What then?"

"I'm certain that her parents will not be here until much later.

Most of the girls return home mid-week, and those who remain have been invited to have tea with Helen. Even if an unexpected caller were to arrive, Mrs. Shepherd is more than capable of sending that person away. No one will bother us."

"Are you truly willing to risk your reputation and that of the school for this fool plan of yours? Well, I cannot be a part of it, not in good conscience. I must be firm in my denial."

Agnes followed him to the foyer before placing a hand on his arm. "Henry, we've known one another for many years. The risk is mine, I know that, and I'm willing to accept that. What they have is special. If you could only understand how much Emma has changed, you would understand why I'm willing to do this. I know you understood at one time in your life."

"Oh, I understand all too well."

"Then you've forgotten. I know you've shared much with the boy, but you truly have forgotten what it's like."

Henry adjusted the buttons on his coat. "I'm sorry, my friend, but I simply cannot agree to such an imprudent plan."

Agnes nodded. There was nothing more she could say. She had learned from Mr. Porter to always believe in hope, and that hope had made her into the woman she was today. But for the first time in a very long time, Agnes wondered if hope would be enough.

*

Emma and Diana clung to one another as the wind howled around them. The cold only worsened the heaviness in Emma's heart. With each step, she came closer to the school, and her spirit waned. Andrew was gone, her fate was now sealed, and there was nothing she could do about it. Knowing it was out of her hands only made matters worse.

"I purchased drinking chocolate and everything needed to prepare it as a special gift for you," Diana said. "I'll ask Mrs. Shepherd to make it for us."

"Thank you," Emma said as they turned onto the road that led to the school. "Perhaps that will warm me up."

After her argument with Andrew, Emma had not wanted to return to the school. Therefore, she and Diana had walked around the village for an hour before finally admitting that it was far too cold to remain out any longer. Now she wished they had returned sooner. Her toes would never warm again!

"Did I do the right thing?" Emma asked. "Should I have left with Andrew, do you think? Staying felt like the right decision, but now I'm unsure."

"I believe so," Diana replied. "It's like you said, your problems will follow you no matter where you go. You may as well face them here. At least then, you'll have your friends to help you."

As Emma reached for the door handle, the door opened, and a tall gentleman exited. Emma had seen him before, but she could not recall his name.

"Ah, Emma, there you are," Mrs. Rutley said from the doorway. "This is Lord Walcott. He's a friend of Lord St. John."

Emma curtsied. "My lord."

"It's a pleasure, Miss Hunter," Lord Walcott said as he lifted his hat to her. "I was hoping to speak to you."

"Why don't you come inside where it's warm," Mrs. Rutley said.

Once the door was closed, Lord Walcott said, "Miss Hunter, it's come to my attention that you've been of help to Lord St. John. Is this true?"

"I suppose so," Emma replied. "Although, he's helped me far more than I've helped him." She shrugged. "But I'm afraid that in the end, no matter how wonderful it has been, it's been for naught. He's left Chatsworth."

"And this bothers you?"

Emma nodded. "In many ways, my lord. I had once believed that what we had was enough to sustain us. Now I know that was wrong. Sometimes in life, we just need money."

Lord Walcott winced and then rubbed his chin. What could he be thinking?

Then he smiled. "It appears that what I believed to be sage advice lacked one important point." He turned to Mrs. Rutley. "I've no doubt now that you were right. I did forget what it was truly like. Proceed as planned."

Emma frowned as the earl gave her a polite nod and walked out the front door. "What did he mean?" she asked Mrs. Rutley.

"Oh, just the mundane task of convincing a man to allow his niece to attend our school," Mrs. Rutley replied. "But it's not important at the moment. Did I hear you say that Lord St. John has gone away?"

Emma nodded. "He has. May I speak to you, Mrs. Rutley?" She gave Diana an apologetic smile. "Alone?"

"I really should practice my French," Diana said, hugging Emma and hurrying away.

Mrs. Rutley turned. "Let's go to my office."

Once they were alone, Emma explained her meeting with Andrew. It was far more difficult than she could have believed, and by the time she finished, she felt depleted.

"I must admit I was tempted to go away with him, but I simply could not."

Mrs. Rutley nodded. "May I ask why you decided to stay?"

"I thought about what you told me, that when one runs from her problems, they tend to follow her. None of us can escape our troubles, can we?"

"No, I'm afraid not," Mrs. Rutley replied. "I know you wish to hear that the grass is always greener elsewhere, but I won't lie to you."

Emma knew Mrs. Rutley always told the truth. Even if it meant hurting someone. "When I was angry with you before, I said I despised you. But that wasn't true. I consider you more than my headmistress. You are a friend. I'm terribly sorry for saying such hateful words to you."

Mrs. Rutley smiled. "I appreciate the apology, and I accept it. We are friends, and we made a promise to one another, did we not? That in time of need, we'll always be there for each other."

"Yes, we did."

"Then rest assured that I'll always be here for you, just as I know you will be for me," Mrs. Rutley said, patting Emma's hand. "Don't forget that."

"I won't," Emma replied. Then a new thought came to mind. "I've learned so much over the past year about what it means to be a woman. At first, I believe it had to do with how I should conduct myself in society. And although that remains true, I've come to realize that it's far more. A woman must use grace, dignity, and strength to rise above that which falls down around her."

"You've become a very wise woman," Mrs. Rutley said. "The path a woman must take in life is never easy, for it is oftentimes clouded, making it difficult to traverse. Those who remain strong in the face of the storm are the ones who will remain standing when those troubles come to an end."

Emma gave a tiny laugh. "Andrew told me a story, a legend, that currently matches my life. I feel like the princess in that story, waiting for her prince to return. No matter what happens, at least I'll have that to remind me of him."

Mrs. Rutley took Emma's hands in hers. "When you first arrived here, you were a meek and quiet girl who allowed others to intimidate and harass you. But now you've become a lovely young woman who has not only done well in her studies but has also become much more confident in herself. I've heard the story about the lost prince, and you should know that the princess never gave up hope, no matter how bad the storm looked. And neither should you."

Emma smiled and rose from her chair. "Although my fate is sealed, do you think there may still be hope?"

The headmistress laughed. "I always think it's wise to never give in to defeat until the last cast of the die."

"Thank you, Mrs. Rutley. For everything."

As Emma reached the staircase, Diana joined her, looking quite excited. "Our drinking chocolate is ready," she said. "And Mrs. Shepherd has promised to tell me more about the Marquess of Magic! Will you join me?"

Emma would have preferred to wallow away her time in bed, but Mrs. Rutley was right. Until the last die was cast, she could not give up that her prince would return.

"Yes, I believe I will," Emma replied, smiling. "Did you happen to mention the unfortunate encounter at the bookstore and the book you selected?"

Diana's cheeks reddened. "No, I did not. Though I adore her, I fear Mrs. Shepherd would be unable to keep that tidbit of information to herself. Would you not agree?"

Emma laughed. "I could not agree with you more!"

CHAPTER 21

M id-afternoon on Thursday, Andrew approached an inn surrounded by a handful of small cottages. With no people about and no sound coming from within, the place seemed to have closed early, and he knew why. Thick snowflakes fell around him and had been falling over the past hour to create a thick, heavy blanket on the ground.

He had spent the last days traveling at a leisurely pace, often finding his riding time that of only a few hours. There was no urgency in his running. Surely, Lord Egerton and his ruffians knew nothing about his leaving. He guided his mount to the tiny stable at the back of the inn.

"What're ye doin' out in the snow, mister?" a young boy of perhaps ten asked as he took the reins from Andrew. "It's dangerous bein' in such cold."

"It is, indeed," Andrew replied. "And it does not appear to be stopping anytime soon."

The boy shook his head. "Papa says it'll keep goin' all night. Maybe even a whole year!"

Andrew glanced around. "What's the name of this tiny village of yours?"

"It don't got a name," the boy said with a shrug. "We jus' call it Home."

"Interesting name," Andrew mused as he placed a coin in the boy's hand.

A gust of wind drove the snowflakes, so they stung his already aching cheeks. He trudged through the accumulated snow to the door of the inn. A wooden sign with the image of a man carrying an ax over his shoulder creaked on a metal rod, naming the inn as The Hearty Woodsman.

The hinges on the door groaned in agony as he entered the common room. The half-dozen tables and the long bar across the back wall told Andrew that the establishment was also a tavern. Good. A few glasses of drink would warm his chilled bones in no time.

A woman stood peering out the front window, mumbling to herself and nibbling on the tips of her fingers. Two men in heavy woolen coats hunched over mugs of ale, their collars pulled up around their ears.

"What're ye havin'?" the barkeeper asked. He had a dark, bushy mustache and beady eyes.

"What do you have to warm me?"

"Well, we ain't a fine establishment, but I've got a decent gin that'll do ye well. But I'd recommend whiskey for this sorta weather. It'll wipe out any cold in ye."

Andrew nodded. "Then whiskey it is."

A door at the back of the room opened, and a woman of perhaps twenty entered with an armful of logs.

"Susanna'll bank the fire," the barkeep said as he set the whiskey on the bar. "Have ye been traveling long?"

"A few days. I'm heading to Scotland."

The barkeep raised brows as thick as his mustache. "Ye've a bit to go yet. And this weather won't help none. I'm bettin' it'll be tomorrow before it breaks."

"The young man outside said the same."

"That's me son, Todd," the barkeep said with a proud smile. "He's a good lad. So, are ye going North for business?"

Andrew threw back his head and downed the measure of whiskey, grimacing. "I am," he replied, pushing the glass forward to indicate he wanted another. He glanced at the woman beside the window.

"That'll be Molly Lanton," the barkeep offered. "Her husband was meant to come home last night but never got there."

"Because of the snow?"

The barkeep nodded. "See those men there?" he asked, indicating the two with their pulled-up collars. "They came from the west, from the very place Albert Lanton's meant to come from. They said there's snow all the way up to yer thighs in places there. Word is that no matter which direction ye go from here, it's bad." He shook his head. "Let's just pray the poor soul's alive."

Andrew lifted the newly filled drink. "May he'll find his way home to the woman he loves," he toasted before he downed that measure in one gulp, as well. "Another. And one of whatever the lady would like."

He turned and leaned an elbow on the counter to stare at the now blazing fire. He could not help but smile as he recalled the large fireplace in the ruins of the castle he had taken Emma to see. The day had been magical, for that was when he realized she was far more than a means to pay his debt. That was the day he had fallen in love with her.

With a quiet chuckle, he recalled how she had referred to the two of them as the prince and princess from the legend he had shared with her. How wrong she had been, for if he were the prince, he would not have run from his troubles. True men, the heroes in such stories, faced evil foes and great obstacles that would cause most men to cower. No, he was no prince nor a hero. He was a coward who refused to face danger.

Guilt washed over him just as it had every time he thought of Emma. He had left her to face a terrible future with a man she abhorred.

But she loved Andrew. And he loved her.

Knowing Lord Egerton only made matters worse, for Andrew could imagine what life would be like once Emma married him. He likely treated his woman as he did those who owed him money—with contempt and distrust.

"Your drinks," the barkeeper said, setting two glasses on the bar.

Andrew thanked him, pushing forward the coins on the counter, and walked over to the woman beside the window.

"I beg your pardon," Andrew said. "Mrs. Lanton, is it?" He handed her the wine. "To calm your nerves."

She gave him a weak smile and took the glass. "Thank you," she whispered.

"I understand your husband was due to return home last night," Andrew said.

"He was," Mrs. Lanton replied. "He sent word at the end of last week that he would be home by Wednesday, and he's never late."

Andrew glanced outside at the swirling snow. "Perhaps he found lodging along the way to wait out the storm? I've heard that travel is difficult at the moment."

The woman shook her head. "Not my Albert. He would never allow any storm, be it rain or snow, to stop him from keeping his word." She turned toward the window. "My husband knows me far too well."

"What do you mean? If you don't mind my asking."

"He knows that I'll be here waiting for him and will not rest until he returns. That's why I'm certain he'll return without fail. And why I'll not leave this spot until he does."

Andrew downed the rest of his whiskey. "Well, I wish you good fortune, Mrs. Lanton," he replied.

The door opened, and a man entered, a brown cap speckled with white flakes pulled down low on his head and a firm grip on the collar of his coat.

"Albert!" Mrs. Lanton shouted as she rushed over to the newcomer. "I knew you'd make it through!"

Mr. Lanton chuckled as he put his arms around his wife. "And I knew you'd not sleep until I did. Let's drink in celebration. I've much to tell you."

Everything around Andrew had a fantastical feel to it, as if he were experiencing a dream. He finally understood. It was the man's love for his wife that made him brave the storm. It was also love that had his wife maintain her watch at the window of the inn. Andrew had that same love for Emma, and he had promised to save her.

Only cowards ran from their problems. The true hero faced any adversary or obstacle that stood in their way. It was about time Andrew did just that. To be the man Emma saw in him. To be the man he truly was.

With renewed vigor, he walked outside, pulling his coat tighter to ward off the chill in the air. "You, Todd," he called to the young stable boy, "bring my horse."

Todd's eyes widened. "But the storm's bad, sir. And it's only gonna get worse. Can't ye wait till it's gone?"

"Not any longer," Andrew said, tossing a coin to the lad. "I must face the storm."

The boy shrugged and brought out the mount. It was not long before the animal was saddled, and Andrew was riding away, bent low over the horse's neck to keep the snow from striking his face. All he could see was a white mist, but he refused to allow it to stop him.

"If it's possible that my love for Emma guides me to her, then let it be."

And as the wind increased, Andrew urged the horse forward, praying he would make it back in time.

Emma stared out the window at the blowing snow. Her thoughts were not on Lord Egerton and the wedding that was soon to come. Instead, she recalled the story Andrew had told her about the prince and princess that were said to have lived in the castle they had visited. Emma was no princess, to be sure, but she had the same burning need to see her prince come riding up the drive.

Snow had fallen over the past two days, but the flakes were small, and patches of green poked through that which had accumulated on the ground. Had Andrew reached his destination before the storm hit? She prayed it was so, for she could not imagine him hiding beneath a hedge or a bale of hay if the storm became too fierce.

Mrs. Rutley had told her not to give up hope, and Emma had taken that advice to heart. Yet Lord Egerton was due to arrive within the hour and her parents later in the day. If Andrew did not come to her aid before then, she would have no choice but to return home and prepare for a life she did not want.

With a heart longing to see Andrew, she placed a hand against the cold crystal of the windowpane. "The storm you face is great," she whispered. "But somehow, if we face it together, it can be overcome."

"Emma," Mrs. Rutley said as she came to stand beside her. "It's time to say goodbye to the others. When you're finished, meet me in my office."

Emma gave her a nod and turned to find her dearest friends—her sisters—waiting for her. Those girls who had not returned home for the holidays were waiting to have tea with Lady St. John. Because she would be leaving, Emma had declined joining them.

"I don't know what to say," Emma whispered. "Only that the bond we share will bring me peace. I'll miss you all so terribly."

Jenny hurried over and threw her arms around Emma. "I'll miss you, too! But you know you can always write to me whenever you wish. You know I'll respond."

"I promise," Emma replied.

Unity came next, her brown eyes shining with unshed tears. "All will be well," she said in Emma's ear.

"Do write," Theodosia said as she hugged Emma.

Ruth gave Emma a mischievous grin. "If he mistreats you, be sure to send word. I'll be the first to arrive to set him straight." She pushed a fist into the palm of her other hand to punctuate her point.

Emma laughed. "I'll keep that in mind," she said.

"Promise me that, no matter what, you'll let me know how you're doing," Diana said.

"As long as you promise the same."

Diana clicked her tongue. "You know I shall," she replied, removing her handkerchief and dabbing at Emma's eyes before her own. "I don't know if Mrs. Rutley will request that I be your chaperone this afternoon, but if she does not, I want to thank you for allowing me to witness such a wonderful romance between you and Lord St. John. It has given me hope that one day I'll find a man willing to love me just as you have."

"I may have found him," Emma said, "but keeping him is quite another matter. But I do thank you for all your help. If it weren't for you, I'd not have had what little time I did with Andrew."

"And I'm sorry it didn't work out for you," Diana said, embracing Emma once more.

Emma smiled. "At least I was given the chance to experience love, even if it was only for a short while."

Watching her friends walk out to the waiting carriage that would take them to Redborrow Estate, Emma frowned. Mrs. Shepherd stood in the doorway to the parlor like a sentry on guard duty. "I'll miss you," Emma said as she hugged the cook.

"And I'll miss you, too. Now, you mind yourself. And I want you to listen very carefully to Mrs. Rutley. You hear?"

Emma furrowed her brow but nodded. Since when did she *not* listen to Mrs. Rutley?

Well, she had no time to consider it. The headmistress was waiting for her in the office.

As she passed the drawing room, she was surprised to see Lord Walcott standing over the large folding table. Two decanters of what she believed was brandy sat on a small table beside it. Did Mrs. Rutley plan to toast Emma's departure? Surely her headmistress was not that cruel.

"Are you packed?" Mrs. Rutley asked as Emma entered her office. She was standing at the large window that overlooked the back garden.

"Yes, Mrs. Rutley," Emma replied.

"The viscount will be here soon," the headmistress said as she walked around her desk to stand in front of Emma. "And although you won't be leaving with him today, it's imperative that you make a wonderful impression while he's here. Do you understand?"

Emma looked down. "Yes, Mrs. Rutley."

"You are to compliment him at every turn. No matter what he says. If he boasts about his trade, applaud him. If he gives an opinion on the weather, agree. If he states that his favorite meal consists of venison and beets, say they are your favorite, too."

Emma grimaced. "But I don't care for beets."

Mrs. Rutley gave her a firm glare. "You'll agree, regardless. I don't care what he says, what position he takes in an argument, you are to agree."

"But I already said I would do so. Do you not trust me to do as I'm told? Have I given you reason to doubt me?"

"You are to remain in my office until exactly half-past one," Mrs. Rutley continued. Emma was uncertain which was worse, the instructions she was given or how the headmistress ignored her questions. "Then you are to go to the drawing room."

"I don't understand. Why am I to wait here? And what does my going to the drawing room have to do with Lord Walcott being there?"

"'Yes, Mrs. Rutley' is the only response I wish to hear."

Swallowing hard, Emma said, "Yes, Mrs. Rutley."

"Good. Now, I have a few more things to see to. Remember, remain here. Don't leave this room for any reason until you are meant to do so."

As the headmistress headed to the door, Emma called out, "Mrs. Rutley, do you care anything for me?"

Mrs. Rutley came to a sudden stop and turned around. "Have you not realized yet that I consider you more a daughter than a student? Of course, I care about you. Why would you ever doubt it?"

"I don't. But why is Lord Walcott preparing drinks in the drawing room? Why would you wish to celebrate what I'm being forced to do?"

The headmistress heaved a heavy sigh. "I won't lie to you. I do wish to celebrate." And without another word, she left the room.

Emma went over and sat in one of the high-back chairs. Her suspicions had been correct, they would celebrate Emma's departure—and Lord Egerton's victory. She could do nothing to stop the sense of betrayal from washing over her.

Yet, that was unfair. Mrs. Rutley's responsibility was to train her young students, and that was what she had done. Emma was much more refined than she'd been upon her arrival, and she had to thank Mrs. Rutley for that. She owed the woman so much.

Which was why she would do exactly as the headmistress requested. It would not be easy. With a sigh, she glanced up at the mantle clock, wishing for the hour to pass by quickly. Perhaps Andrew would come and rescue her in time.

Where was he? Was it snowing there as it was here? Surely, he was safe at an inn or in the fine home of a member of the peerage with whom he was acquainted. She would rather marry Lord Egerton than to hear that Andrew had gotten hurt, somehow.

Was that the bell at the front door? Perhaps it was Andrew come to save her!

Emma hurried to the door and listened. It was not the voice of the man she loved but rather that of the viscount. With her shoulders drooping, she returned to the chair and dropped in it dejectedly. The hands on the clock inched by, and she placed her chin in her hands, her elbows resting on her knees. Mrs. Gouldsmith would have chastised her severely for her posture, but she could not have cared less at the moment.

She sat upright. What was the noise coming from the drawing room? One moment, there were shouts of anger and the next, cries of joy. What was happening?

When the appointed hour finally arrived, Emma leaped from the chair and hurried out into the corridor. Mrs. Shepherd stood outside the drawing room, and she gave Emma an encouraging smile, opening the door for her.

When Emma entered the room, she came to a sudden stop, her eyes growing wide in surprise. Mrs. Rutley sat at the folding table, Lord Egerton on one side of her and Lord Walcott on the other. A large square of green baize had been placed over the table surrounded by four short planks that had been formed into a square.

"Five," Lord Egerton cried as his dice flew across the table.

Games of chance? What an odd form of celebration! And at the school of all places? The parents would be irate if they knew the headmistress was allowing men to gamble there! Mrs. Rutley would be run out of town for certain.

"It seems you lose again, Walcott. Will you not admit defeat yet?"

Lord Walcott snorted. "No. We'll play again. I've the funds to go all night if need be."

"Then I'll remain all night and take them," Lord Egerton said with a laugh that made the tiny hairs at the nape of Emma's neck stand on end. He noticed Emma and grinned. "Oh, wonderful! Now you'll be able to see what I do best!"

Mrs. Rutley gave her a tiny nod.

"I've no doubt that you'll prevail, my lord," Emma said in her best dulcet tones. "You cannot lose no matter what you do, I'm sure."

This made Lord Egerton's grin widen. "You've trained the girl well, Mrs. Rutley." He motioned to Emma. "Sit. You standing there is distracting me."

Emma did as he bade and watched as they played. Although the men rolled the dice, Mrs. Rutley collected them from the table and dispersed them to the man whose turn was next as if she had been doing it for years. Truly, Emma did not know her headmistress at all!

After some time, Lord Walcott raised his hands. "I believed I was quite good at this game, but with each round I win, I lose three. I'll be bankrupt come midnight."

"Are you wishing to forfeit?" Lord Egerton asked. "Perhaps we can raise the stakes and allow you to lose quicker, so you can return home sooner."

The door opened, and Emma gasped when Andrew entered. Snow covered his coat and hat, and his nose and cheeks were rosy from the cold. Shadows beneath his eyes said he had not slept.

With joy in her heart, Emma stood. "Andrew, you came!"

He smiled at her as he removed his overcoat. "I faced the storm," he replied. "I refused to allow it to stop me from finding you."

Emma's heart warmed. Her prince had returned!

Yet the storm was far from over as Lord Egerton joined them.

CHAPTER 22

Approaching the front door of Courtly Manor, Andrew knew he had faced a storm that had yet to cease. Despite the fact that the snow was much lighter here than it was when he had left the inn early this morning, rain should have been pounding the ground around him. Wind ought to have been sending him careening across the drive. Then it would match the storm in his heart.

He would go to see Lord Walcott and ask for his aid, but first, he wished to speak to Emma.

When he knocked on the door, he stifled a groan when Mrs. Shepherd answered. He prayed there would be no need to convince the cook that he should be granted entry.

To his surprise, Mrs. Shepherd gave him a stern gaze and said, "'Bout time you showed up, my lord. Get yourself into the drawing room. They've been waitin' for you."

"Waiting for me? Who? What's going on, Mrs. Shepherd?"

Without so much as a second thought, the cook grabbed him by the arm and pushed him toward the corridor just past the stairs. "Hurry along, now, my lord. Right down there. You'll figure out soon enough. Just get goin'."

Andrew rubbed his frozen hands together as he walked to the

drawing room, stunned by the cook's strange behavior. When he stepped inside the room, he came to an abrupt stop. Had the cold weather brought about hallucinations? In the middle of the room sat a table, Lord Walcott and Lord Egerton on either end. Were they playing hazard?

He was unsure which was worse, Mrs. Rutley allowing the men to game at the school, or the fact that it was she who was dispersing the dice!

To add to his shock, Emma sat watching as the men gamed! Had the world gone mad?

He hurried over and smiled down at her. Let the others enjoy their gaming. He only had eyes for Emma. "I faced the storm," he said, the love for her more than he could bear. "It could not stop me from returning to you, just as I promised."

"What's this?" Lord Egerton barked as he walked over to join them. "What are you doing here, boy? You should be off making money to pay what you owe me." He looked from Andrew to Emma and back again, a smirk forming on his lips. "Ah, I see now. You two are acquainted. Or is it more than a mere acquaintance?" He turned a glare on Emma. "Your father will hear of this. And once we're wed, we'll have a very long talk about your behavior."

"You'll do no such thing," Andrew said, stepping between Emma and the viscount. "You don't care for her as I do. There are many women you could marry but not her. I'll make any payment you require to set her free."

Lord Egerton laughed. "Payment? You cannot pay the debt you already owe me. How on earth will you be able to pay for anything else?"

Lord Walcott stood on unsteady legs. "I remem... rember... remember a time when men were willing to wager a woman's hand at the gaming tables. Ah, the memories." With the hand holding a glass of brandy, he pointed, causing the amber liquid to slosh over the rim. He did not seem to notice. "You ought to do that, Egerton. Teach this boy a lesson he'll never forget!" He hiccuped and fell back in his chair with a decided *thunk*.

"I don't need you telling me what to do, Walcott," Lord Egerton hissed. "Besides, why would I extend such a wager? He already owes me more money that he could ever hope to pay. What could he possibly use as collateral to place such an expensive bet?"

Andrew gave Lord Walcott an incredulous stare. "I won't play against him. I've seen the incredible luck he possesses."

"And I've seen you lose," the viscount said, giving him a thoughtful look. "You know, her father is to receive my country cottage in Dover as a part of our agreement. Combine that with the money you owe me—with interest, of course—and we're speaking of a great deal of money you don't have. Well, boy, what are you willing to wager for her hand? Redborrow Estate? That's really all you have left, is it not?"

The earl pulled himself from his chair with great effort once more, only to fall against the wall behind him. "I'll put up the money on his..." He hiccuped. "On his behalf."

Lord Egerton shook his head. "No, I don't think so. Let the boy suffer in the years to come because he was unable to put up his own money." He barked a laugh and returned to the table. "Let's get back to our game. I'd like time to speak to my future wife before I leave."

"Told you he's not as wealthy as he proclaims," Lord Walcott slurred to Mrs. Rutley. "It's why he's only willing to play for his opponents' coats and twenty-pound wagers! He's all bravado and bluster."

Lord Egerton growled. "What was that about my financial situation, Walcott? How dare you spread such lies!"

The earl belched. "I've encountered your type all too often. All that grand talk meant to impress those of lower standing. Like the headmistress here." He jerked a thumb toward Mrs. Rutley and then leaned in closer to the viscount. "Don't worry," he said in what was likely meant to be a whisper but was not, "I'll not reveal your secret to anyone."

Andrew closed his gaping mouth. What had gotten into Lord Walcott? He was making a fool of himself! He had never been one to show such disrespect to any woman, let alone Mrs. Rutley.

Lord Egerton's face had gone from red to puce. "You'll regret those words, you drunken half-wit! I'll wager the girl's hand *and* the money the boy owes me. Make certain your offer is worthy, Walcott. An estate of worth!" He then turned to Emma. "Watch and learn what happens to those who speak against me, so you don't step out of line."

Emma nodded. "I know that anyone who does will soon regret their words, my lord."

"Ha! You see that, boy? She knows her place already. And she knows I can't lose."

When Emma nodded, Andrew's heart clenched. Had she already given up on him?

"One more thing," the viscount said as he pointed at Andrew. "I wish to play against this dolt. What a victory it will be to watch you lose her for a second time!"

Andrew could only shake his head in disbelief. It was not that he did not wish to win Emma's hand, but given his luck in comparison to that of Lord Egerton, his chances were slim. That was the reason he had sworn off gaming altogether.

Mrs. Rutley, who had walked over to a nearby writing table, placed a document on the table for Lord Walcott to sign.

"Very good," the headmistress said and then turned to Lord Egerton. "And do you have the contract for the hand of Miss Hunter?"

The viscount pulled a paper from his pocket and slammed it on the table. "I want to read that document beforehand."

"Of course," Mrs. Rutley said, turning the paper so Lord Egerton could peruse it.

Lord Walcott stumbled over to Andrew, spilling more brandy along the way.

"I can't win against this man," Andrew hissed. "All I'll end up with is more debt, and I don't like the idea of owing you money."

The earl clasped a hand on Andrew's shoulder and leaned in close. Andrew had to strain to hear his words. "As I'm your benefactor, I've some favorite numbers I would like you to call. I've a sense for these things, you know. I have an idea how to let you know when to call which..." He explained each number and its corresponding signal. "Don't deviate. Watch for my signal, and you'll win."

"Walcott, you're drunk—"

"Do. Not. Deviate." He punctuated each word with a harsh finger in Andrew's chest.

Andrew could do nothing but nod as Mrs. Rutley called him over.

"You know the rules of hazard, correct?" she asked.

"I do."

"Good. Now, each of you roll to determine who starts. This is the best of seven rounds, is that not correct, Lord Egerton?"

"Seven or seven hundred, it does not matter," the viscount said, snatching a die from Mrs. Rutley. "Four!" he called before throwing the die.

"Three," Mrs. Rutley said as she scooped up the die from the table. "Lord St. John, your turn."

With his heart racing and his mouth dry, Andrew glanced at Lord Walcott, who held his glass out in front of him.

"Five," Andrew called and held his breath as the die tumbled across the table.

"Five it is." Mrs. Rutley placed the set of dice in Andrew's hand. "You may begin, my lord."

———

Emma watched in disbelief as Lord Egerton and Lord Walcott signed their names to the document Mrs. Rutley provided. Although her headmistress skirted the rules from time to time, what she had allowed here today shook Emma to her core.

The rights to her hand had been sold to the viscount, and now those same rights were being wagered against money Andrew did not have. How could Mrs. Rutley allow Lord Walcott to make such an irresponsible wager in his current state? He could barely remain standing!

Glancing at Andrew, her heart ached for the worry on his features. By his own admission, he had lost his fortune playing such games. Could his luck turn for the better? She prayed it to be so!

In the stories of old, the prince was tasked with slaying the dragon, which Lord Egerton certainly was. How strange that this battle would not require lances nor broadswords. Instead, the conflict would require a pair of dice.

Emma had no idea how this game was played, but apparently

Andrew had won the initial toss with the number he called. At least he was able to play first. She tiptoed closer to the table to watch.

"Early luck, my boy," Lord Egerton said with a laugh. "This is what happened the last time we played, and you lost."

Andrew made no comment as he called out the number seven.

"Seven it is!" Mrs. Rutley said when the dice stopped rolling, and Andrew grinned.

With each call and throw, the knot in Emma's stomach tightened. It was far too early to guess the outcome, but thus far, Andrew was doing well. Or so she supposed.

"You'd best win!" Lord Walcott said, swaying on his feet. "Or I'll allow Egerton to help me collect the money I've loaned you for this."

"You'll collect your own money," Lord Egerton snapped.

"Six," Andrew called out.

"Ah, you see," the viscount said with a grin. "The boy will lose. Mark my words."

Andrew dropped his head, and Lord Walcott groaned at the four pips that showed on the dice. A moment later, Lord Egerton was declared the winner of that match, and Emma tightened her grip. When had she taken hold of her skirts?

Lord Egerton glowered at Andrew before calling, "Five!" He tossed the dice and cursed when the pips showed eight.

Mrs. Rutley swooped in and collected the dice, giving them to Andrew. As the minutes ticked by, Emma believed she had a rudimentary understanding of the game. Each man called a number, rolled the pair of dice, and if he matched the pips with his called number, he won that match.

What shocked Emma the most, however, was the headmistress. Never had she seen anyone with such efficient movements. Perhaps this ability came from writing numerous letters.

"This is ludicrous!" Lord Egerton snapped when his throw was three pips off his call. "I need another drink." He poured himself more brandy without so much as asking permission from Mrs. Rutley. Based on the viscount's demeanor, he was not doing as well as he had expected. He drank his brandy in one gulp and slammed the glass on the table. "Last one, boy. Go ahead and lose. Your luck has come to an end, I assure you."

This was it, the deciding match. If Andrew failed this toss, all would be lost, including Lord Walcott's contribution. Emma's future lay in the roll of the dice.

Andrew shook the dice in his hand. "Seven," he said and let loose the dice. It was as if time itself stood still, as if a sudden freeze blanketed the room. Each bounce of the tiny cubes was exaggerated, taking hours to flip and roll across the table until they finally, blessedly, stopped.

"No!" Lord Egerton shouted as Mrs. Rutley performed her usual scoop of the dice. "Impossible! Give me those dice, woman!"

Mrs. Rutley gave him a flat stare. "Are you accusing me of cheating, my lord?" she asked.

"We'll see," he said as he took the dice from her hand and threw them. They landed on a total of four. Cursing, he grabbed them and tossed again. Six. "Blast it! Let's play again, the stakes doubled."

Andrew shook his head. "No. I believe I'm done."

"Then I'll—"

"Honor your agreement," Lord Walcott said, his voice lacking its previous notes of intoxication. "No one in Chatsworth is respected more than I. Honor your agreement, Egerton, or the wrath of the *ton* will be far greater than any henchmen you employ."

Lord Egerton stormed out of the room, a string of curses following in his wake.

Emma ran to Andrew and allowed him to gather her in his arms.

"I faced the storm," he said again. "What you said was true, running was not the answer. I'm sorry."

"You've nothing to apologize for," she said as she looked up into his dark eyes. "Were you aware this game would be played today? Or that Lord Walcott would be willing to back your wagers?"

Andrew shook his head. "I came to speak to you, and then I planned to search out Walcott. Before I knew it, I was tossing dice. I swore to you that I would never play again. That promise has been broken, but from this day forward, I give you my word that it will not happen again." He brushed away a tear from her cheek. "The storm outside was great, but the one inside me is far greater. You're the one who made me realize that."

"It was you who made me believe in myself," Emma said. "And although your leaving hurt, in my heart, I knew you would return. Is that not what a prince does? He doesn't stop until he's reunited with the one he loves."

They embraced again, and Emma wanted nothing more than to remain in his arms forever.

"My lord," Mrs. Rutley said as she approached them. "I've never seen such a display of luck in a game of chance. How did you accomplish such a feat?"

"Walcott asked me to play his favorite numbers and told me when to use them. I thought it no more than a drunken idea, but it worked!"

Mrs. Rutley smiled. "It most certainly did. Now, I hate to be a burden, but if you would please help Lord Walcott clear the room of any evidence of what took place here before Emma's parents arrive, I'd be grateful."

"Oh yes, of course," Andrew said. "And thank you, Mrs. Rutley."

As he walked away, Emma turned to the headmistress. "I don't understand what just occurred. Oh, I'm pleased, quite pleased, but I'm at a loss as to what to think about it all."

"Your hand and heart are now secure," Mrs. Rutley said as she patted Emma's hand. "Is there anything else that must be understood?"

"No, I suppose not," Emma replied, her heart filled with happiness. "There is one thing, however. I never knew you played games of chance. Was it something you've done often in the past?"

Mrs. Rutley glanced behind her and then whispered, "Don't share this with anyone, but I paid Lord Walcott for an hour of private lessons, and the only time he had available was today. I believed we had plenty of time before everyone was to arrive, but then Lord Egerton was early and asked to play, as well." She shrugged. "I believe I learned a valuable lesson today—that perhaps the school is not the best place to receive lessons in gaming! But it did all work out for the best."

Emma smiled. "Indeed, it did. And you were correct. Fate was out of my hands." Then a thought occurred to her. "It was actually in the roll of the dice, just as you said."

"It surely was," Mrs. Rutley said. "Come. Let's go to the parlor where we can wait for your parents."

Andrew soon joined them. "Walcott's gone home," he said when Mrs. Rutley asked. "He said that he's had enough excitement for one day."

Mrs. Shepherd brought them a tea tray, and Emma and Andrew discussed their future, and Emma could not have been happier. Her sisters returned not long after, and soon the room buzzed with excited conversation.

When the clock struck five, the door opened, and Emma's father walked into the room.

"We're finally here," Sir Henry said, stepping aside to allow Lady Hunter to enter. "That snow to the north is the worst I've experienced in years. I'm just glad we were able to make it all the way here." He came to an abrupt stop and frowned. "Where's Lord Egerton? And who's this man smiling at my daughter like a cat with a cornered mouse?"

Mrs. Rutley stood. "Sir Henry and Lady Hunter, there has been a slight change in arrangements."

"What do you mean 'a slight change in arrangements'?" her father asked.

"Please," Mrs. Rutley said. "If you and your wife will just take a seat, I'll explain everything. Diana and Unity, would you allow them to take your places, please?"

As if in a huff, Emma's father took the two girls' places on the sofa, her mother beside him.

"I'm afraid that Lord Egerton does not mean to honor his agreement with you. The exact facts are a bit muddled, but he left the contract the two of you signed and said that he no longer wishes to marry Emma."

"But why give it to you?" her father asked. "Why not wait to speak to me directly?"

Mrs. Rutley shrugged. "Given the uncertainty of the weather, I imagine he was concerned about waiting too long to begin his journey back to London. But I assure you, I made certain all was in order before he left."

"And what about this man?"

"Father, Mother, this is my fiancé." Emma said, her cheeks heating.

"Your fiancé?" her father asked in clear confusion. "But Lord Egerton and I had an agreement up until today."

The headmistress intervened. "Sir Henry and Lady Hunter, I would like you to meet Andrew, Baron St. John. He and Miss Hunter met at a recent gathering, and they have grown quite fond of one another."

"It's a pleasure to meet you, sir," Andrew said, offering Emma's father his hand. "And I apologize for not asking you for her hand first, but as you were traveling, I had no desire to wait to propose."

"I'm still unsure of what transpired," her father said. "Lord Egerton seemed more than anxious to marry my daughter. Why the change of heart?"

For a moment, Emma thought her father would refuse the new arrangement. But that worry soon fell away when Andrew began to speak.

"Sir Henry, if I may briefly explain," Andrew said. "Lord Egerton and I have had many, shall we say, transactions as of late that proved unsuccessful. We discussed various methods of righting the situation. When he learned of my admiration for your daughter, he decided it was in his and Emma's best interest to step aside." Before her father could respond, Andrew added, "Though this has no doubt come as a shock, I believe you'll find this new agreement beneficial to both you and your daughter."

"I'll admit, I didn't expect this news." Sir Henry rubbed his chin, embarrassment staining his cheeks. "The problem is I did have certain *arrangements* of the financial nature with the earl."

"Of course, sir." Andrew produced the document Lord Egerton had signed. "I understand that the viscount promised you an estate in Dover in exchange for your daughter's hand. As you can see, you will still receive the house when she and I marry, for he included it in the agreement we made. His solicitors will contact you once you return home to go over the finer details. Rest assured, you fulfilled your part of the bargain, so whatever debt you may have owed him is now paid in full. If that was the case, of course."

"Well," Emma's father said as he looked at her mother, "it seems as if we all win with this arrangement."

Emma stifled a laugh. Her father had no idea how true that statement was!

"We should leave first thing after the storm ends, so we can prepare for your wedding," her father said. "If that's what His Lordship wishes."

Andrew smiled down at Emma. "I'd love nothing more," he said. "Six weeks, just after Twelfth Night, would be a wonderful time for a wedding, don't you think?"

Nodding, Emma found herself unable to stop smiling. "That would be lovely."

Her father rose. "Why don't you tell me about yourself," he said, leading Andrew to a side table and pouring them each a glass of brandy. One he likely needed more than Andrew.

Emma looked at each of her friends. "I don't know what to say. I'm sad that I'll be leaving you all, but I'm so happy knowing what my future holds."

"Don't be sad," Diana said. "Leave with your father and know we'll always be here for you."

The others nodded their agreement.

Diana stood. "I say we give them time alone. Come, girls, we must dress for dinner."

Grumbling, the others each hugged Emma before leaving the room.

"Are your bags packed?" Emma's father asked as he walked up to her.

"They are, Father."

He nodded. "At least the snow's not too bad here. We should be able to leave by tomorrow if the roads are passable. But I doubt it will be an issue."

Emma turned to look at Andrew and smiled. "No, I don't believe it will," she said.

Andrew grinned. "It most certainly will not. I'll write to you soon."

At her father's carriage, Emma turned to look back once more. She whispered a goodbye to Andrew. Then her gaze fell on Mrs. Rutley. All her headmistress had done for her over the years, how she had helped her, came rushing through her mind. It had been Mrs. Rutley who gave Emma hope for a better day. Who had convinced her that neither her father's finances nor her height could determine who she was as a woman. Who had arranged for Emma to meet Andrew. Who had been there to listen to Emma's worries.

Emma wiped away a tear. Yes, Mrs. Rutley had done so much for her.

"Thank you," Emma mouthed to her headmistress.

Although there were many memories at the school, Emma would never forget one last image of Mrs. Rutley placing a hand over her heart and whispering back, "You're most welcome."

EPILOGUE

Once Emma and Andrew were married, they returned to Redborrow Estate, where they lived for two years. She called on her old friends often at the school, those who remained, and also spent a great deal of time visiting with Mrs. Rutley. Emma had seen Julia and Diana twice since then, their bond as strong as ever.

Not only did Andrew save his estate, but he also kept his promise to never game again. With the guidance of Henry, Lord Walcott, the estate soon prospered more than any of them could imagine, allowing Emma and Andrew to purchase a lovely home in Cornwall.

Five years after their wedding, Emma found herself peering out the parlor window of the estate. An unusual storm had hit Cornwall, and large flakes of snow fluttered to the ground, much like they had that final day at the school. It was nights like this that Emma wished that those who had made the pact around the tree could be together once again. Yet, all now lived in various parts of the country and had their own busy lives to lead, making reunions impossible.

"What are you doing?" Andrew asked, startling her.

"Thinking."

He joined her at the window. Emma still found him as handsome as the first time she had seen him in that alleyway off Rake Street, and his gaze could make her cheeks burn even today.

"About what?" he asked as he wrapped his arms around her.

Emma leaned the back of her head against his chest. "About the school I once attended. The friends I made. The day you came for me in a storm much like this."

Andrew nodded. "What a day that was," he said with a laugh. "I had never witnessed Walcott act so reckless before, nor have I seen it since."

"I hope Mrs. Rutley has stopped those lessons," Emma said. "I do adore her, of course, and I'm thankful that her lesson brought us together, but it really is unbecoming of a headmistress to be gambling like that."

He leaned down and kissed her. "Well, we have a certain young girl waiting for a story," he said, taking her hand. "Shall we?"

Emma nodded, and they went to their daughter's bedroom. At four, she had Emma's dark hair and eyes. Andrew always said she was a younger version of Emma. Lying on the bed with the blanket up to her chin, Elizabeth Agnes St. John was simply adorable.

"Is it time for our story, mum?"

Emma sat on the edge of the bed and smiled. "Of course. In fact, I have a new story to tell you tonight, one you've never heard before."

Elizabeth's eyes went wide. "Oh! What's it about?"

Glancing up at Andrew, who stood beside her, Emma said, "It's the story about a prince and princess and what happened to them on a night very much like tonight. The prince was lost in a storm. But the princess loved him as much as he loved her, so she knew he would come and save her."

<hr />

Chatsworth England, 1825

Emma St. John wiped tears from her eyes upon seeing the smile her headmistress wore. "And that's the story of a baron lost in a storm, the young woman who waited for him to return, and the love they share to this day."

"Such a lovely tale," Mrs. Rutley whispered. "And I'm thankful I was able to witness its unfolding."

Emma smiled. "I've often thought of how everything worked out as it did. How you arranged for Andrew's mother and me to meet. The lies Andrew and I had to work through. The early return of Lord Egerton. Even the lesson you had arranged with Lord Walcott." She shook her head. "It all came together so well, but I cannot seem to fathom how Andrew was able to win."

"What do you mean?" Mrs. Rutley asked.

"He had lost everything because of the dice, and yet, somehow, he won that night." She gave a small laugh. "I still can't believe how much his luck changed at such an opportune moment."

Mrs. Rutley repositioned herself on the pillow. "Do you remember when I told you that you could not control your fate?"

"I do. You said that it was out of my hands, that fate was in the casting of the dice. I remember thinking how strange that such a figurative statement had become so literal."

"Fate was indeed out of your hands," Mrs. Rutley said, smiling. "But it was not out of mine."

Emma frowned. "What do you..." Her words fell when Mrs. Rutley opened her hand to reveal a pair of dice.

"They are weighted, my dear. One is meant to land on two and the other five. Everything was set up to appeal to the viscount's insatiable greed. Lord Walcott was not there to give me lessons, nor was he intoxicated. It was all an elaborate ruse."

With wide eyes, Emma gasped. "That's why you told me to compliment Lord Egerton that day! So, he would be less likely to notice what was going on. But how could you have been so certain that Andrew would return? He hadn't even decided to do so."

"I didn't know. But like you, I had hoped that he would come to his senses. Everything was ready, but that was one aspect of it I could not control. That was fate. It was his love for you that drove him through that storm. That was the part of the story that was in your hands, not mine."

Emma leaned over and hugged Mrs. Rutley. "Thank you," she whispered.

And like she had done twenty years earlier, her headmistress replied, "You're most welcome."

Mrs. Rutley then closed her eyes, and Emma watched the steady rise and fall of the covers. Pulling the blanket up to Mrs. Rutley's chin, Emma stood and wiped a tear from her eye.

Julia embraced her. "That was a beautiful story, my friend. I'm so glad I was able to hear it."

"Now we wait for the others," Emma said.

And as if by magic, the door opened and a head with a mop of blonde curls peeked inside.

Like Emma, Julia, and Mrs. Rutley, Diana had aged, but she was still as lovely as ever.

"My friends... sisters," Diana whispered. "It's so good to see you again. How's Mrs. Rutley?"

"She's resting now," Emma replied. "But when she wakes, she'll wish to speak to you, for she wishes to hear a story. And if you don't mind, Julia and I would like to listen as well."

THE END

Thank you for reading *Baron of Rake Street*!

Find out what happens between Diana and Lord Barrington in Book Three of the *Sisterhood of Secrets Series*, **Marquess of Magic**. Coming May 2022.

Have you already read book 1? If not, read Julia's story in *Duke of Madness*!

THE SISTERHOOD OF SECRETS

  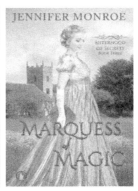

While waiting for book 3 to be released, check out other books by Jennifer Monroe or dive into one of the latest releases by WOLF Publishing: *Once Upon an Achingly Beautiful Kiss* by *USA Today* Bestselling Author Bree Wolf.

THE WHICKERTONS IN LOVE

ALSO BY JENNIFER MONROE

Sisterhood of Secrets

#1 Duke of Madness

#2 Baron of Rake Street

#3 Marquess of Magic

Secrets of Scarlett Hall

Victoria Parker Regency Mysteries

Regency Hearts

Defiant Brides

ABOUT JENNIFER MONROE

 Jennifer Monroe writes clean Regency romances you can't resist. Her stories are filled with first loves and second chances, dashing dukes, and strong heroines. Each turn of the page promises an adventure in love and many late nights of reading.

With over twenty books published, her nine-part series, The Secrets of Scarlett Hall, which tells the stories of the Lambert Children, remain a favorite with her readers.

Connect with Jennifer:

www.jennifermonroeromance.com

facebook.com/JenniferMonroeAuthor

instagram.com/authorjennifermonroe

bookbub.com/authors/jennifer-monroe

amazon.com/Jennifer-Monroe/e/B07F1MRXDN

Made in the USA
Coppell, TX
22 December 2024